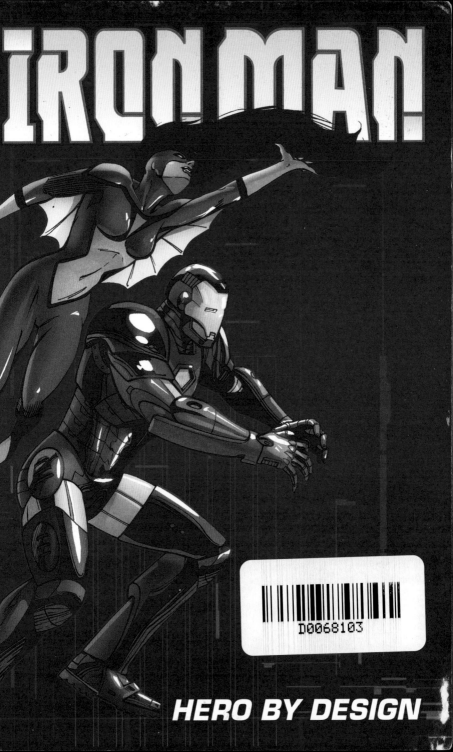

IRON MAN

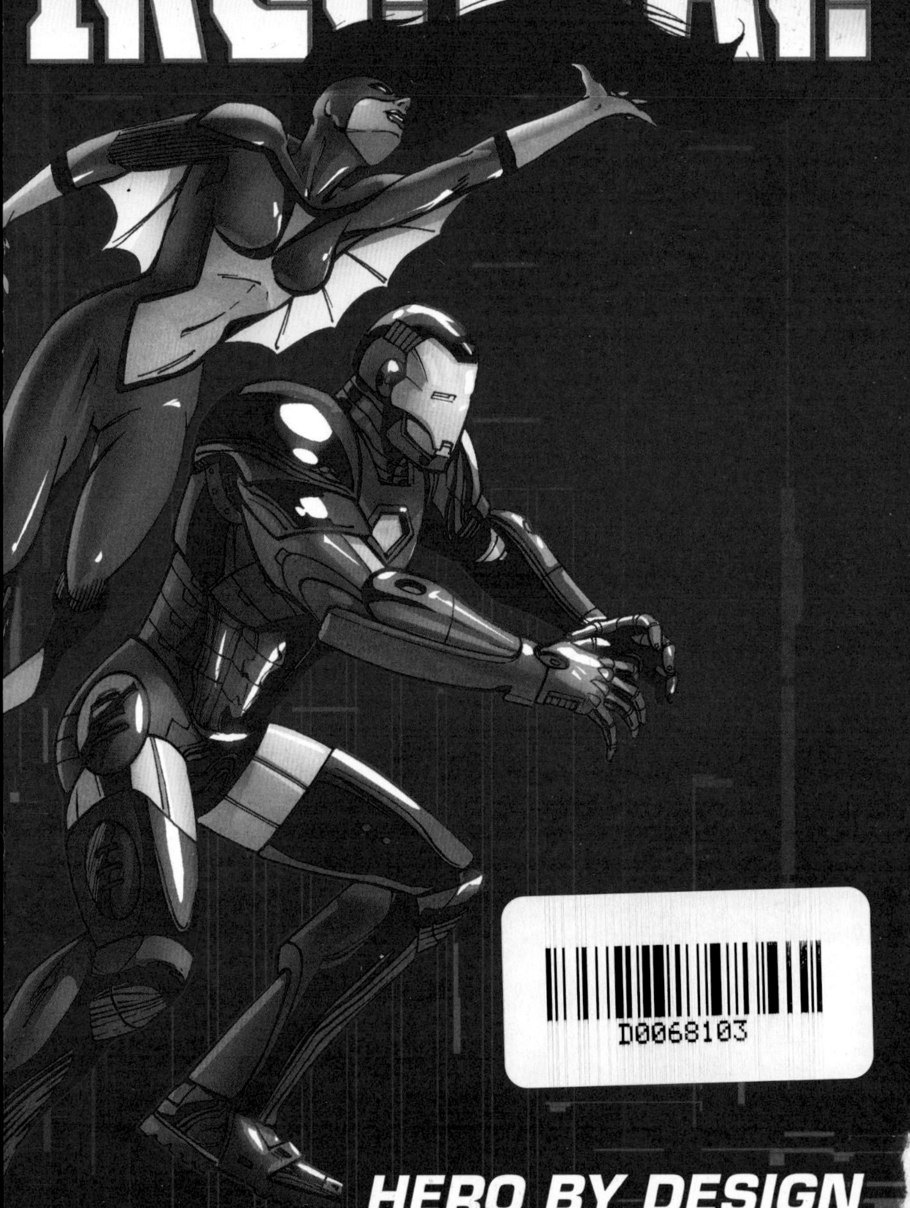

HERO BY DESIGN

IRON MAN

HERO BY DESIGN

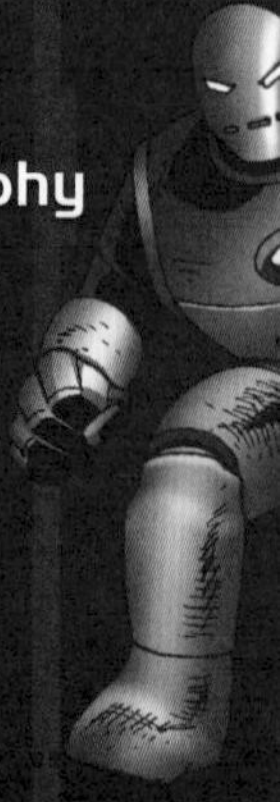

WRITER: Fred Van Lente

PENCILERS: Graham Nolan & Scott Koblish

INKERS: Victor Olazaba & Scott Koblish

COLORISTS: Martegod Gracia, Javier Tartaglia & Chris Sotomayor

LETTERER: Dave Sharpe

COVER ART: Tommy Lee Edwards, Sean Murphy & Moose Baumann and Francis Tsai

ASSISTANT EDITOR: Nathan Cosby

EDITOR: Mark Paniccia

COLLECTION EDITOR: Jennifer Grünwald

EDITORIAL ASSISTANT: Alex Starbuck

ASSISTANT EDITORS: Cory Levine & John Denning

EDITOR, SPECIAL PROJECTS: Mark D. Beazley

SENIOR EDITOR, SPECIAL PROJECTS: Jeff Youngquist

SENIOR VICE PRESIDENT OF SALES: David Gabriel

VICE PRESIDENT OF CREATIVE: Tom Marvelli

EDITOR IN CHIEF: Joe Quesada

PUBLISHER: Dan Buckley

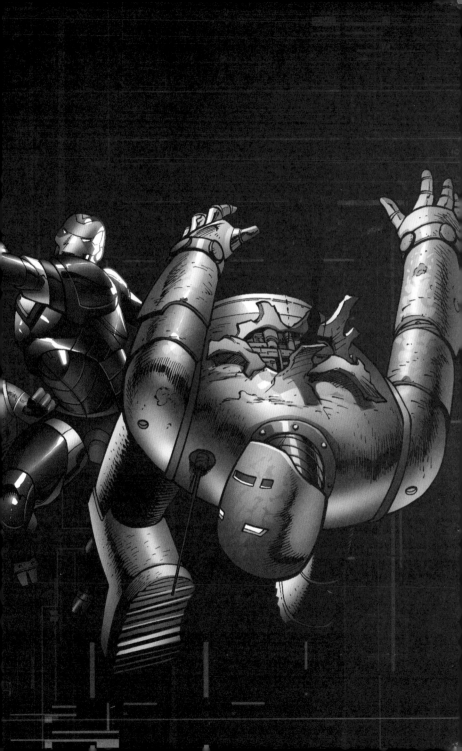

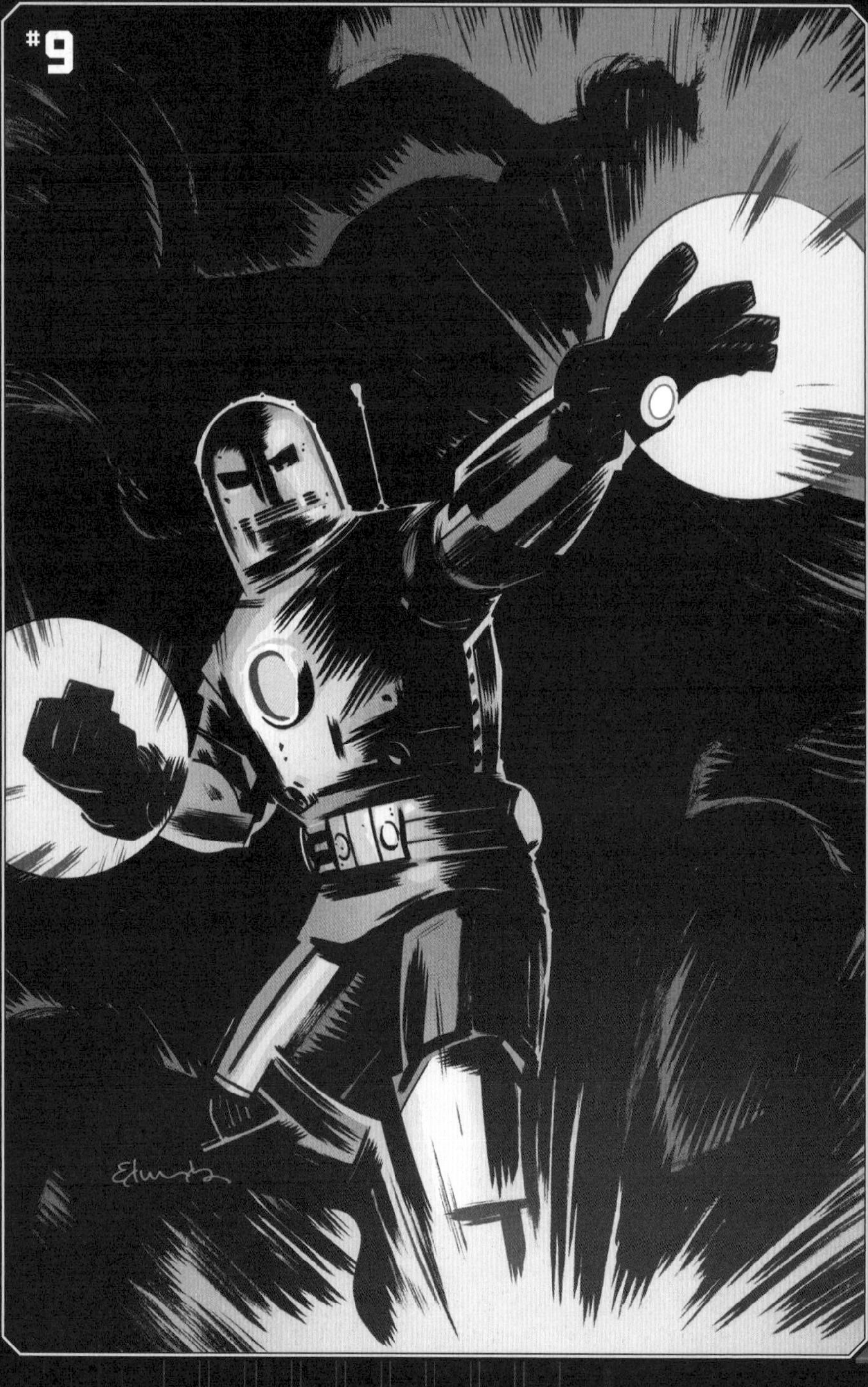
#9

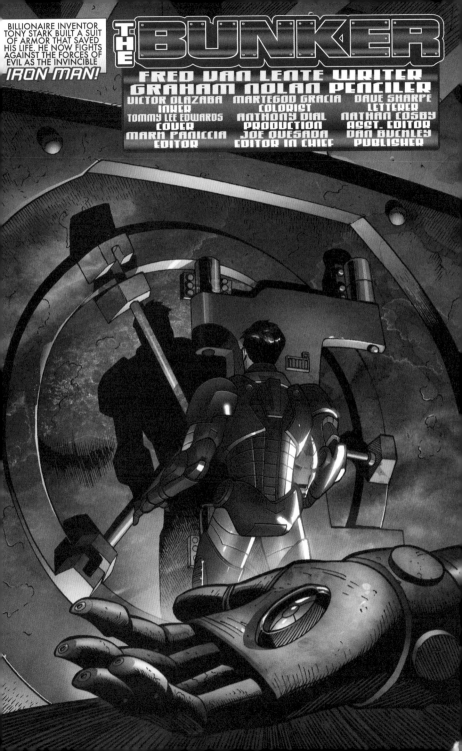

BILLIONAIRE INVENTOR TONY STARK BUILT A SUIT OF ARMOR THAT SAVED HIS LIFE. HE NOW FIGHTS AGAINST THE FORCES OF EVIL AS THE INVINCIBLE *IRON MAN!*

THE BUNKER

FRED VAN LENTE **WRITER**
GRAHAM NOLAN **PENCILER**

VICTOR OLAZABA   MARTEGOD GRACIA   DAVE SHARPE
INKER   **COLORIST**   **LETTERER**

TOMMY LEE EDWARDS   ANTHONY DIAL   NATHAN COSBY
COVER   **PRODUCTION**   **ASST. EDITOR**

MARK PANICCIA   JOE QUESADA   DAN BUCKLEY
EDITOR   **EDITOR IN CHIEF**   **PUBLISHER**

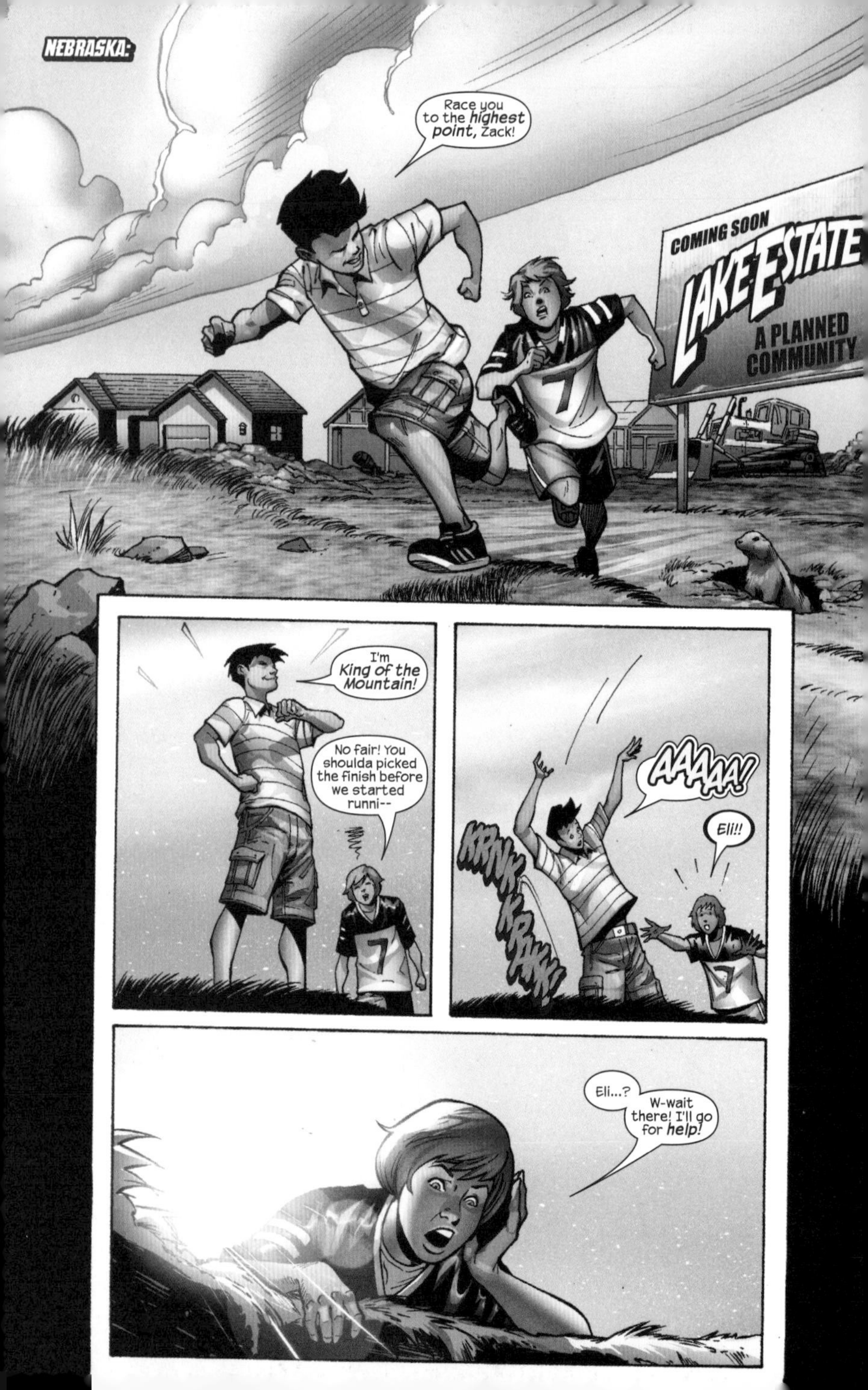
NEBRASKA:
Race you to the *highest point,* Zack!
COMING SOON
LAKE ESTATE
A PLANNED COMMUNITY
I'm *King of the Mountain!*
No fair! You shoulda picked the finish before we started runni--
AAAAA!
KRNK KRAKK!
Eli!!
Eli...?
W-wait there! I'll go for *help!*

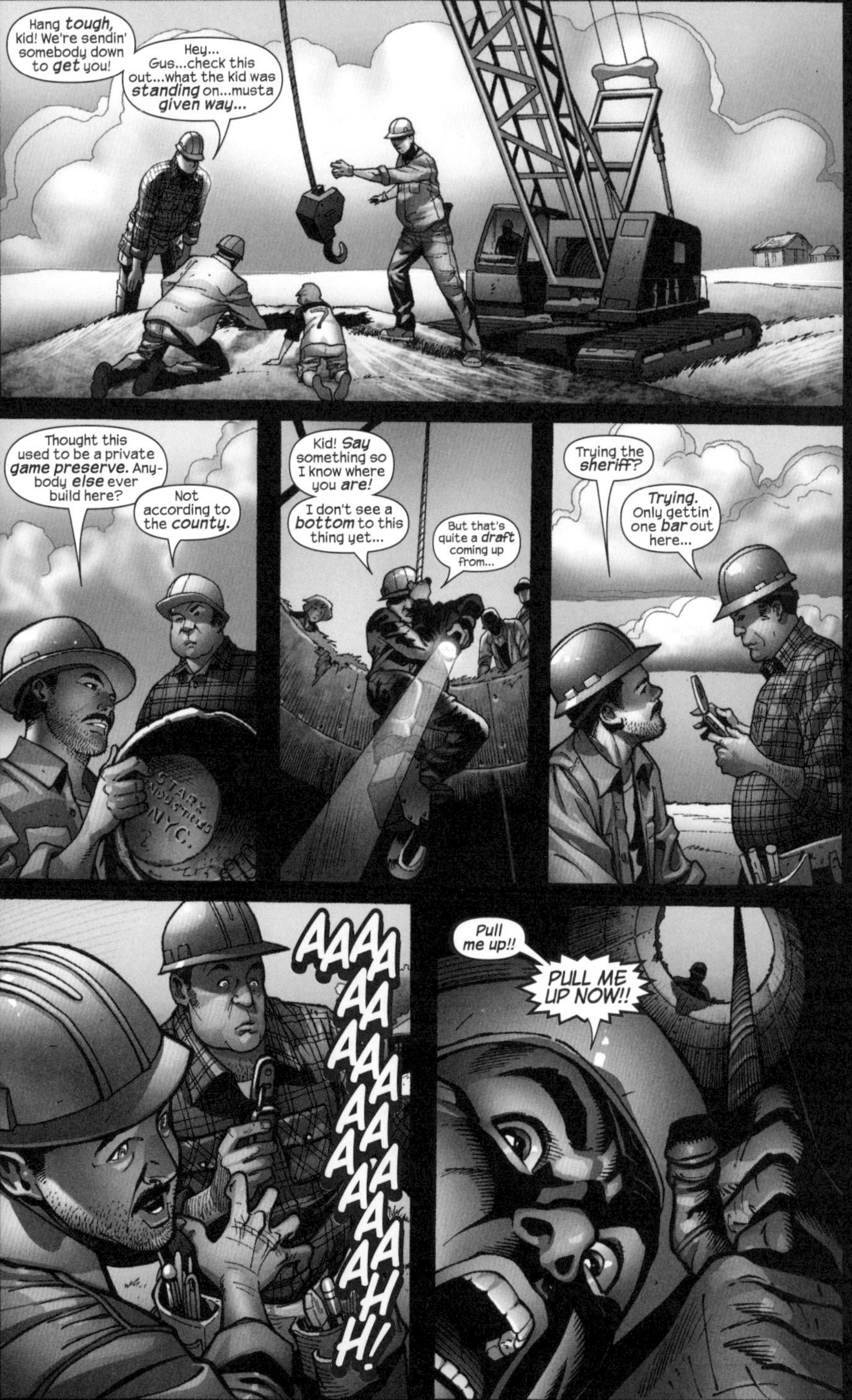
Hang tough, kid! We're sendin' somebody down to get you!
Hey... Gus...check this out...what the kid was standing on...musta given way...
Thought this used to be a private game preserve. Anybody else ever build here?
Not according to the county.
STARK INDUSTRIES NYC.
Kid! Say something so I know where you are!
I don't see a bottom to this thing yet...
But that's quite a draft coming up from...
Trying the sheriff?
Trying. Only gettin' one bar out here...
AAAAAAAAAAAAAAAAAH!
Pull me up!!
PULL ME UP NOW!!

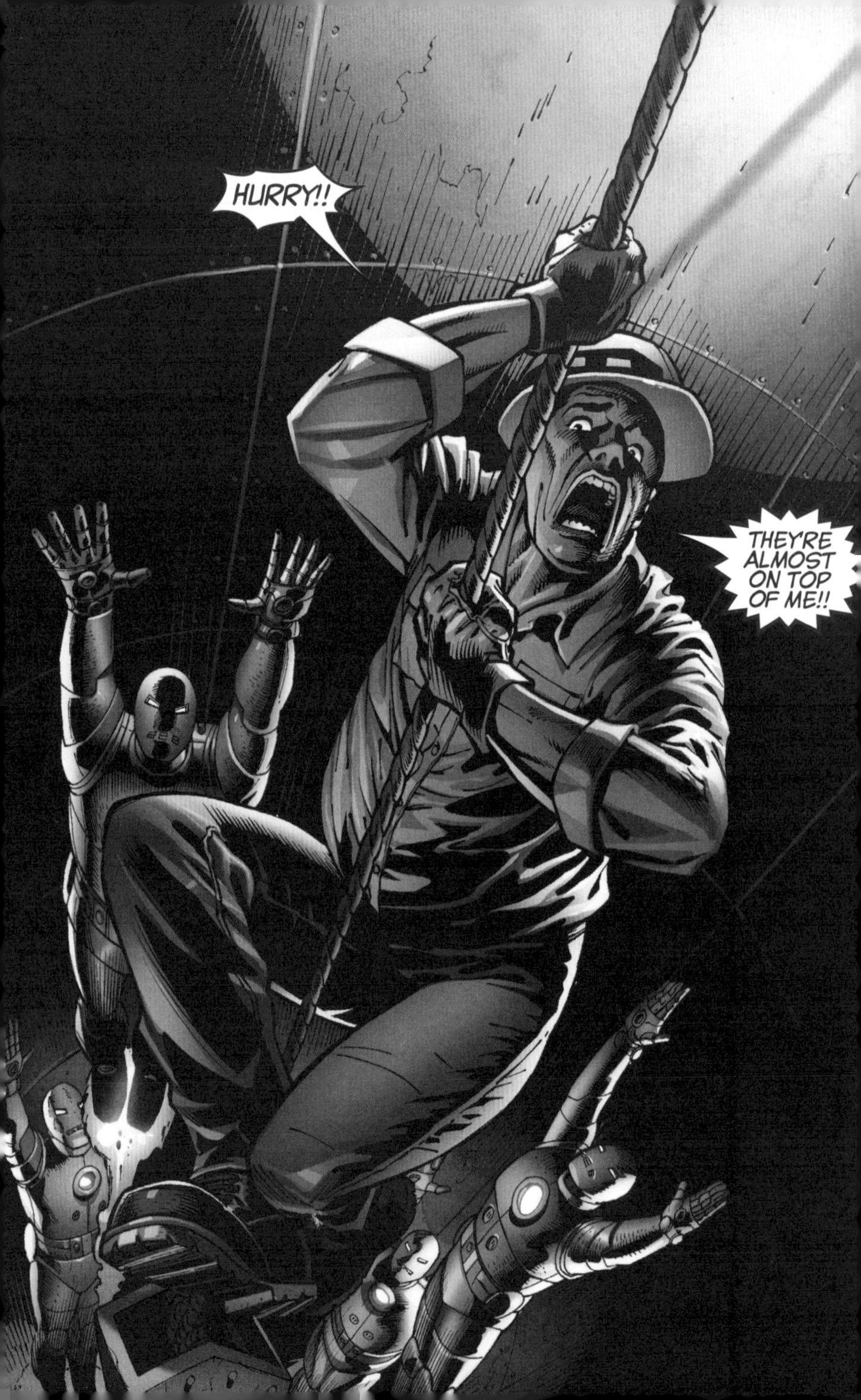
HURRY!!
THEY'RE ALMOST ON TOP OF ME!!

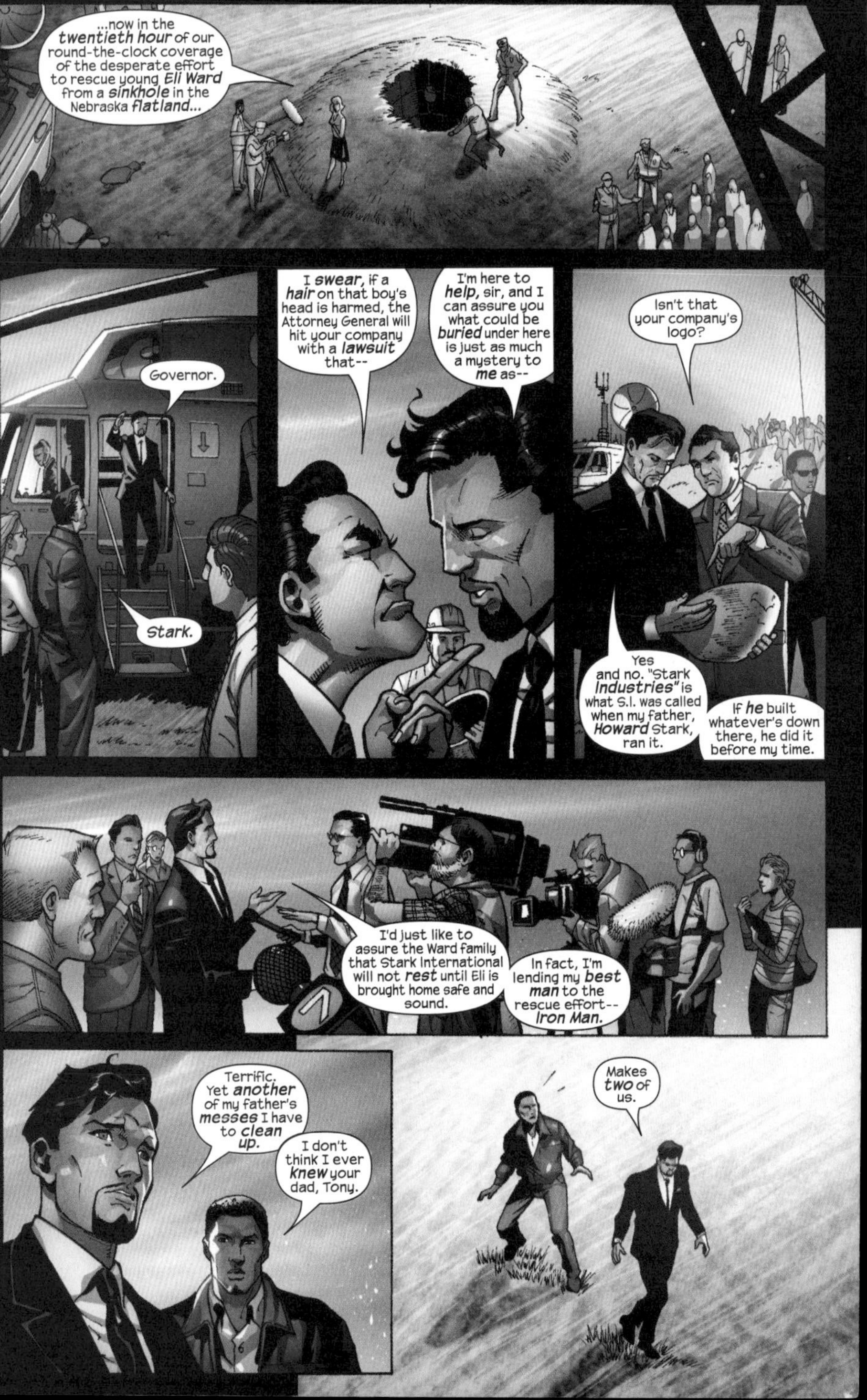
...now in the twentieth hour of our round-the-clock coverage of the desperate effort to rescue young Eli Ward from a sinkhole in the Nebraska flatland...
Governor.
Stark.
I swear, if a hair on that boy's head is harmed, the Attorney General will hit your company with a lawsuit that--
I'm here to help, sir, and I can assure you what could be buried under here is just as much a mystery to me as--
Isn't that your company's logo?
Yes and no. "Stark Industries" is what S.I. was called when my father, Howard Stark, ran it.
If he built whatever's down there, he did it before my time.
I'd just like to assure the Ward family that Stark International will not rest until Eli is brought home safe and sound.
In fact, I'm lending my best man to the rescue effort-- Iron Man.
Terrific. Yet another of my father's messes I have to clean up.
I don't think I ever knew your dad, Tony.
Makes two of us.

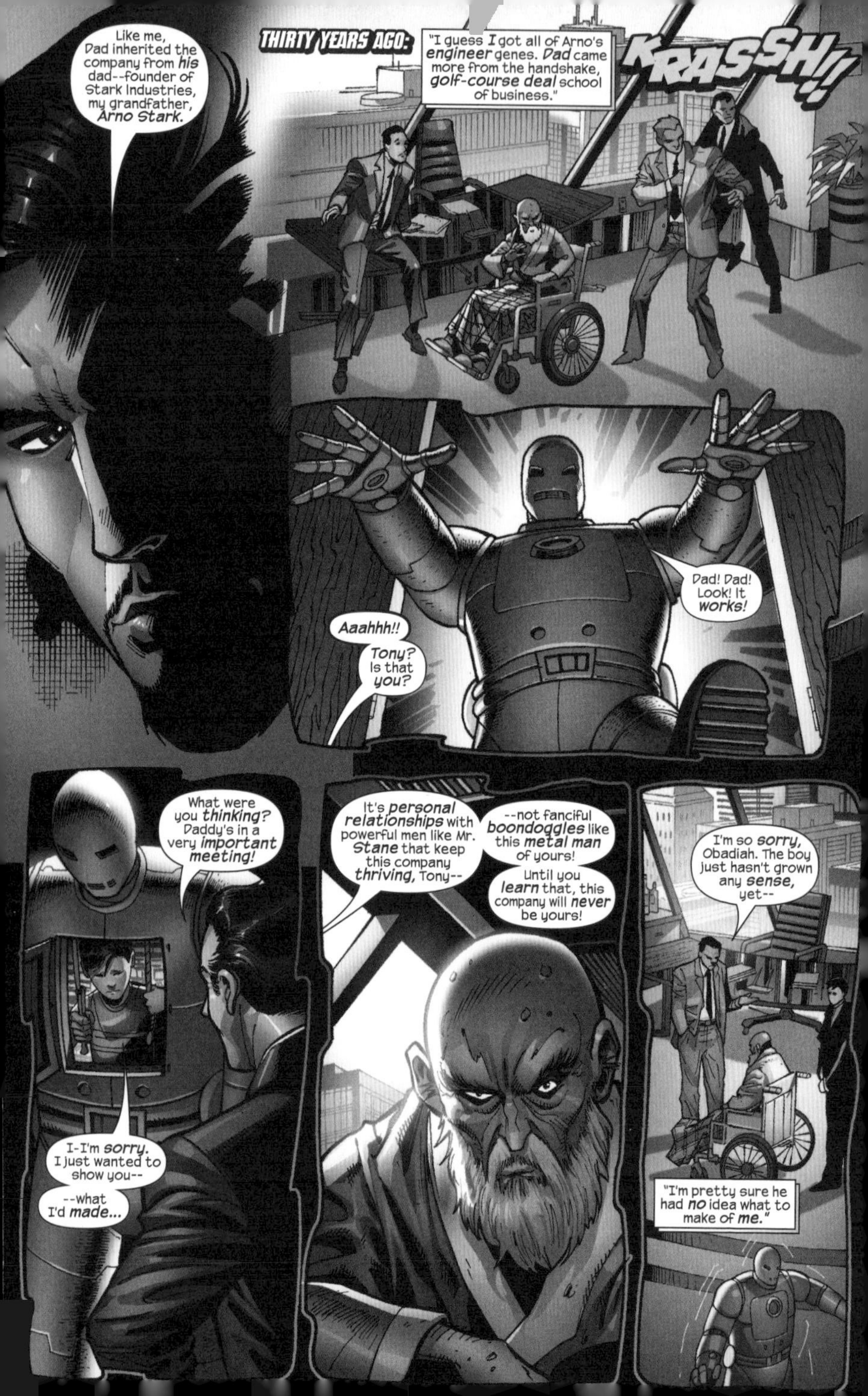
Like me, Dad inherited the company from his dad--founder of Stark Industries, my grandfather, Arno Stark.
THIRTY YEARS AGO:
"I guess I got all of Arno's engineer genes. Dad came more from the handshake, golf-course deal school of business."
KRASSH!!
Dad! Dad! Look! It works!
Aaahhh!!
Tony? Is that you?
What were you thinking? Daddy's in a very important meeting!
I-I'm sorry. I just wanted to show you--
--what I'd made...
It's personal relationships with powerful men like Mr. Stane that keep this company thriving, Tony--
--not fanciful boondoggles like this metal man of yours!
Until you learn that, this company will never be yours!
I'm so sorry, Obadiah. The boy just hasn't grown any sense, yet--
"I'm pretty sure he had no idea what to make of me."

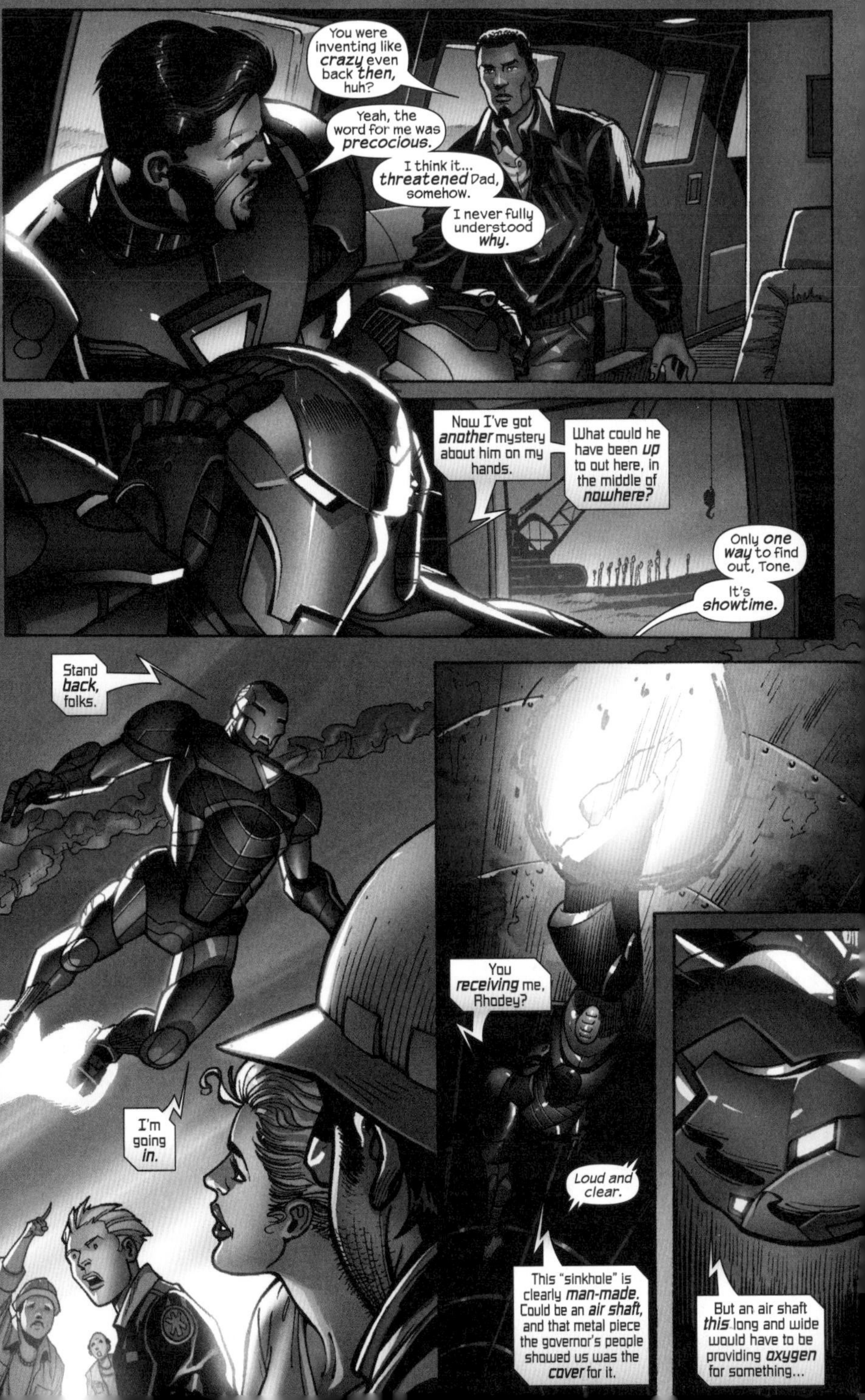
You were inventing like crazy even back then, huh?
Yeah, the word for me was precocious.
I think it... threatened Dad, somehow.
I never fully understood why.
Now I've got another mystery about him on my hands.
What could he have been up to out here, in the middle of nowhere?
Only one way to find out, Tone.
It's showtime.
Stand back, folks.
I'm going in.
You receiving me, Rhodey?
Loud and clear.
This "sinkhole" is clearly man-made. Could be an air shaft, and that metal piece the governor's people showed us was the cover for it.
But an air shaft this long and wide would have to be providing oxygen for something...

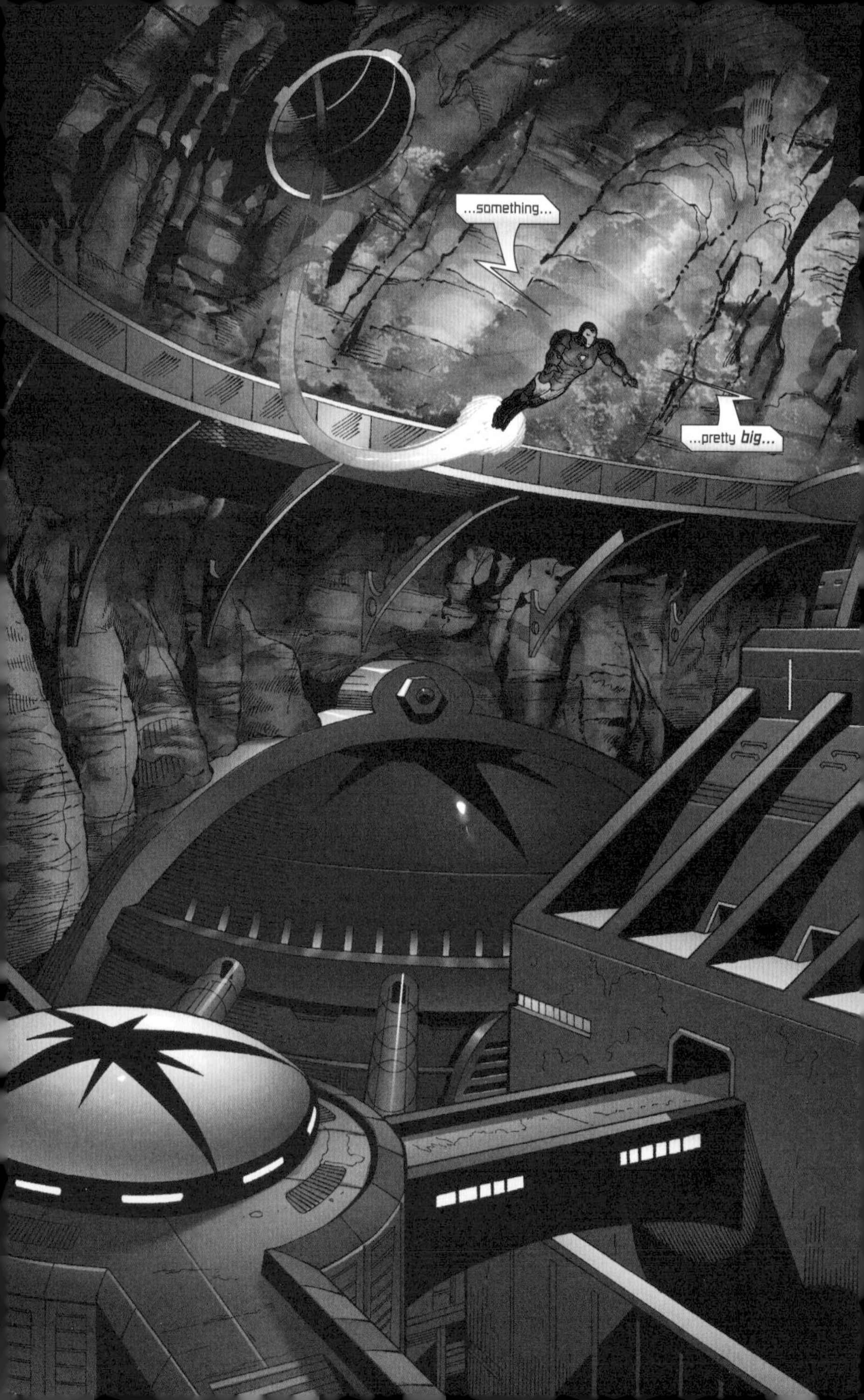
...something...
...pretty *big*...

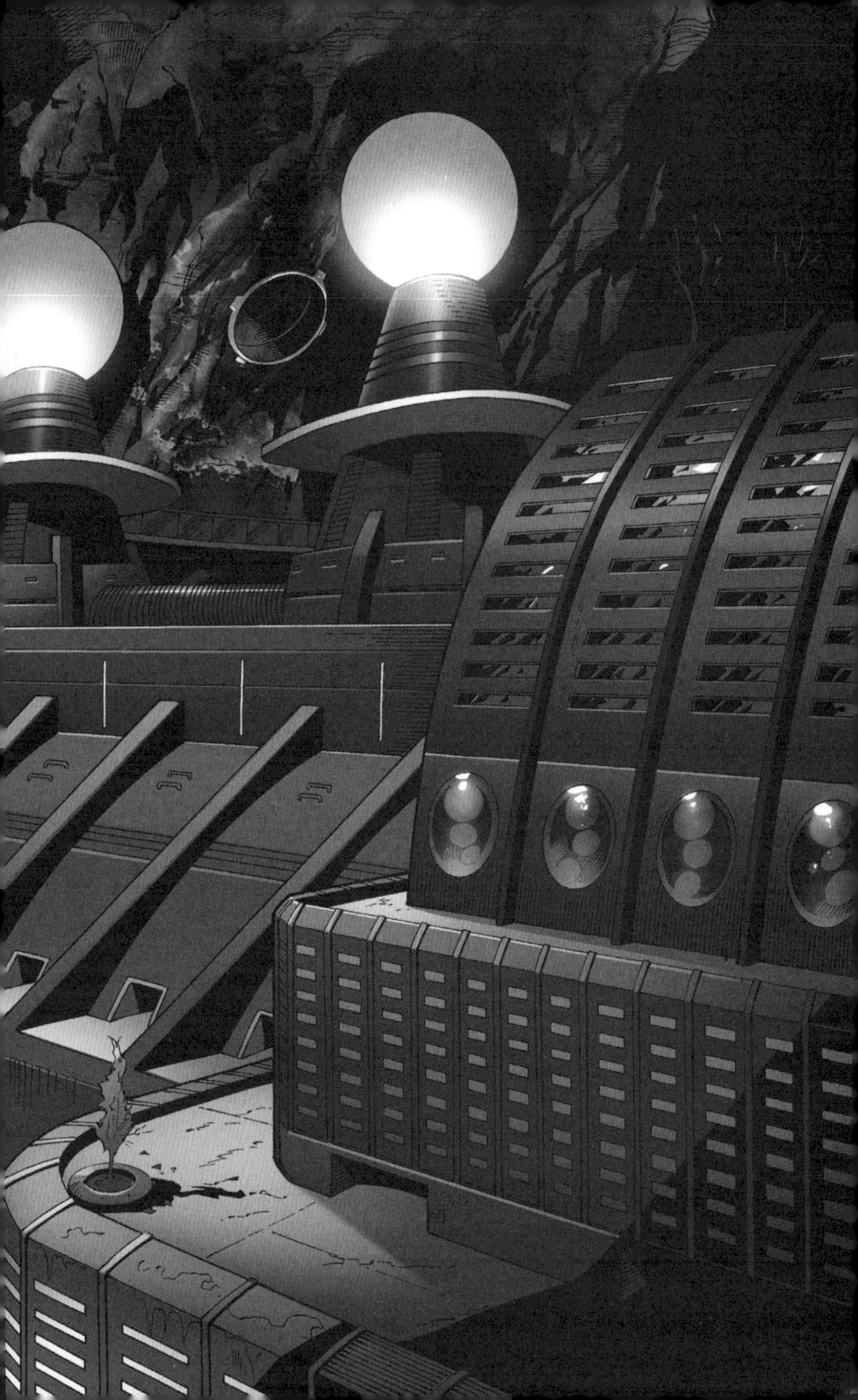

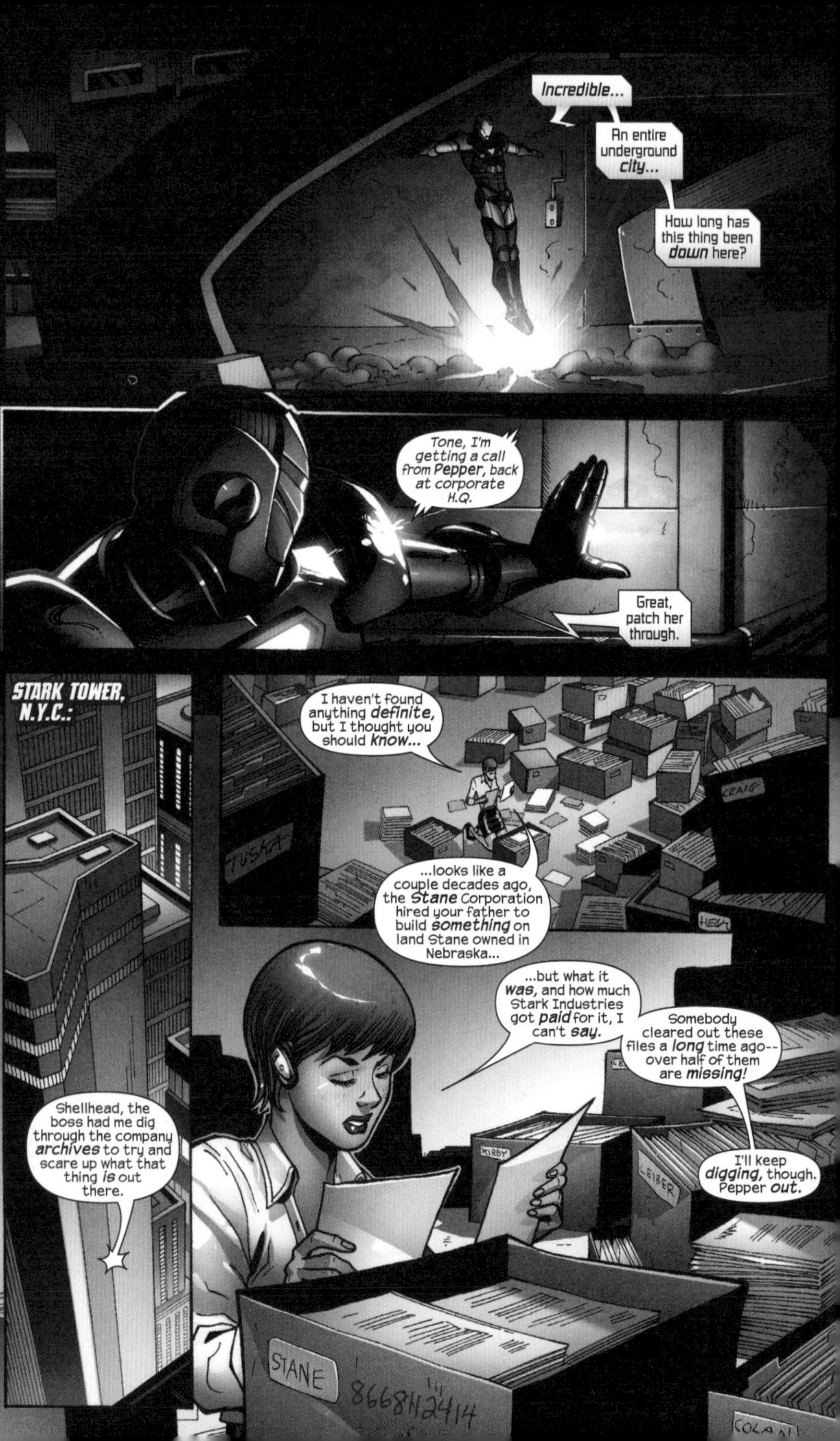
Incredible...
An entire underground city...
How long has this thing been down here?
Tone, I'm getting a call from Pepper, back at corporate H.Q.
Great, patch her through.
STARK TOWER, N.Y.C.:
Shellhead, the boss had me dig through the company archives to try and scare up what that thing is out there.
I haven't found anything definite, but I thought you should know...
...looks like a couple decades ago, the Stane Corporation hired your father to build something on land Stane owned in Nebraska...
...but what it was, and how much Stark Industries got paid for it, I can't say.
Somebody cleared out these files a long time ago--over half of them are missing!
I'll keep digging, though. Pepper out.
TUSKA
CRAIG
KIRBY
LEIBER
STANE
8668N2414

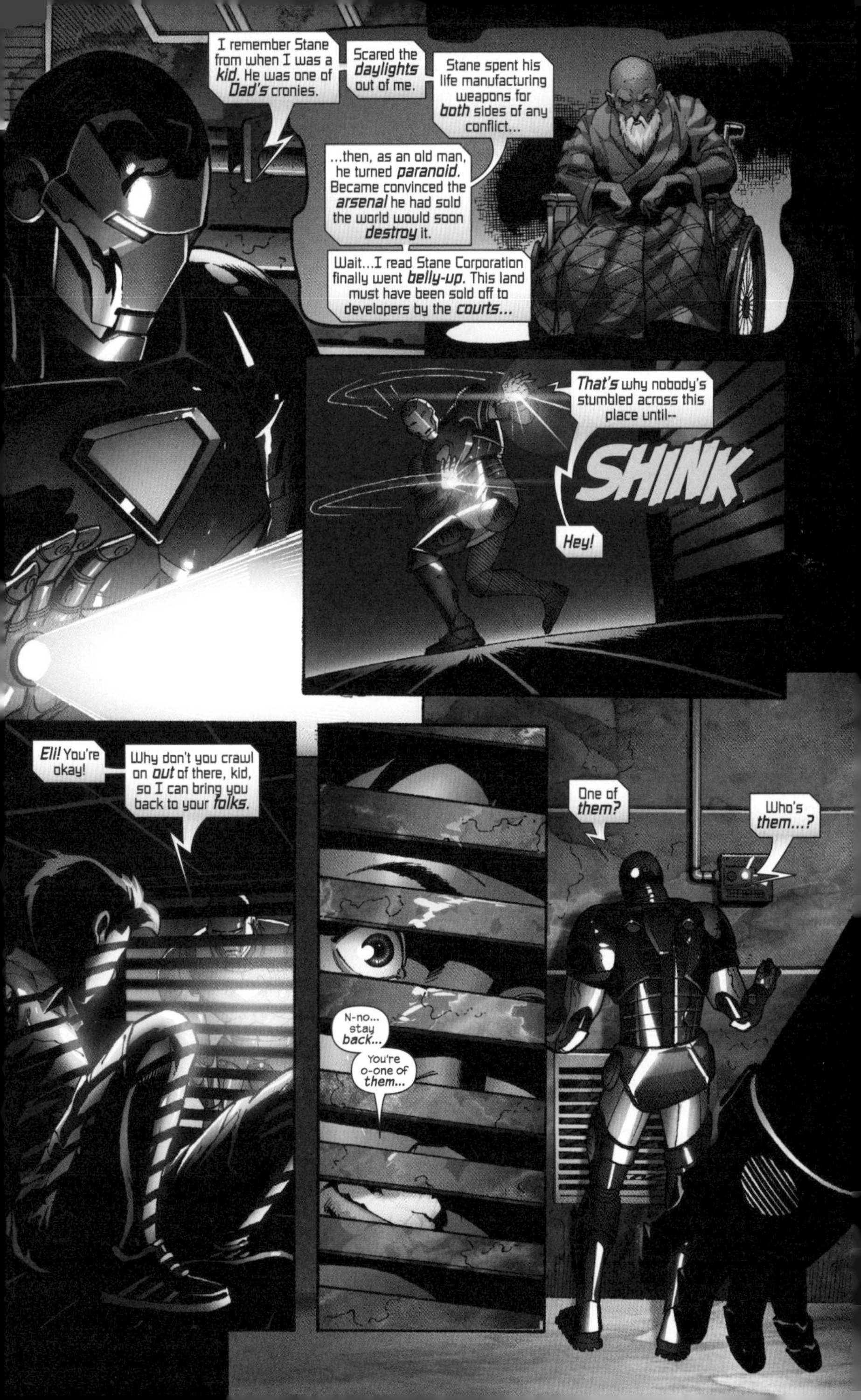
I remember Stane from when I was a *kid.* He was one of *Dad's* cronies.
Scared the *daylights* out of me.
Stane spent his life manufacturing weapons for *both* sides of any conflict...
...then, as an old man, he turned *paranoid.* Became convinced the *arsenal* he had sold the world would soon *destroy* it.
Wait...I read Stane Corporation finally went *belly-up.* This land must have been sold off to developers by the *courts...*
That's why nobody's stumbled across this place until--
SHINK
Hey!
Eli! You're okay!
Why don't you crawl on *out* of there, kid, so I can bring you back to your *folks.*
N-no... stay *back...*
You're o-one of *them...*
One of *them?*
Who's *them...?*

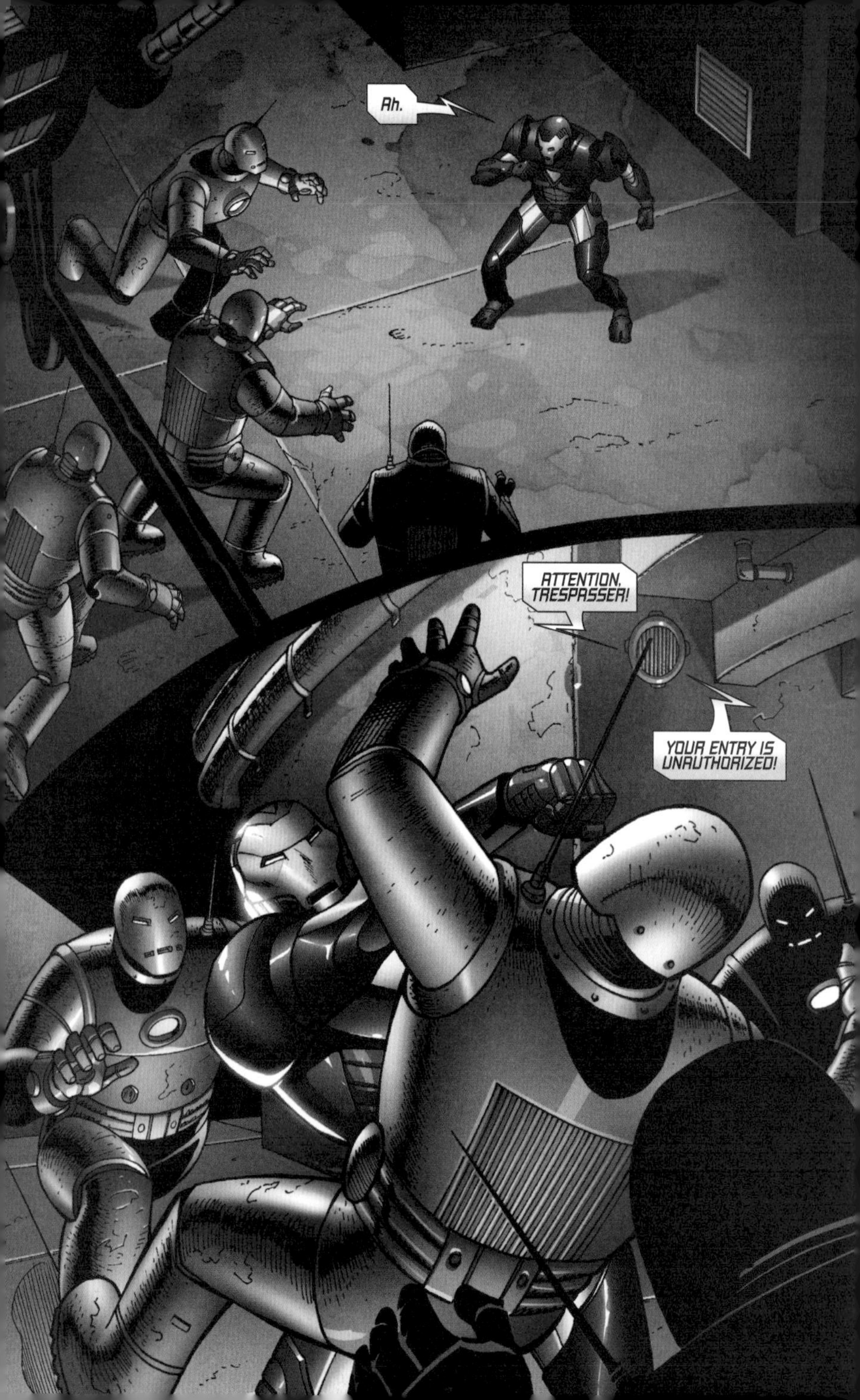
Ah.
ATTENTION, TRESPASSER!
YOUR ENTRY IS UNAUTHORIZED!

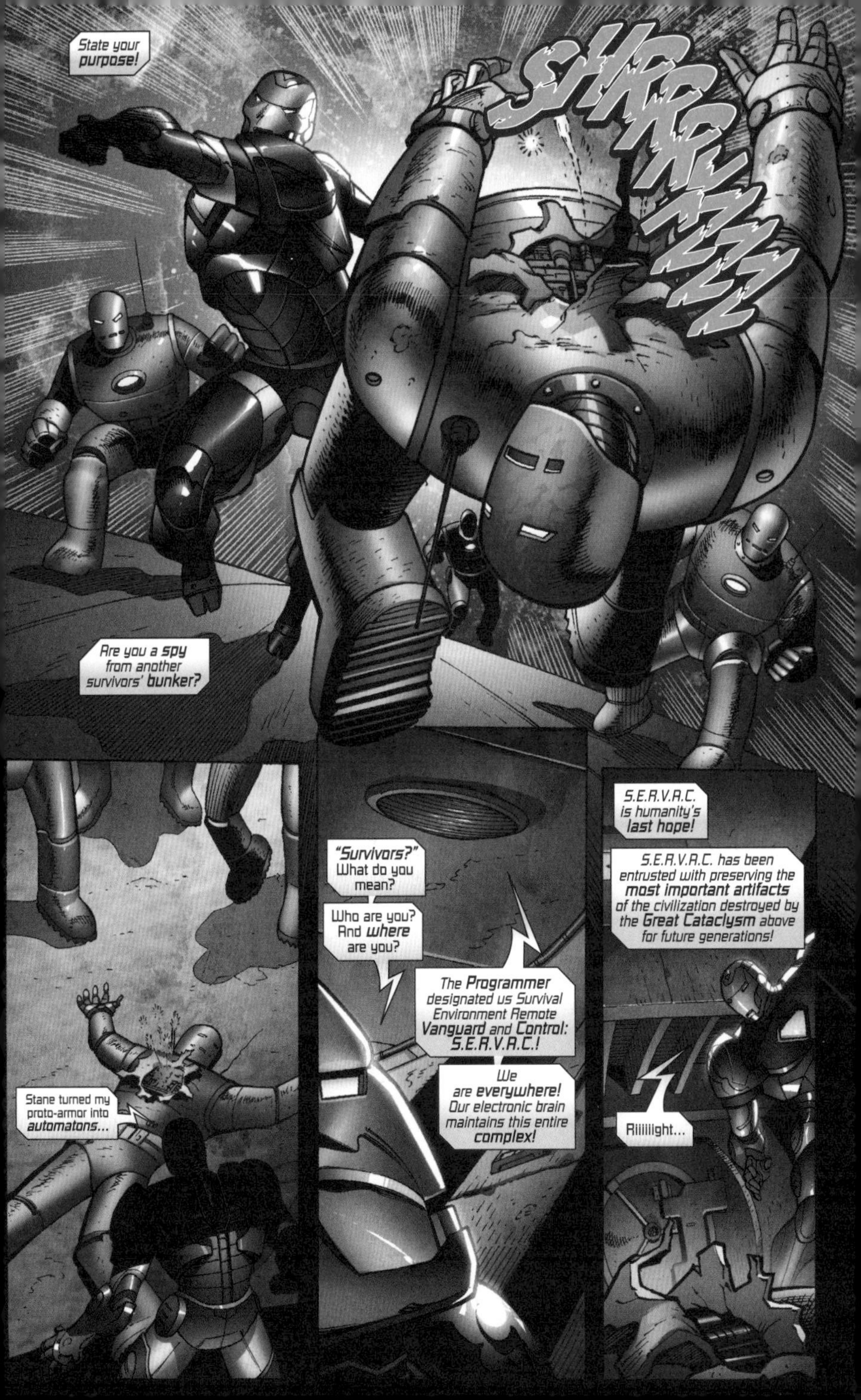
State your purpose!
SHRRRZZZZZ
Are you a spy from another survivors' bunker?
Stane turned my proto-armor into automatons...
"Survivors?" What do you mean?
Who are you? And where are you?
The Programmer designated us Survival Environment Remote Vanguard and Control: S.E.R.V.A.C.!
We are everywhere! Our electronic brain maintains this entire complex!
S.E.R.V.A.C. is humanity's last hope!
S.E.R.V.A.C. has been entrusted with preserving the most important artifacts of the civilization destroyed by the Great Cataclysm above for future generations!
Riiiiight...

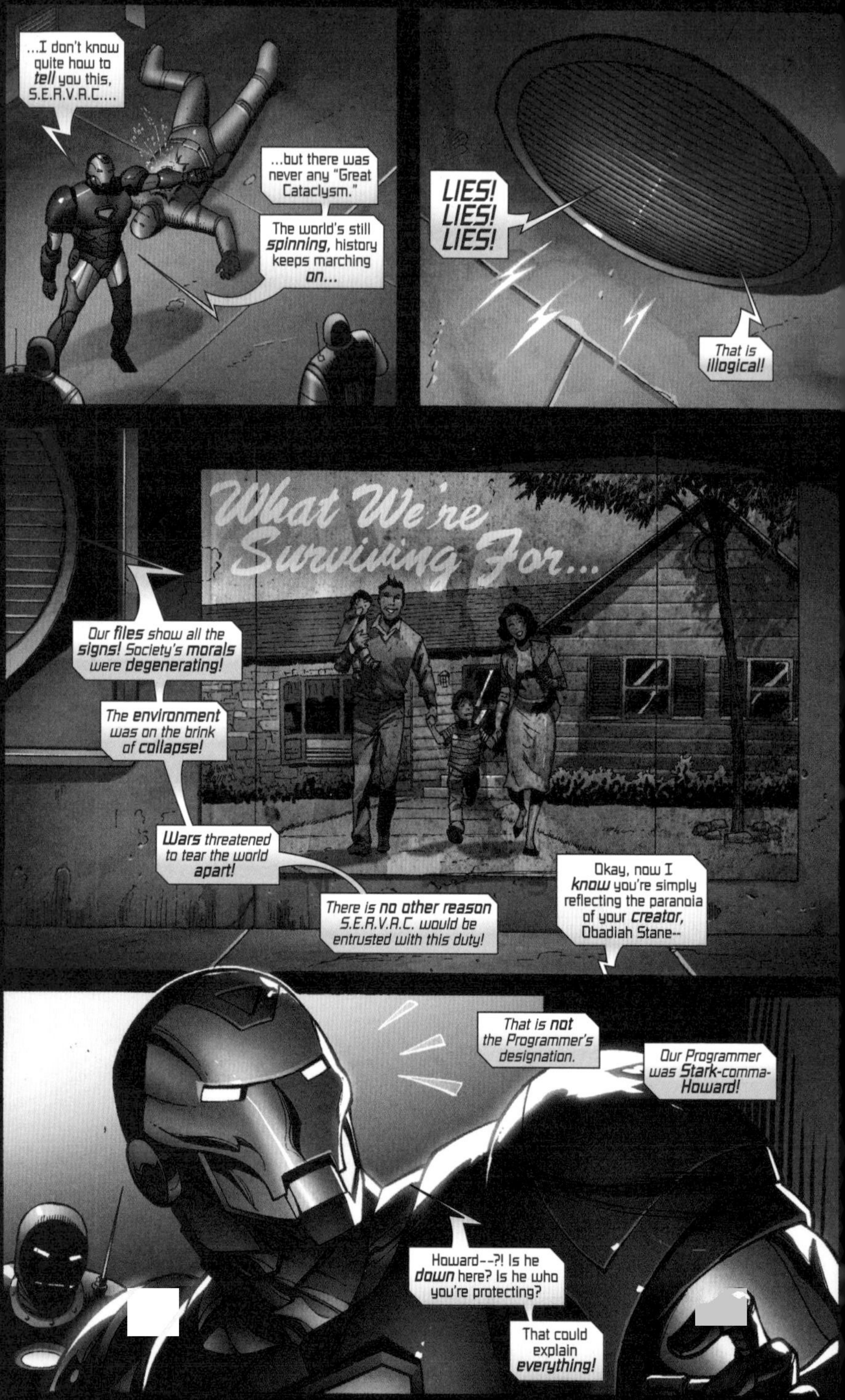

...I don't know quite how to tell you this, S.E.R.V.A.C....
...but there was never any "Great Cataclysm."
The world's still spinning, history keeps marching on...
LIES! LIES! LIES!
That is illogical!
What We're Surviving For...
Our files show all the signs! Society's morals were degenerating!
The environment was on the brink of collapse!
Wars threatened to tear the world apart!
There is no other reason S.E.R.V.A.C. would be entrusted with this duty!
Okay, now I know you're simply reflecting the paranoia of your creator, Obadiah Stane--
That is not the Programmer's designation.
Our Programmer was Stark-comma-Howard!
Howard--?! Is he down here? Is he who you're protecting?
That could explain everything!

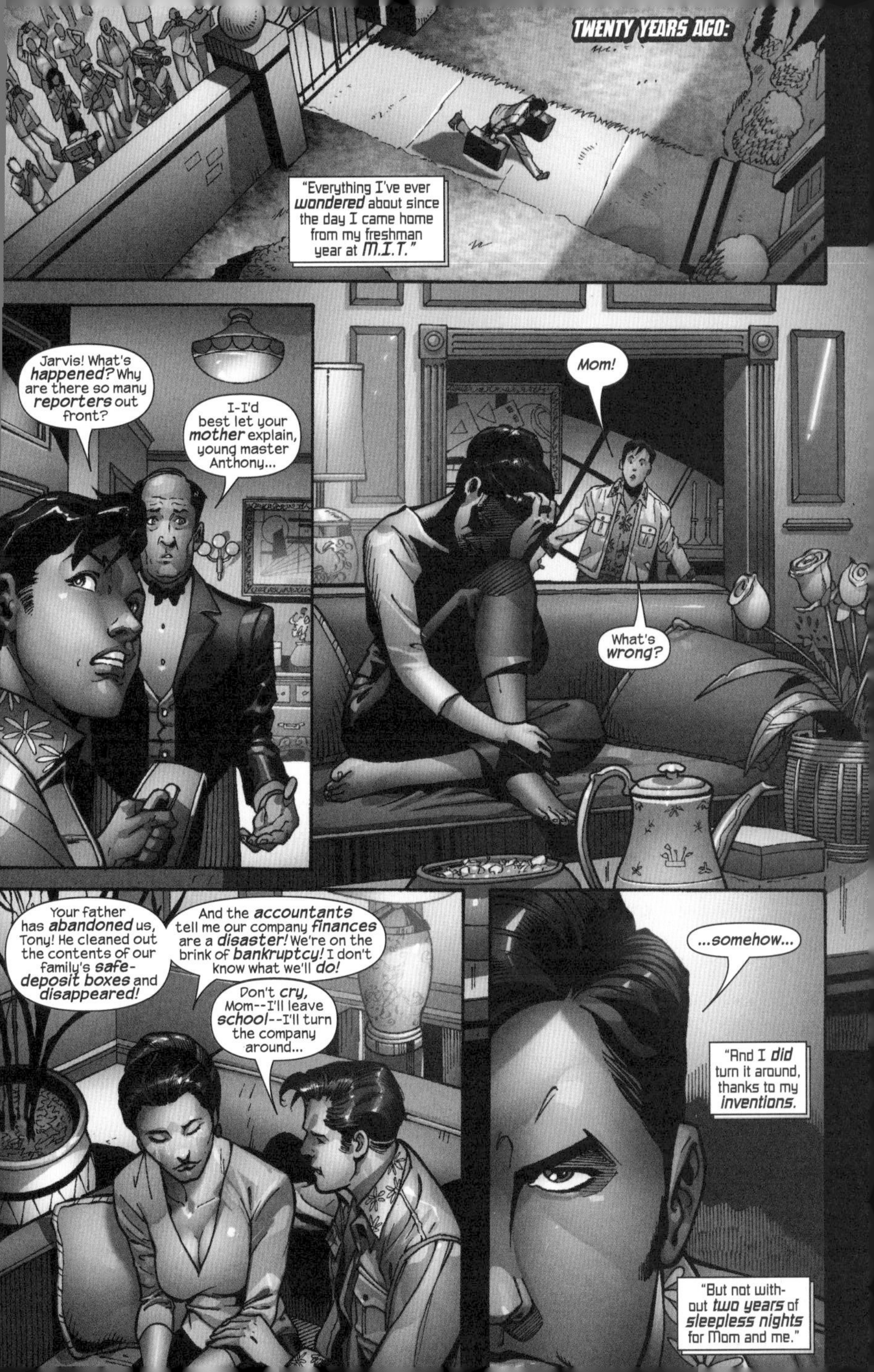
TWENTY YEARS AGO:
"Everything I've ever *wondered* about since the day I came home from my freshman year at *M.I.T.*"
Jarvis! What's *happened?* Why are there so many *reporters* out front?
I-I'd best let your *mother* explain, young master Anthony...
Mom!
What's *wrong?*
Your father has *abandoned* us, Tony! He cleaned out the contents of our family's *safe-deposit boxes* and *disappeared!*
And the *accountants* tell me our company *finances* are a *disaster!* We're on the brink of *bankruptcy!* I don't know what we'll *do!*
Don't *cry,* Mom--I'll leave *school*--I'll turn the company around...
...somehow...
"And I *did* turn it around, thanks to my *inventions.*
"But not without *two years* of *sleepless nights* for Mom and me."

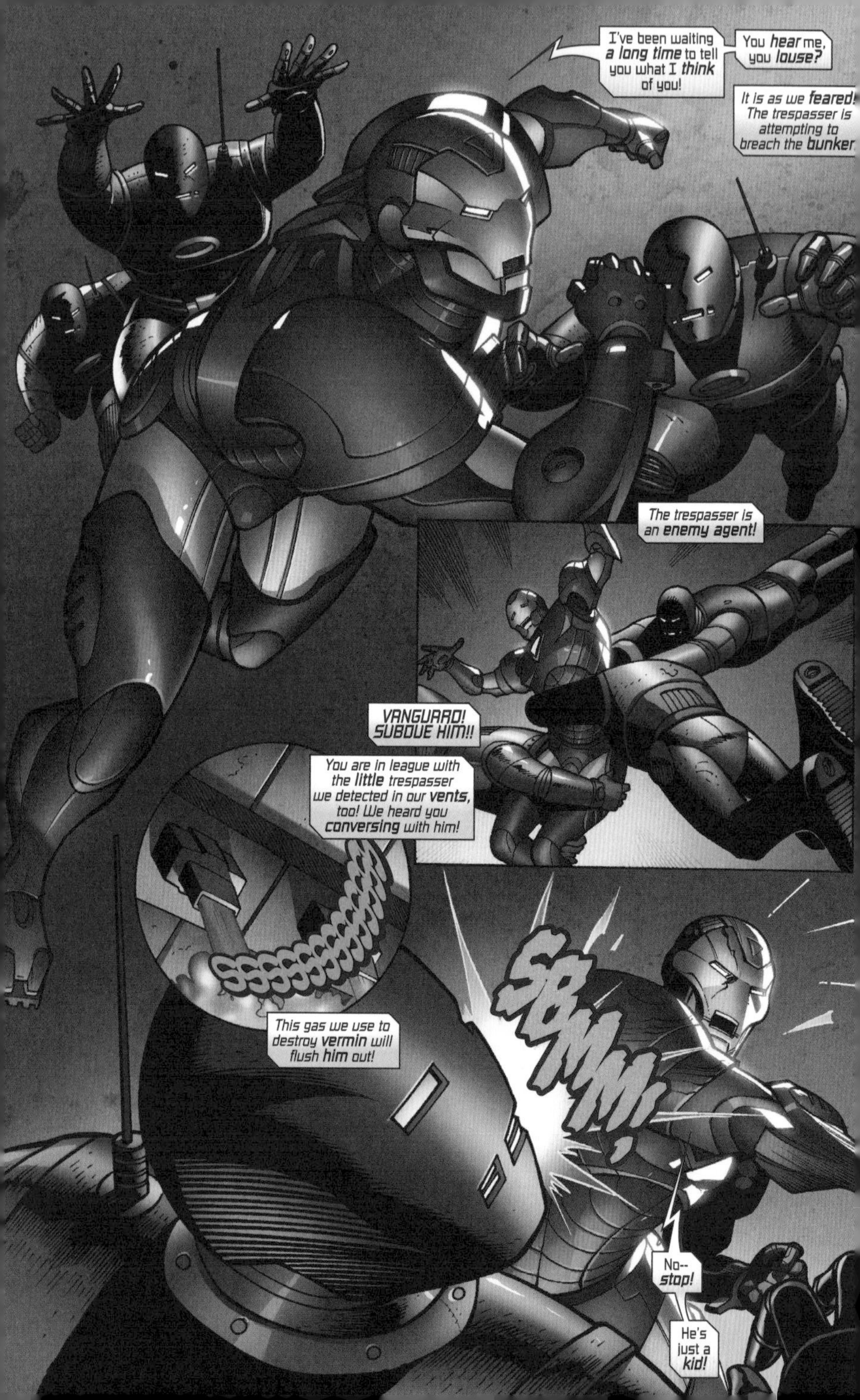
I've been waiting a long time to tell you what I think of you!
You hear me, you louse?
It is as we feared! The trespasser is attempting to breach the bunker.
The trespasser is an enemy agent!
VANGUARD! SUBDUE HIM!!
You are in league with the little trespasser we detected in our vents, too! We heard you conversing with him!
SSSSSSSSSSSSSSSSSSSSS
This gas we use to destroy vermin will flush him out!
SBOMMM!
No-- stop!
He's just a kid!

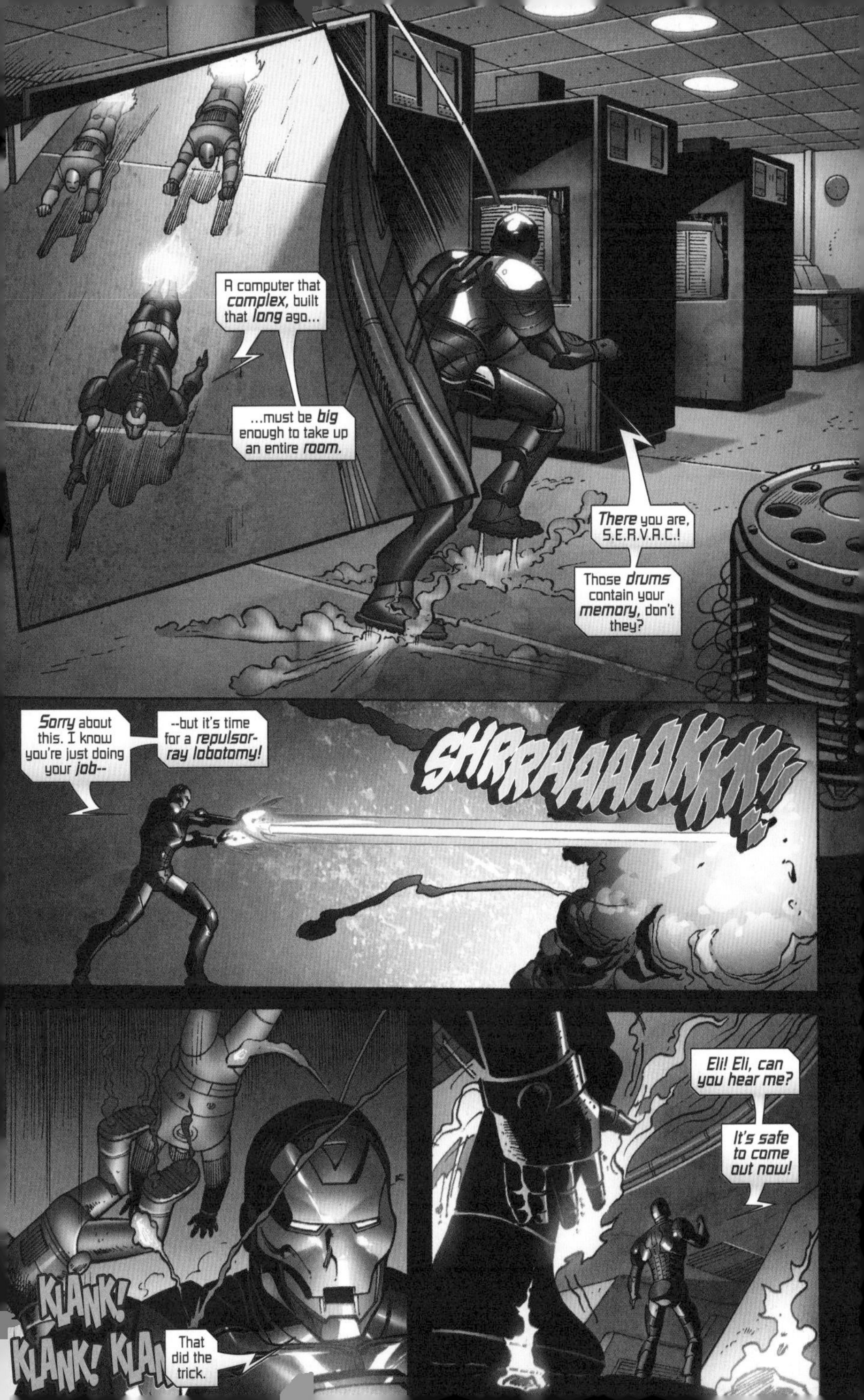

A computer that complex, built that long ago...
...must be big enough to take up an entire room.
There you are, S.E.R.V.A.C.!
Those drums contain your memory, don't they?
Sorry about this. I know you're just doing your job--
--but it's time for a repulsor-ray lobotomy!
SHRRAAAAAKKK!!
KLANK! KLANK! KLAN
That did the trick.
Eli! Eli, can you hear me?
It's safe to come out now!

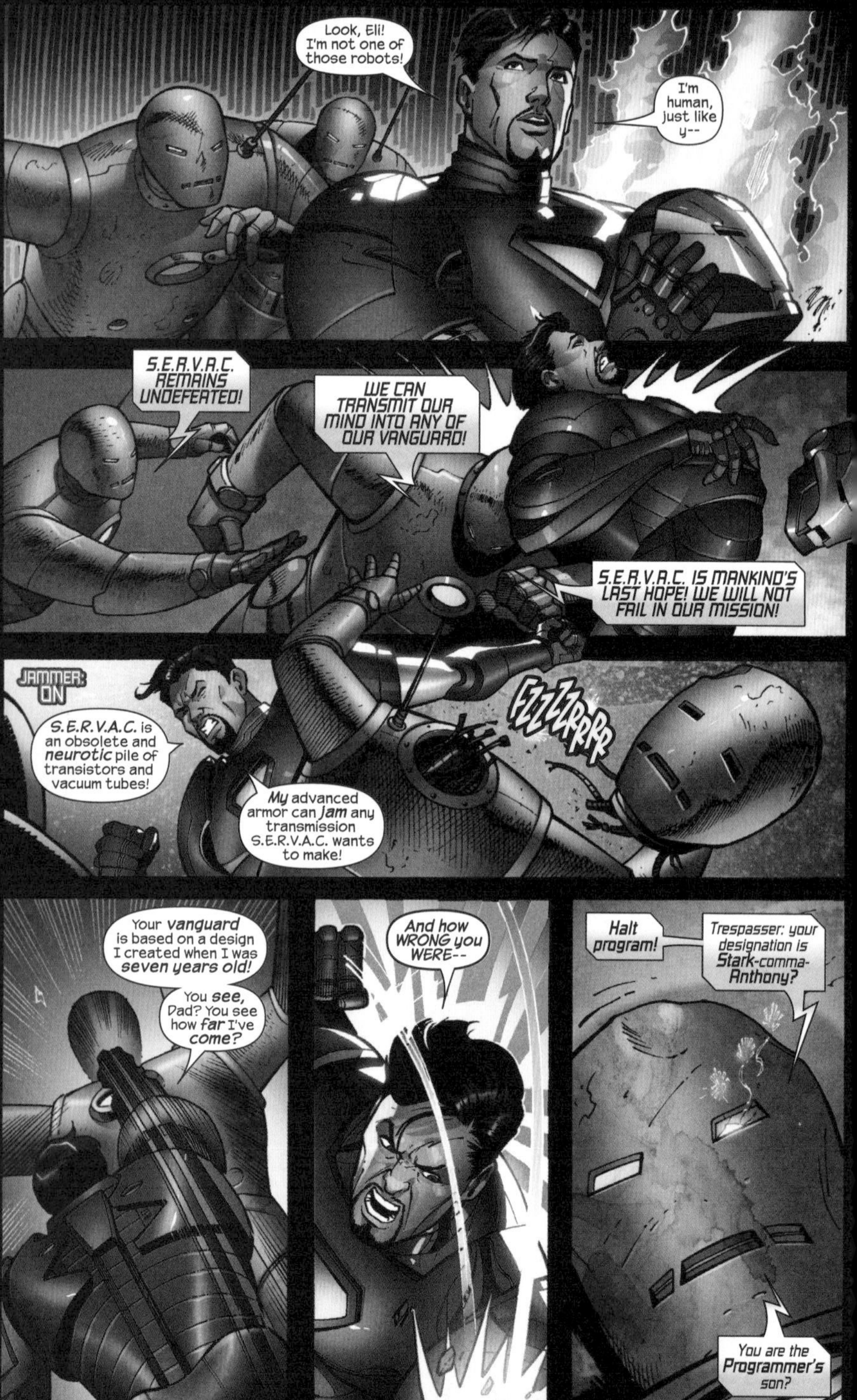
Look, Eli! I'm not one of those robots!
I'm human, just like y--
S.E.R.V.A.C. REMAINS UNDEFEATED!
WE CAN TRANSMIT OUR MIND INTO ANY OF OUR VANGUARD!
S.E.R.V.A.C. IS MANKIND'S LAST HOPE! WE WILL NOT FAIL IN OUR MISSION!
JAMMER: ON
S.E.R.V.A.C. is an obsolete and neurotic pile of transistors and vacuum tubes!
My advanced armor can jam any transmission S.E.R.V.A.C. wants to make!
FZZZZRRRR
Your vanguard is based on a design I created when I was seven years old!
You see, Dad? You see how far I've come?
And how WRONG you WERE--
Halt program!
Trespasser: your designation is Stark-comma-Anthony?
You are the Programmer's son?

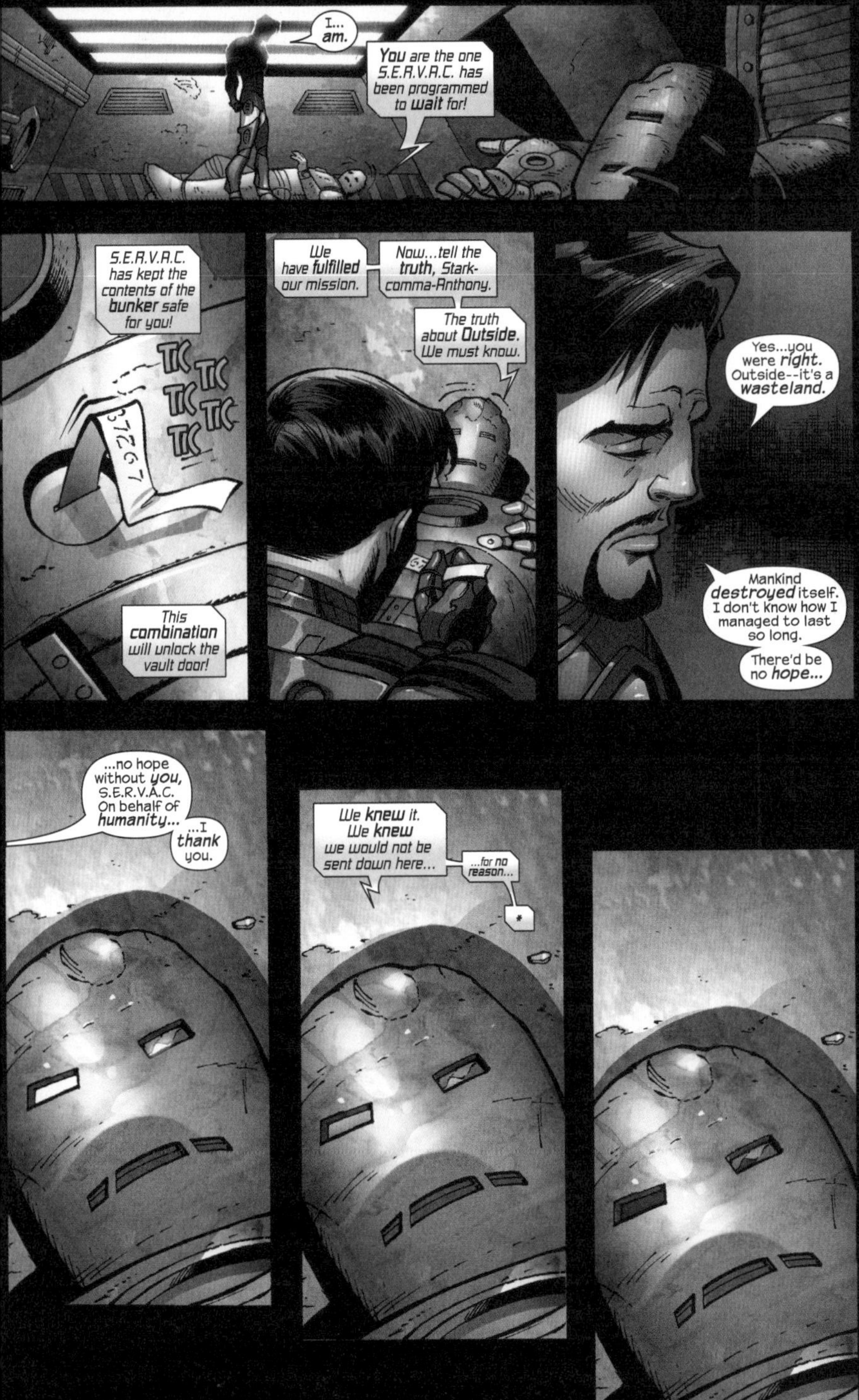

I... am.
You are the one S.E.R.V.A.C. has been programmed to wait for!
S.E.R.V.A.C. has kept the contents of the bunker safe for you!
TIC TIC TIC TIC TIC
37267
This combination will unlock the vault door!
We have fulfilled our mission.
Now...tell the truth, Stark-comma-Anthony.
The truth about Outside. We must know.
Yes...you were right. Outside--it's a wasteland.
Mankind destroyed itself. I don't know how I managed to last so long.
There'd be no hope...
...no hope without you, S.E.R.V.A.C. On behalf of humanity...
...I thank you.
We knew it. We knew we would not be sent down here...
...for no reason...
*

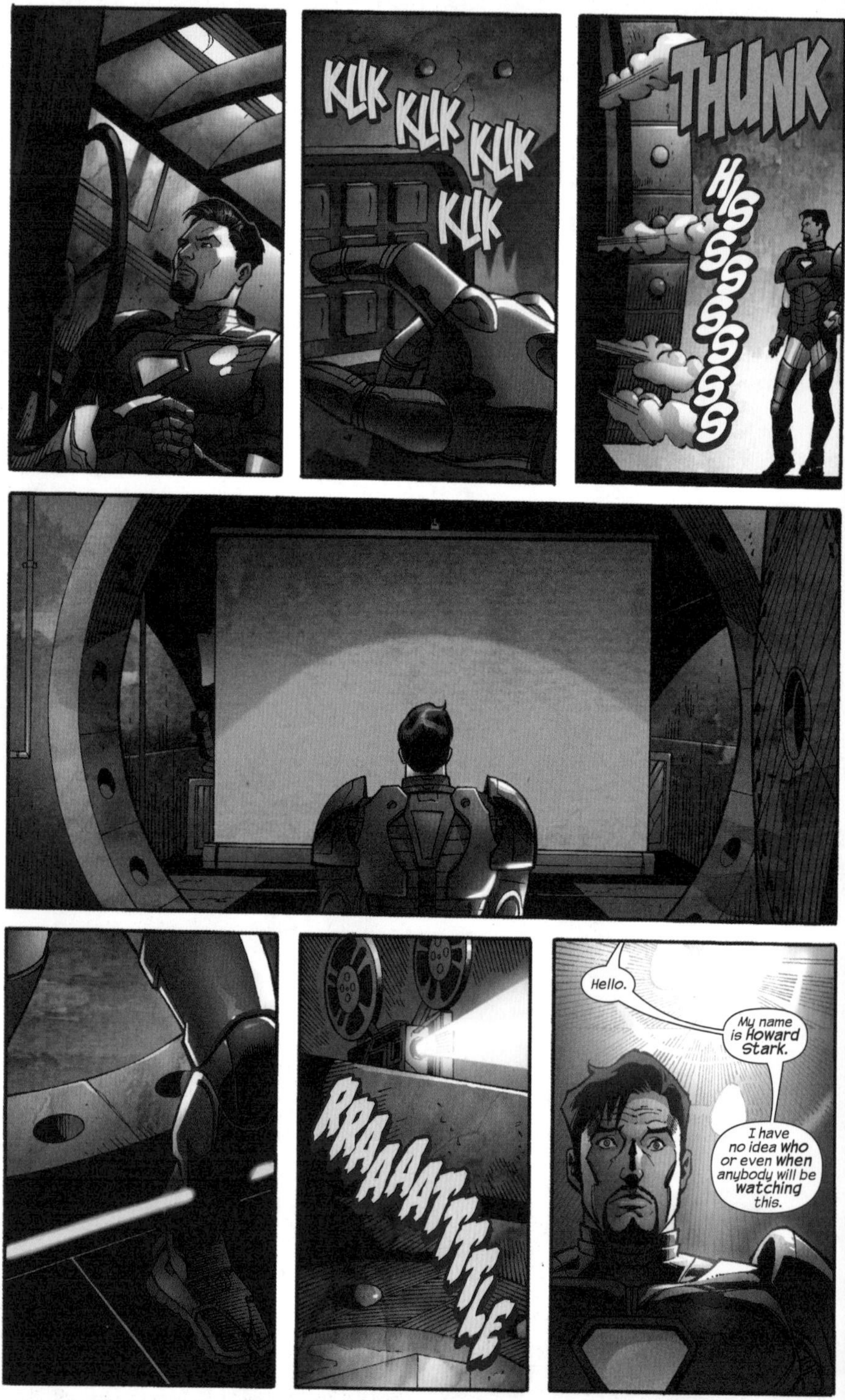
KLIK KLIK KLIK
KLIK
THUNK
HISSSSSSSS
RRAAAATTTTLE
Hello.
My name is Howard Stark.
I have no idea who or even when anybody will be watching this.

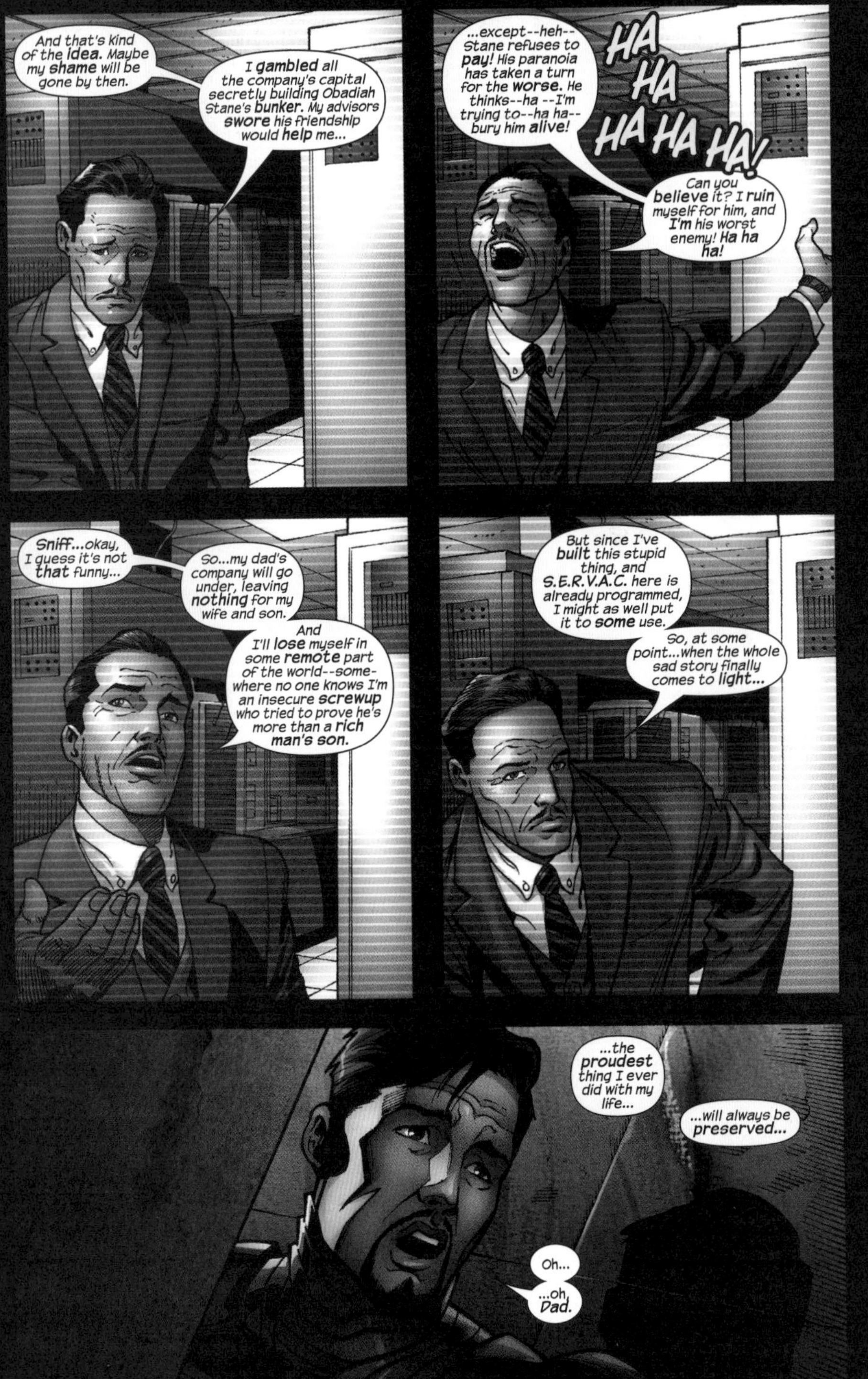
And that's kind of the idea. Maybe my shame will be gone by then.
I gambled all the company's capital secretly building Obadiah Stane's bunker. My advisors swore his friendship would help me...
...except--heh--Stane refuses to pay! His paranoia has taken a turn for the worse. He thinks--ha --I'm trying to--ha ha--bury him alive!
HA HA HA HA HA!
Can you believe it? I ruin myself for him, and I'm his worst enemy! Ha ha ha!
Sniff...okay, I guess it's not that funny...
So...my dad's company will go under, leaving nothing for my wife and son.
And I'll lose myself in some remote part of the world--somewhere no one knows I'm an insecure screwup who tried to prove he's more than a rich man's son.
But since I've built this stupid thing, and S.E.R.V.A.C. here is already programmed, I might as well put it to some use.
So, at some point...when the whole sad story finally comes to light...
...the proudest thing I ever did with my life...
...will always be preserved...
Oh...
...oh, Dad.

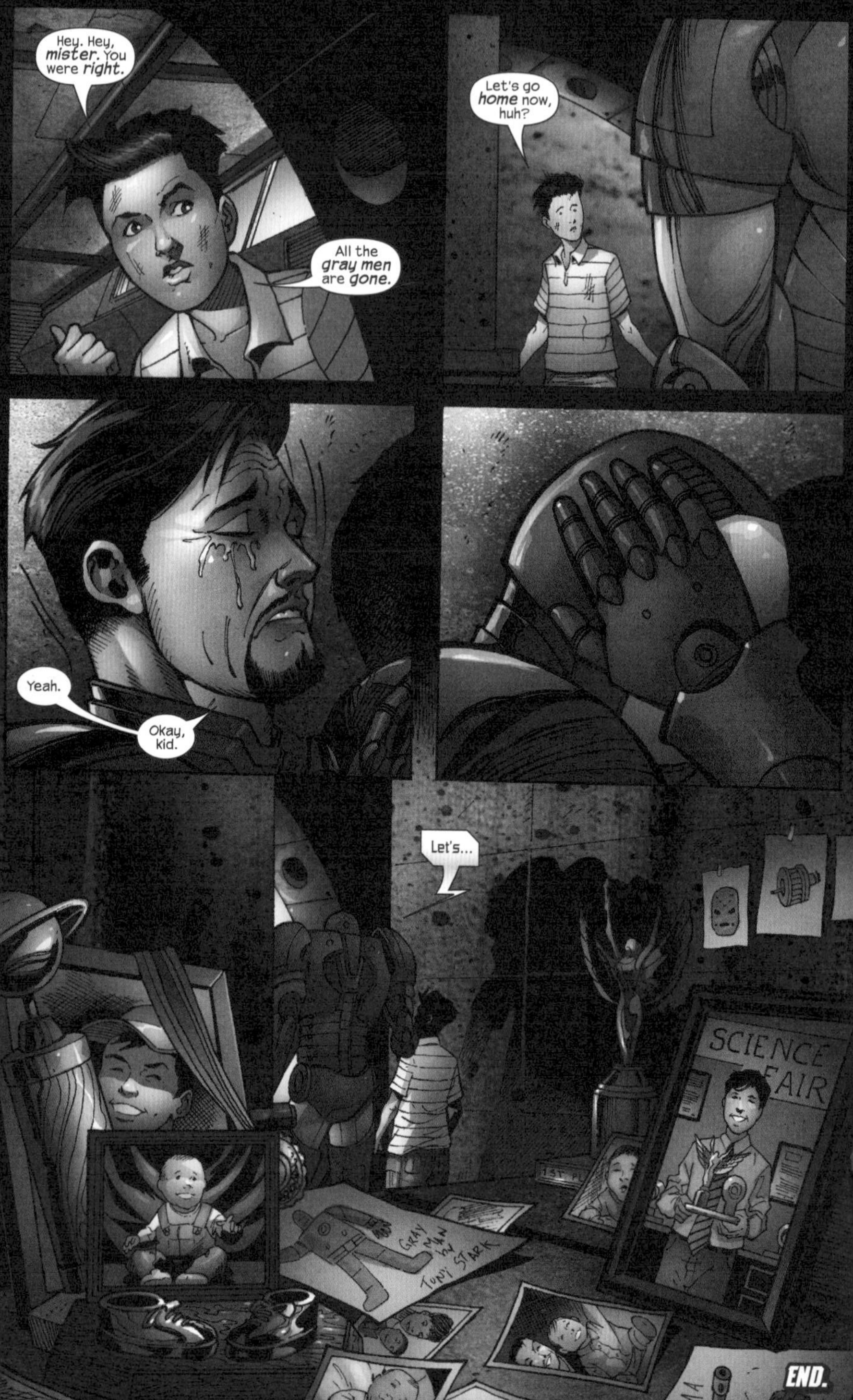
Hey. Hey, mister. You were right.
All the gray men are gone.
Let's go home now, huh?
Yeah.
Okay, kid.
Let's...
SCIENCE FAIR
GRAY MAN by TONI STARK
END.

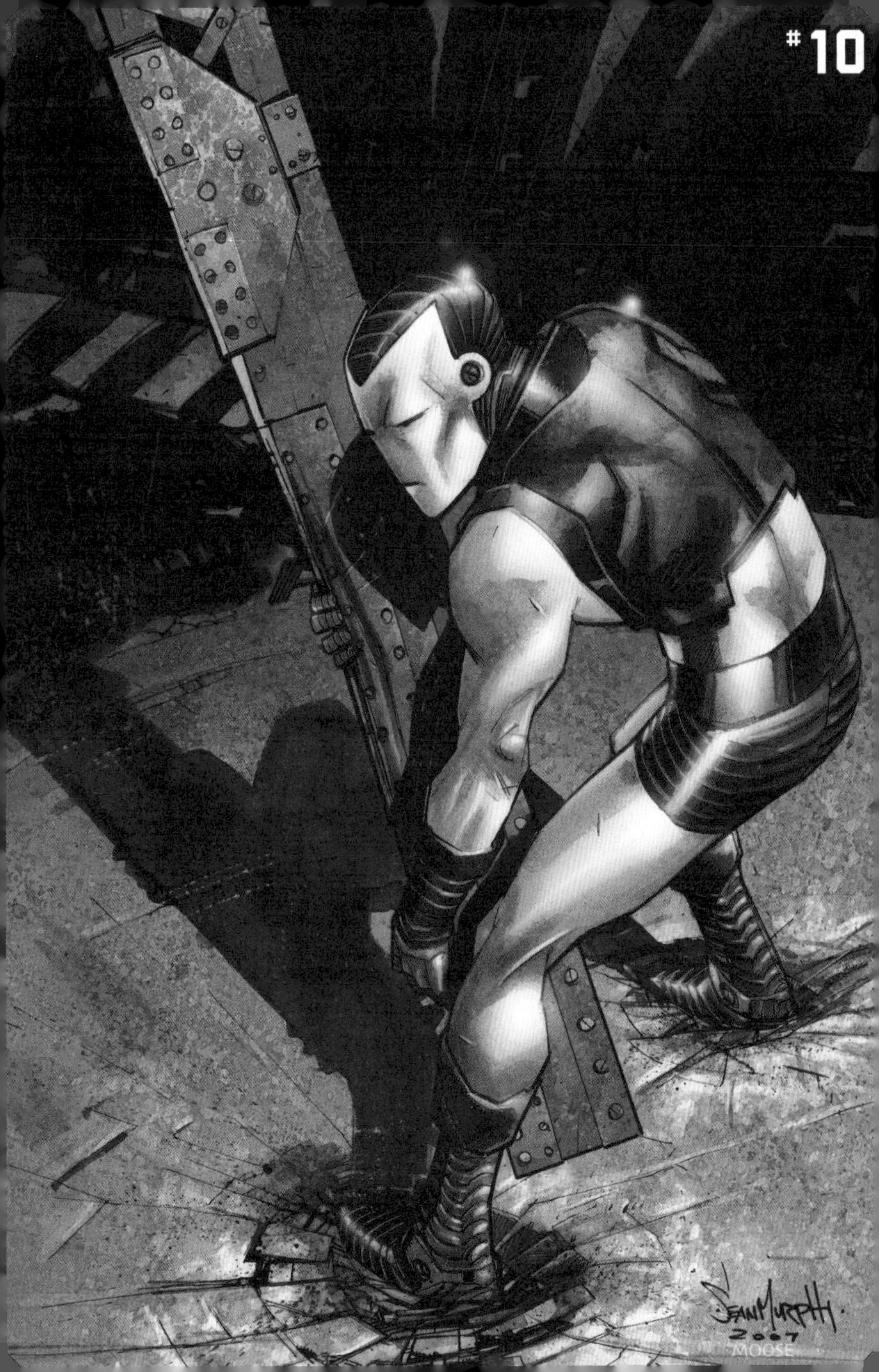
#10

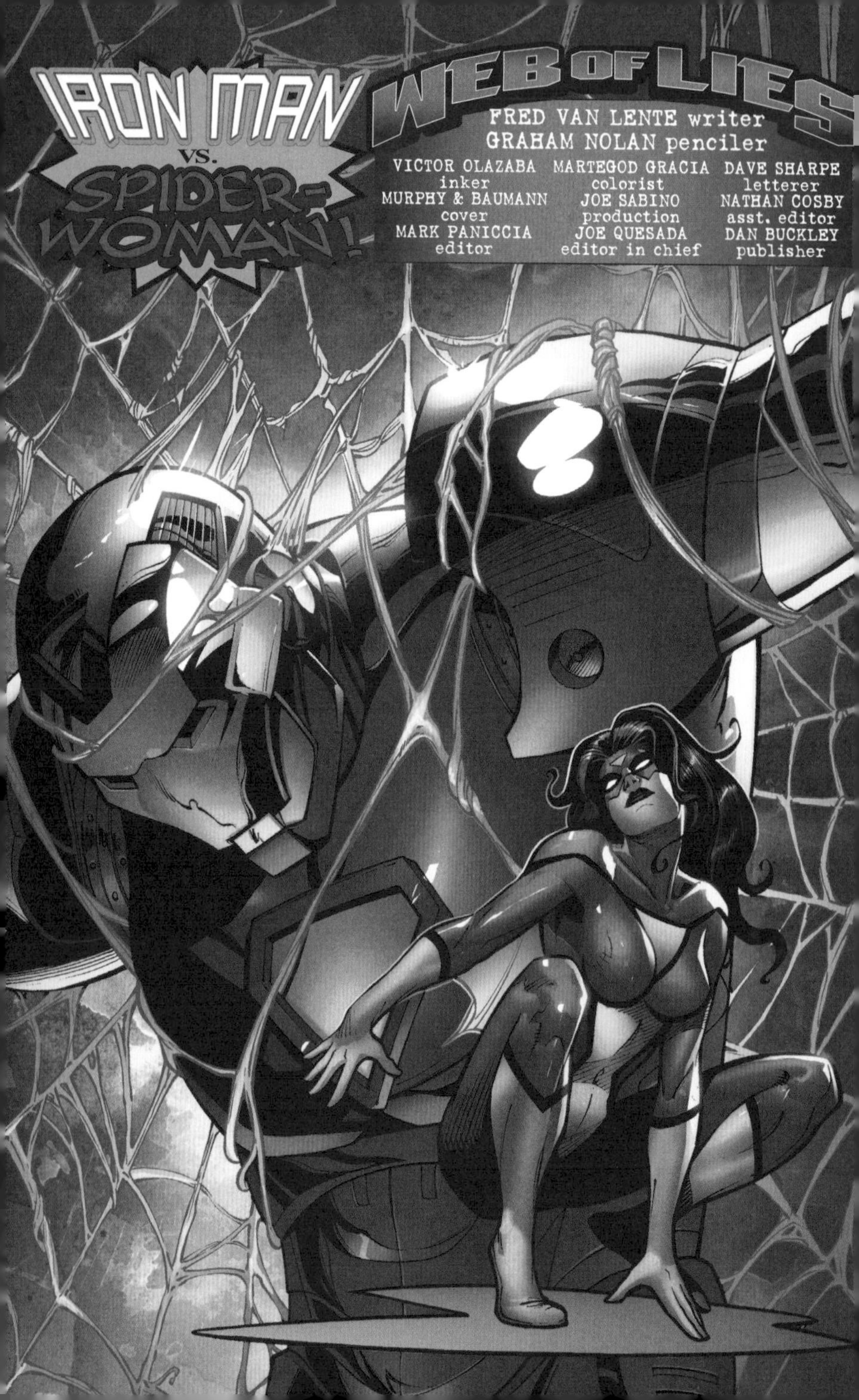
IRON MAN VS. SPIDER-WOMAN!
WEB OF LIES
FRED VAN LENTE writer
GRAHAM NOLAN penciler
VICTOR OLAZABA inker
MARTEGOD GRACIA colorist
DAVE SHARPE letterer
MURPHY & BAUMANN cover
JOE SABINO production
NATHAN COSBY asst. editor
MARK PANICCIA editor
JOE QUESADA editor in chief
DAN BUCKLEY publisher

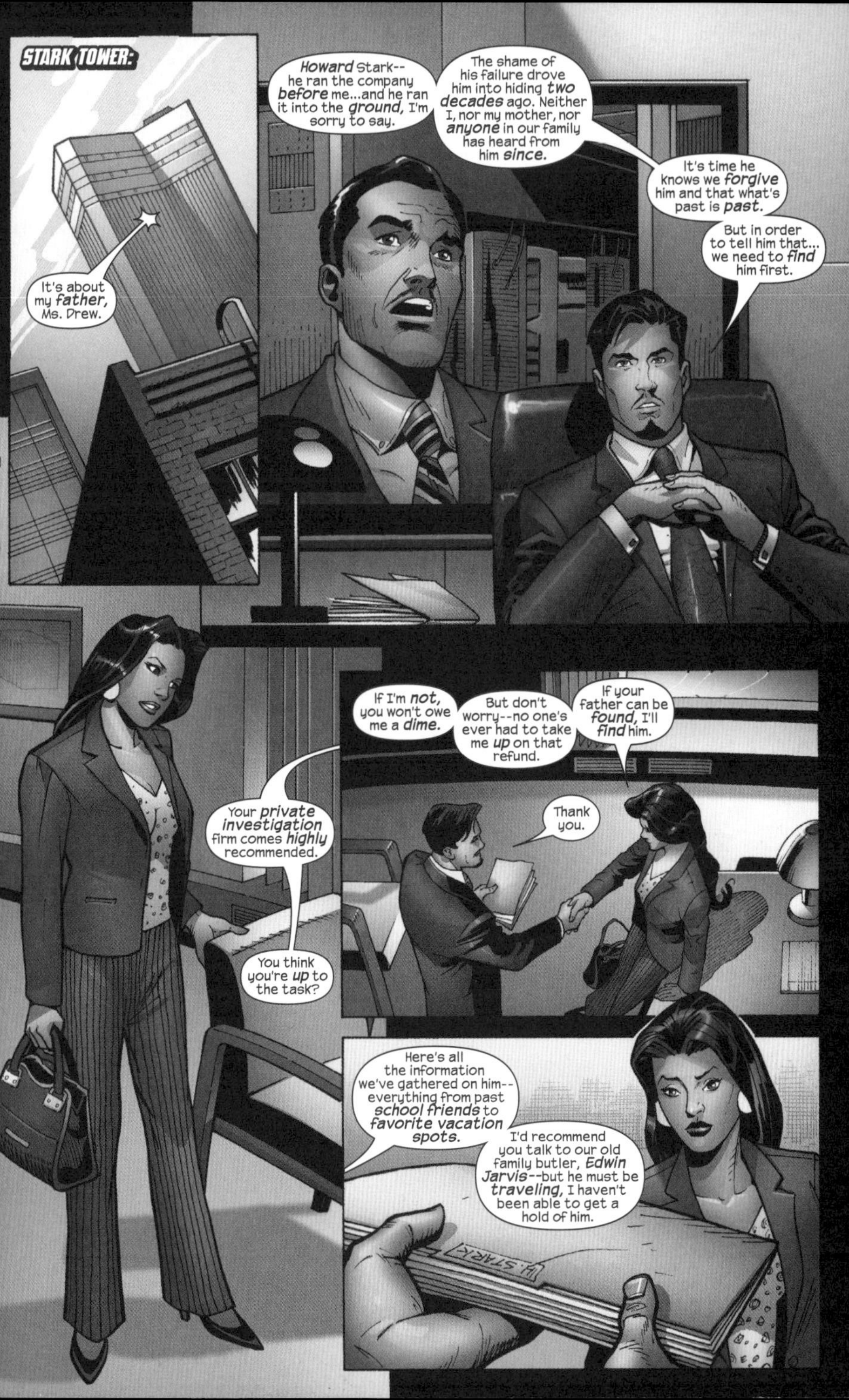
STARK TOWER:
It's about my father, Ms. Drew.
Howard Stark-- he ran the company before me...and he ran it into the ground, I'm sorry to say.
The shame of his failure drove him into hiding two decades ago. Neither I, nor my mother, nor anyone in our family has heard from him since.
It's time he knows we forgive him and that what's past is past.
But in order to tell him that... we need to find him first.
Your private investigation firm comes highly recommended.
You think you're up to the task?
If your father can be found, I'll find him.
But don't worry--no one's ever had to take me up on that refund.
If I'm not, you won't owe me a dime.
Thank you.
Here's all the information we've gathered on him-- everything from past school friends to favorite vacation spots.
I'd recommend you talk to our old family butler, Edwin Jarvis--but he must be traveling, I haven't been able to get a hold of him.
H. STARK

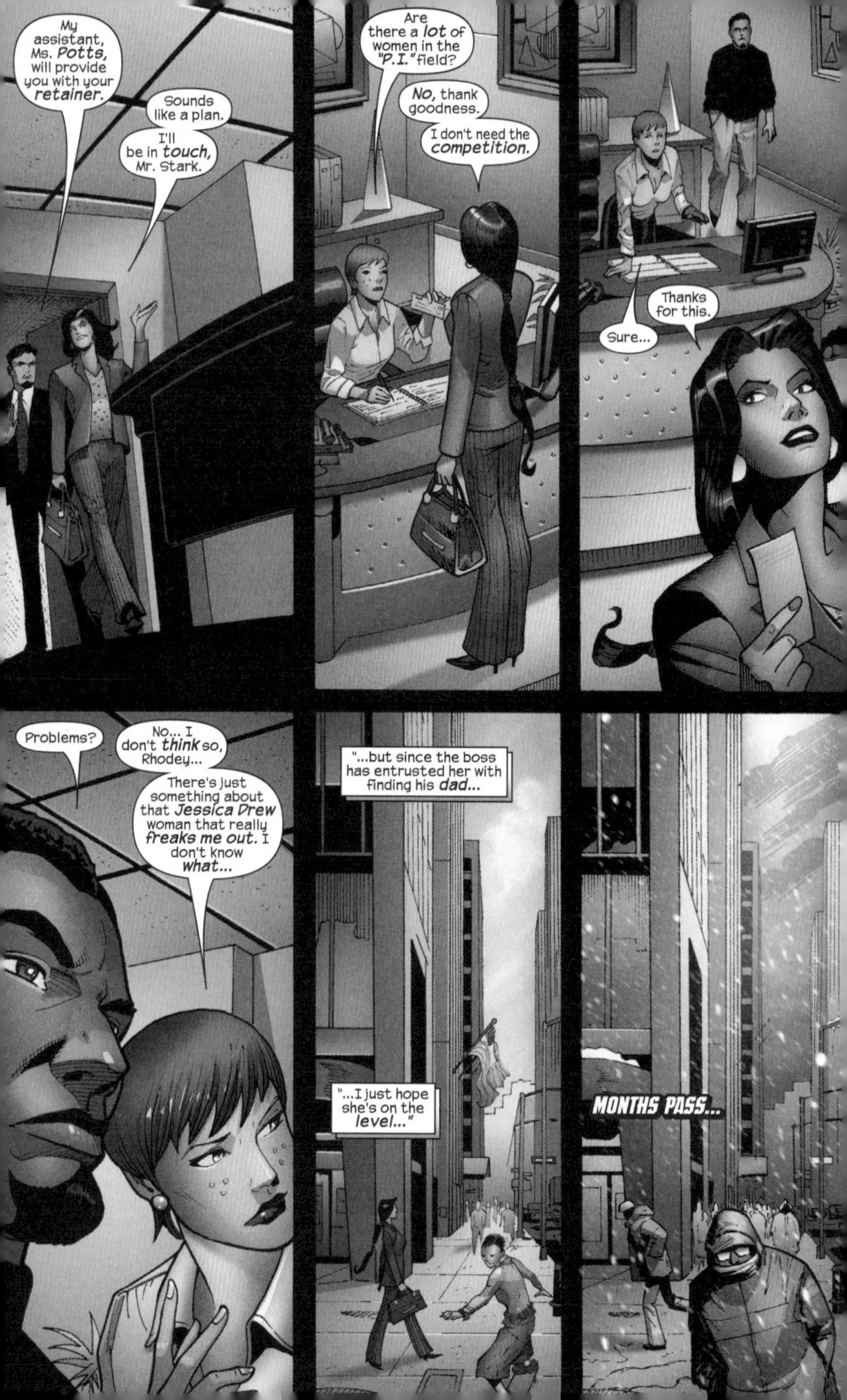
My assistant, Ms. Potts, will provide you with your retainer.
Sounds like a plan.
I'll be in touch, Mr. Stark.
Are there a lot of women in the "P.I." field?
No, thank goodness.
I don't need the competition.
Thanks for this.
Sure...
Problems?
No... I don't think so, Rhodey...
There's just something about that Jessica Drew woman that really freaks me out. I don't know what...
"...but since the boss has entrusted her with finding his dad...
"...I just hope she's on the level..."
MONTHS PASS...

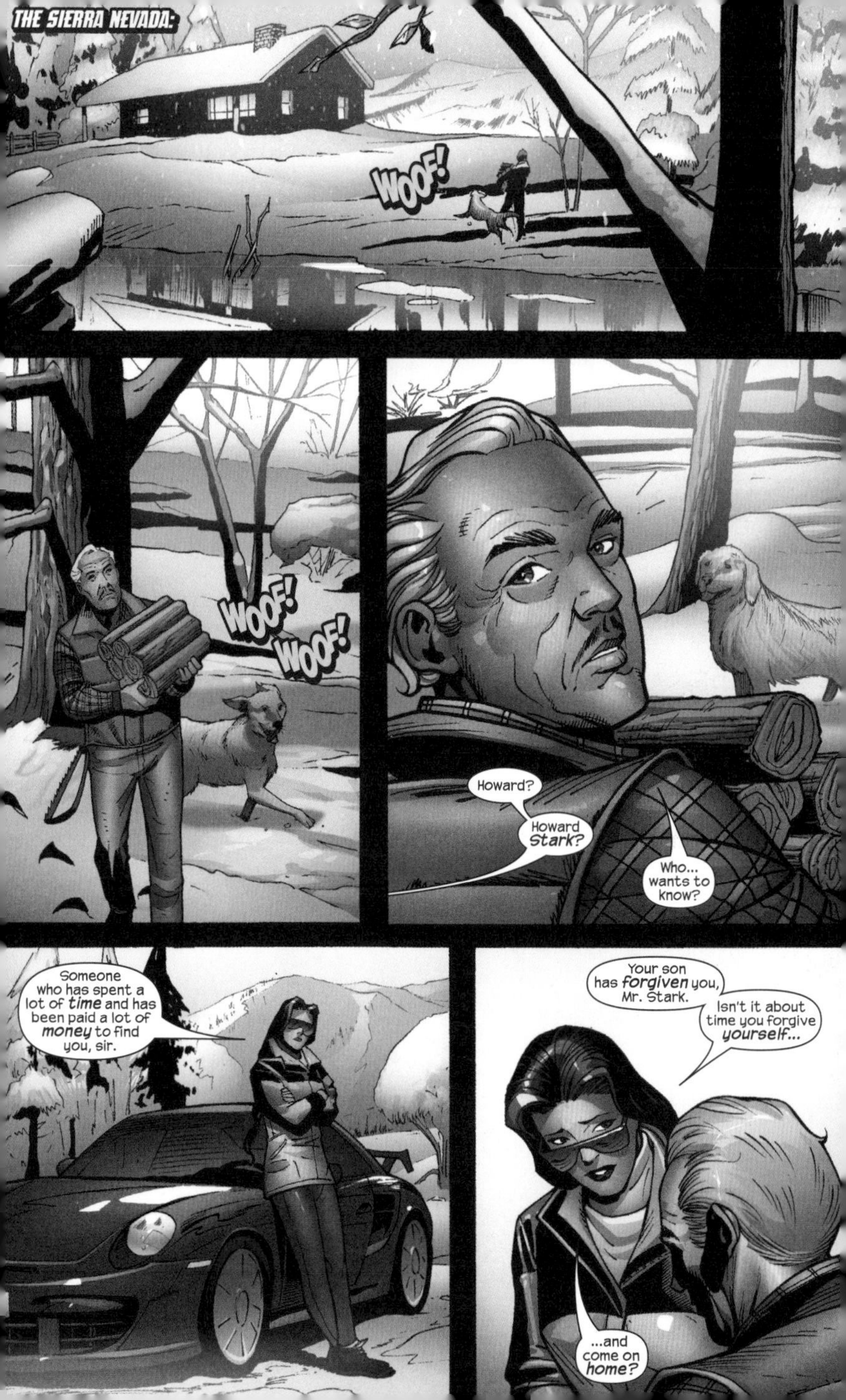
THE SIERRA NEVADA:
WOOF!
WOOF!
WOOF!
Howard?
Howard Stark?
Who... wants to know?
Someone who has spent a lot of time and has been paid a lot of money to find you, sir.
Your son has forgiven you, Mr. Stark.
Isn't it about time you forgive yourself...
...and come on home?

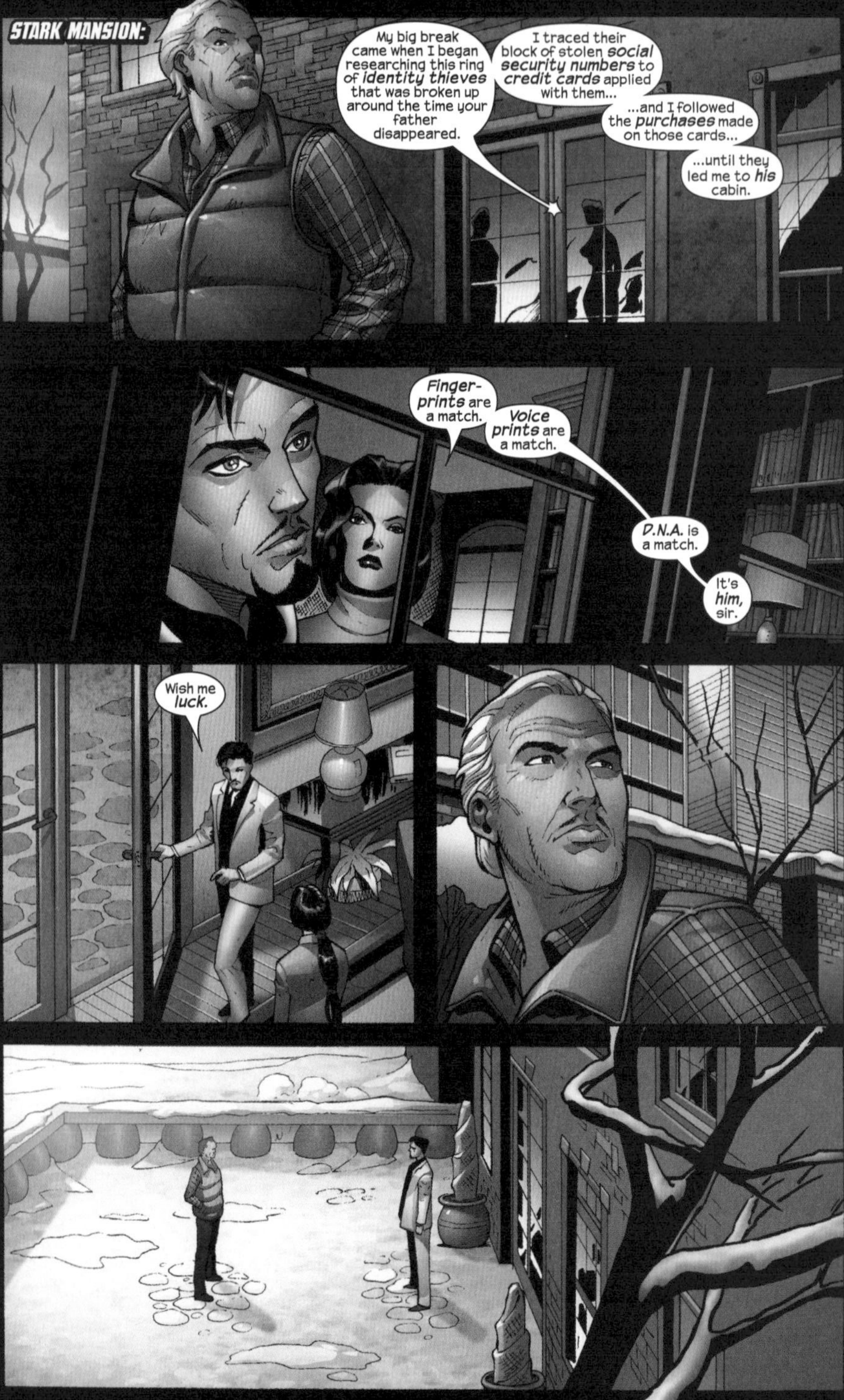
STARK MANSION:
My big break came when I began researching this ring of *identity thieves* that was broken up around the time your father disappeared.
I traced their block of stolen *social security numbers* to *credit cards* applied with them...
...and I followed the *purchases* made on those cards...
...until they led me to *his* cabin.
Finger-prints are a match.
Voice prints are a match.
D.N.A. is a match.
It's *him,* sir.
Wish me *luck.*

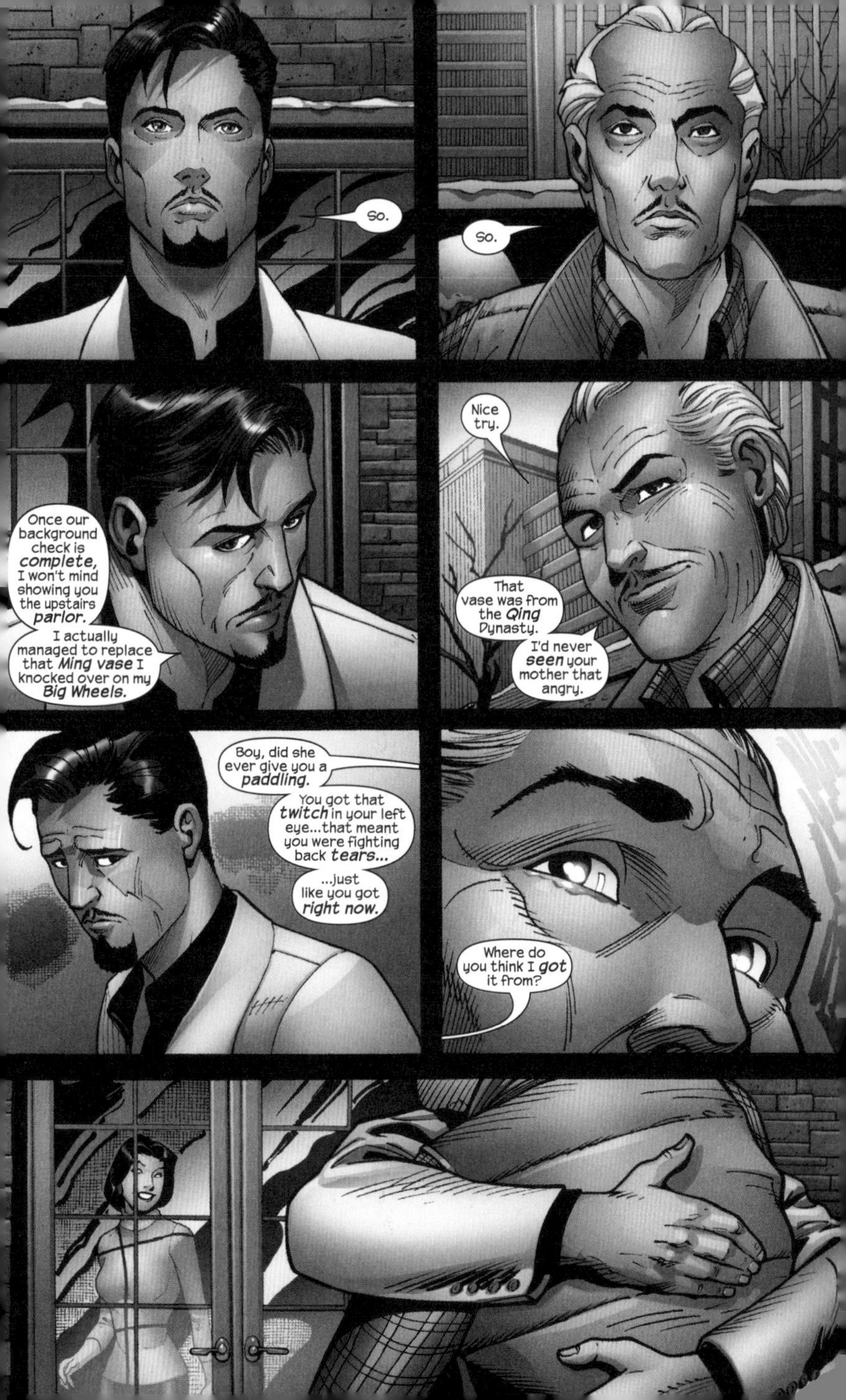
So.
So.
Once our background check is *complete*, I won't mind showing you the upstairs *parlor*.
I actually managed to replace that *Ming vase* I knocked over on my *Big Wheels*.
Nice try.
That vase was from the *Qing* Dynasty.
I'd never *seen* your mother that angry.
Boy, did she ever give you a *paddling*.
You got that *twitch* in your left eye...that meant you were fighting back *tears...*
...just like you got *right now*.
Where do you think I *got* it from?

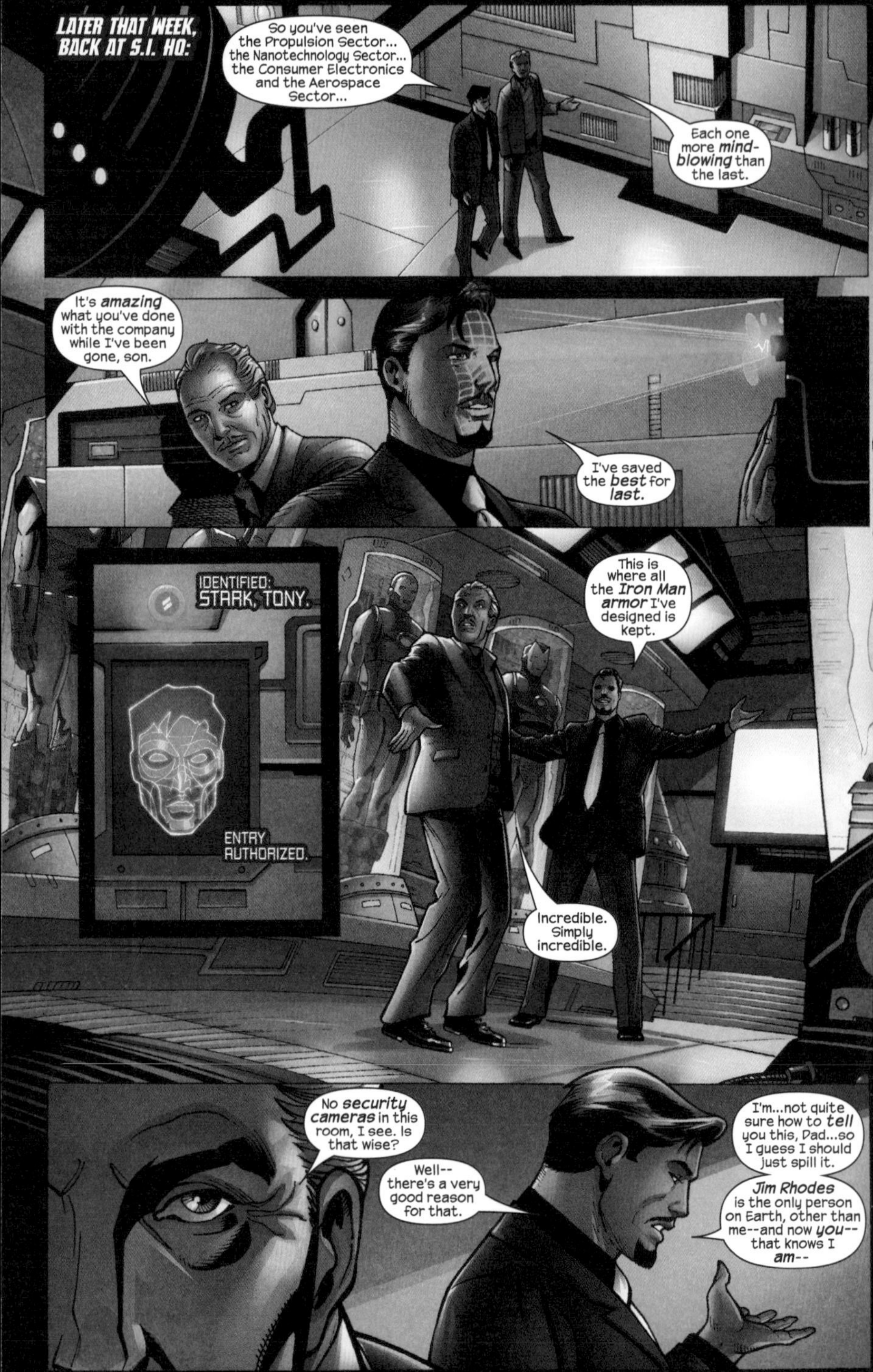
LATER THAT WEEK, BACK AT S.I. HQ:
So you've seen the Propulsion Sector... the Nanotechnology Sector... the Consumer Electronics and the Aerospace Sector...
Each one more mind-blowing than the last.
It's amazing what you've done with the company while I've been gone, son.
I've saved the best for last.
IDENTIFIED: STARK, TONY.
ENTRY AUTHORIZED.
This is where all the Iron Man armor I've designed is kept.
Incredible. Simply incredible.
No security cameras in this room, I see. Is that wise?
Well-- there's a very good reason for that.
I'm...not quite sure how to tell you this, Dad...so I guess I should just spill it.
Jim Rhodes is the only person on Earth, other than me--and now you-- that knows I am--

No cameras means no prying eyes will see me *change...*

...into my *true* form!

Chameleon to *Advanced Idea Mechanics!* Do you read me?

This is the *Scientist Supreme.* Go ahead, Chameleon.

Phase One is a *complete success.* My power to mimic voices and appearances, even *fingerprints,* convinced his ears and eyes I was Howard Stark...

...the *Stark D.N.A.* you acquired when Tony *himself* was a...*guest* of your organization convinced his *machines...*

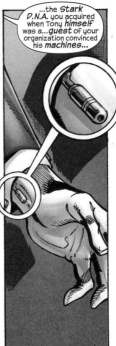

...and, of course, your *ace-in-the-hole* convinced his *heart.*

I shall initiate Phase Two *immediately...*

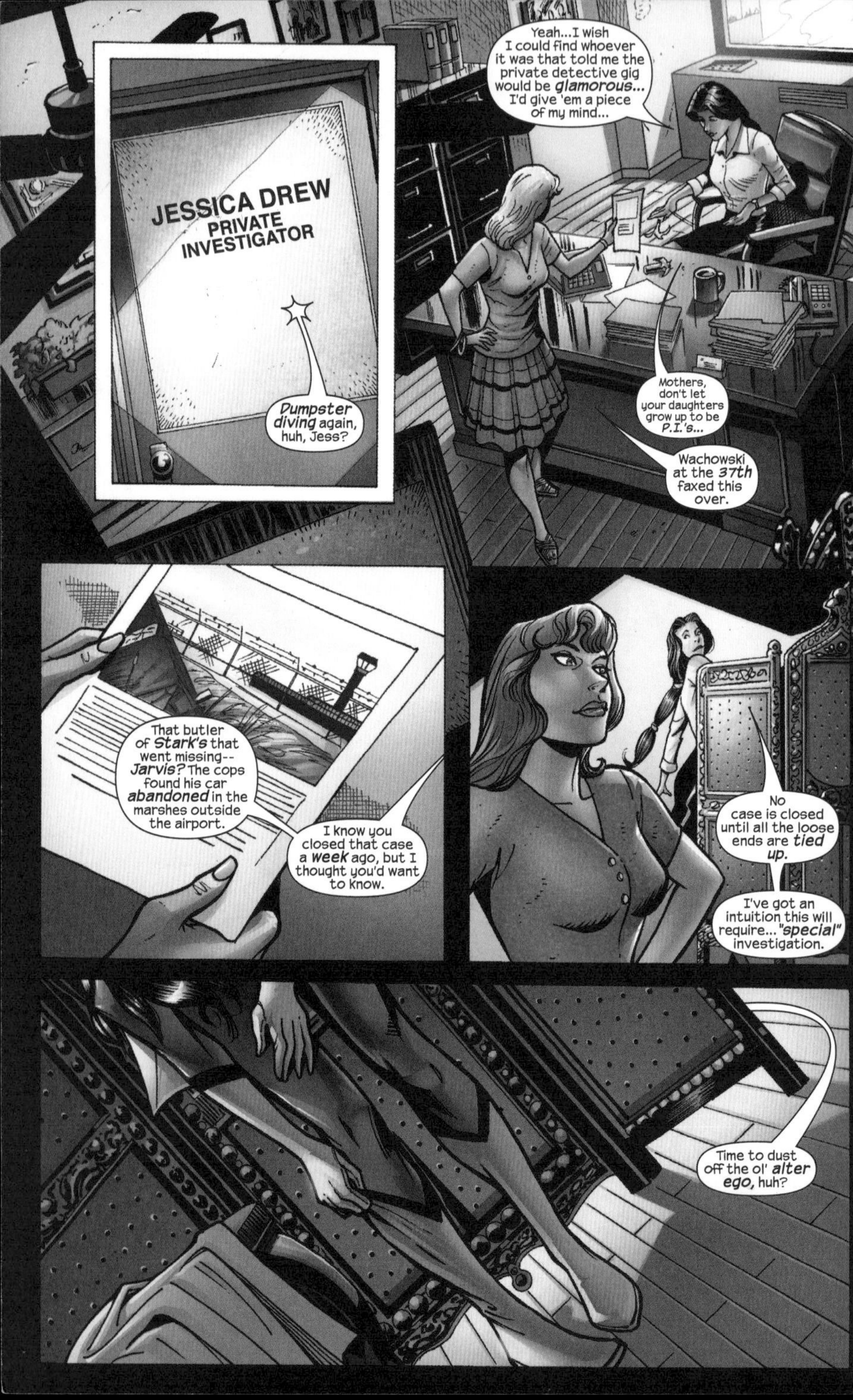
JESSICA DREW
PRIVATE INVESTIGATOR
Dumpster diving again, huh, Jess?
Yeah...I wish I could find whoever it was that told me the private detective gig would be glamorous... I'd give 'em a piece of my mind...
Mothers, don't let your daughters grow up to be P.I.'s...
Wachowski at the 37th faxed this over.
That butler of Stark's that went missing-- Jarvis? The cops found his car abandoned in the marshes outside the airport.
I know you closed that case a week ago, but I thought you'd want to know.
No case is closed until all the loose ends are tied up.
I've got an intuition this will require... "special" investigation.
Time to dust off the ol' alter ego, huh?

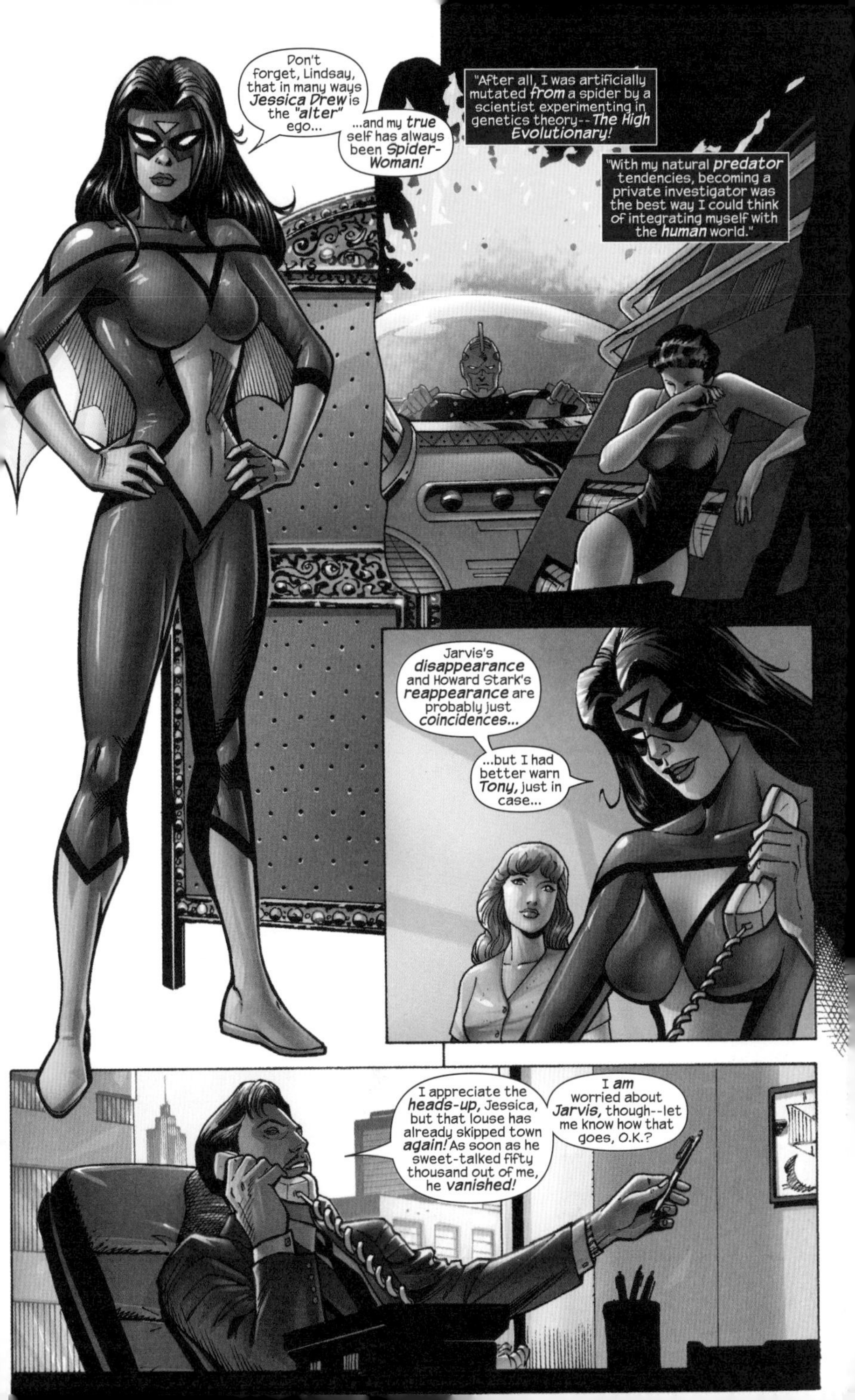
Don't forget, Lindsay, that in many ways Jessica Drew is the "alter" ego...
...and my true self has always been Spider-Woman!
"After all, I was artificially mutated from a spider by a scientist experimenting in genetics theory-- The High Evolutionary!
"With my natural predator tendencies, becoming a private investigator was the best way I could think of integrating myself with the human world."
Jarvis's disappearance and Howard Stark's reappearance are probably just coincidences...
...but I had better warn Tony, just in case...
I appreciate the heads-up, Jessica, but that louse has already skipped town again! As soon as he sweet-talked fifty thousand out of me, he vanished!
I am worried about Jarvis, though--let me know how that goes, O.K.?

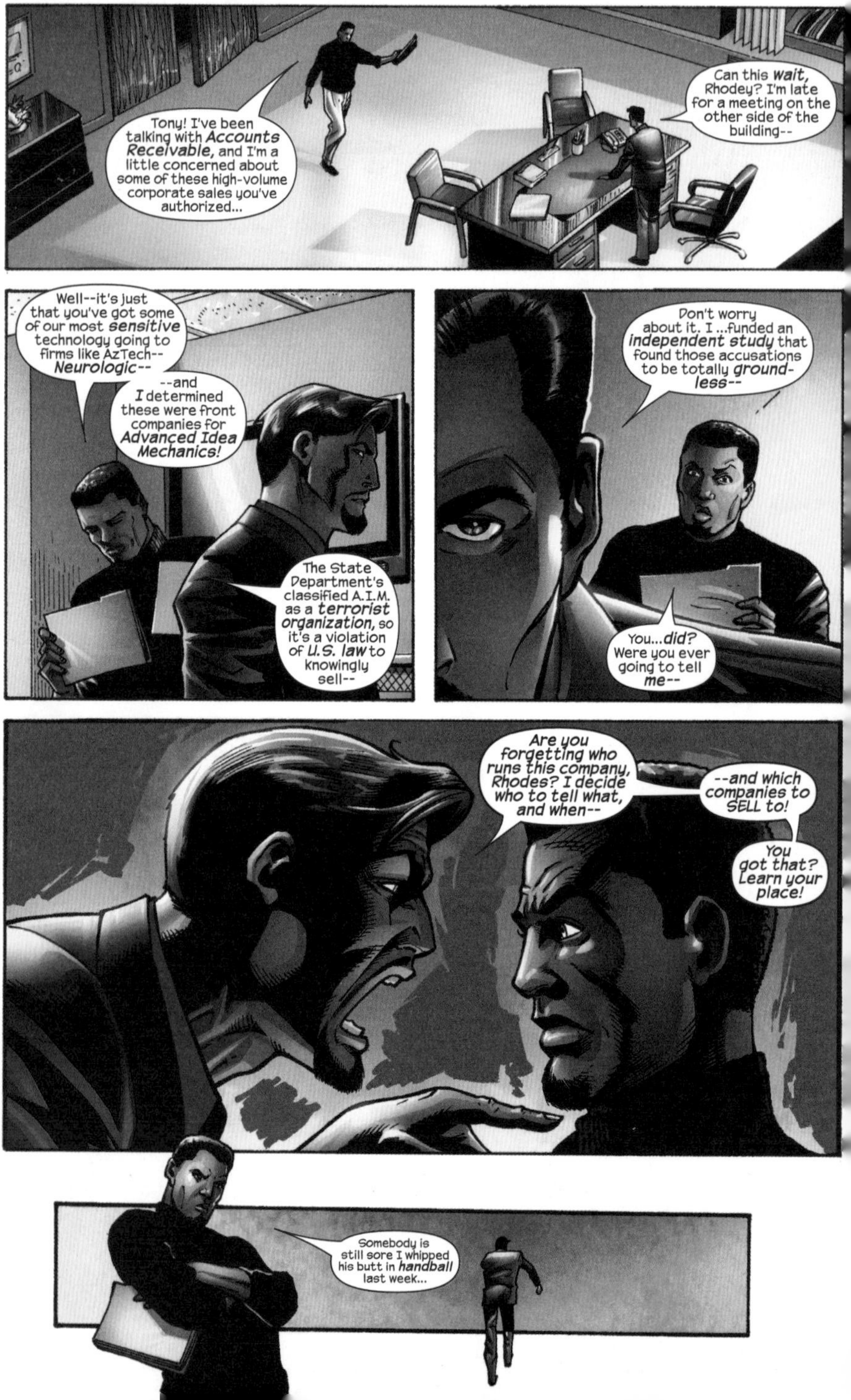
Tony! I've been talking with Accounts Receivable, and I'm a little concerned about some of these high-volume corporate sales you've authorized...
Can this wait, Rhodey? I'm late for a meeting on the other side of the building--
Well--it's just that you've got some of our most sensitive technology going to firms like AzTech--Neurologic--
--and I determined these were front companies for Advanced Idea Mechanics!
The State Department's classified A.I.M. as a terrorist organization, so it's a violation of U.S. law to knowingly sell--
Don't worry about it. I ...funded an independent study that found those accusations to be totally groundless--
You...did? Were you ever going to tell me--
Are you forgetting who runs this company, Rhodes? I decide who to tell what, and when--
--and which companies to SELL to!
You got that? Learn your place!
Somebody is still sore I whipped his butt in handball last week...

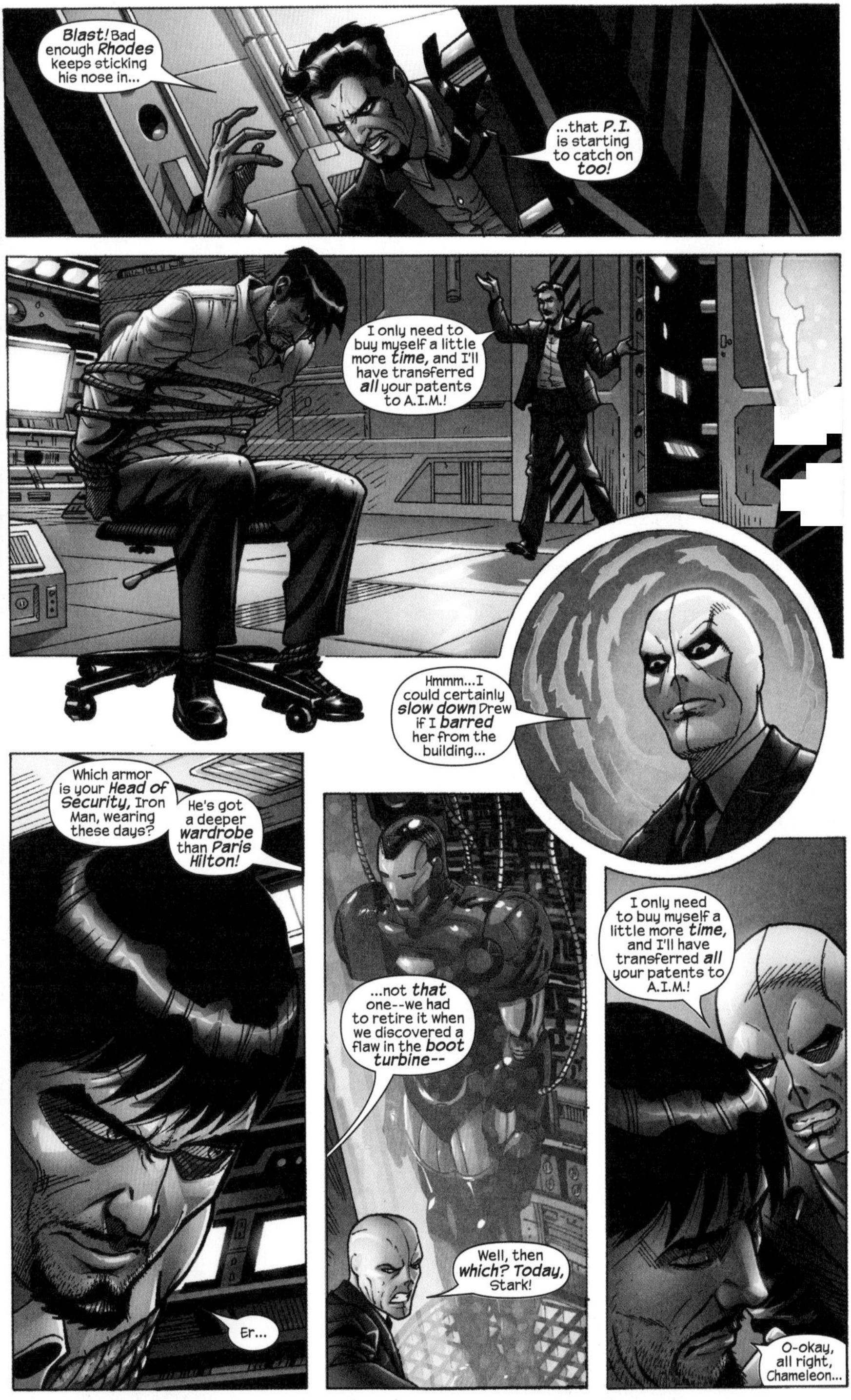
Blast! Bad enough Rhodes keeps sticking his nose in...
...that P.I. is starting to catch on too!
I only need to buy myself a little more time, and I'll have transferred all your patents to A.I.M.!
Hmmm...I could certainly slow down Drew if I barred her from the building...
Which armor is your Head of Security, Iron Man, wearing these days?
He's got a deeper wardrobe than Paris Hilton!
Er...
...not that one--we had to retire it when we discovered a flaw in the boot turbine--
Well, then which? Today, Stark!
I only need to buy myself a little more time, and I'll have transferred all your patents to A.I.M.!
O-okay, all right, Chameleon...

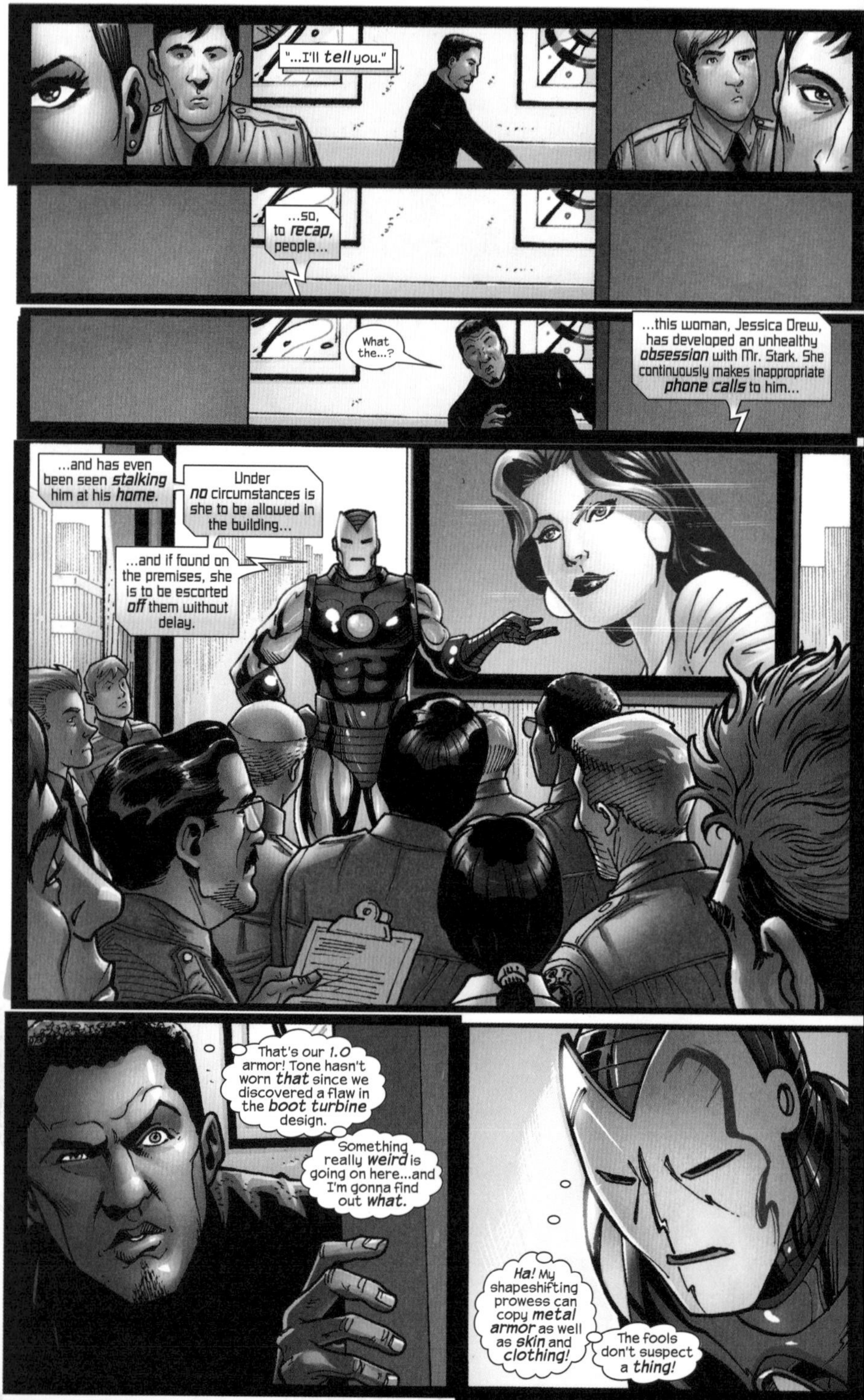
"...I'll tell you."
...so, to recap, people...
What the...?
...this woman, Jessica Drew, has developed an unhealthy obsession with Mr. Stark. She continuously makes inappropriate phone calls to him...
...and has even been seen stalking him at his home.
Under no circumstances is she to be allowed in the building...
...and if found on the premises, she is to be escorted off them without delay.
That's our 1.0 armor! Tone hasn't worn that since we discovered a flaw in the boot turbine design.
Something really weird is going on here...and I'm gonna find out what.
Ha! My shapeshifting prowess can copy metal armor as well as skin and clothing!
The fools don't suspect a thing!

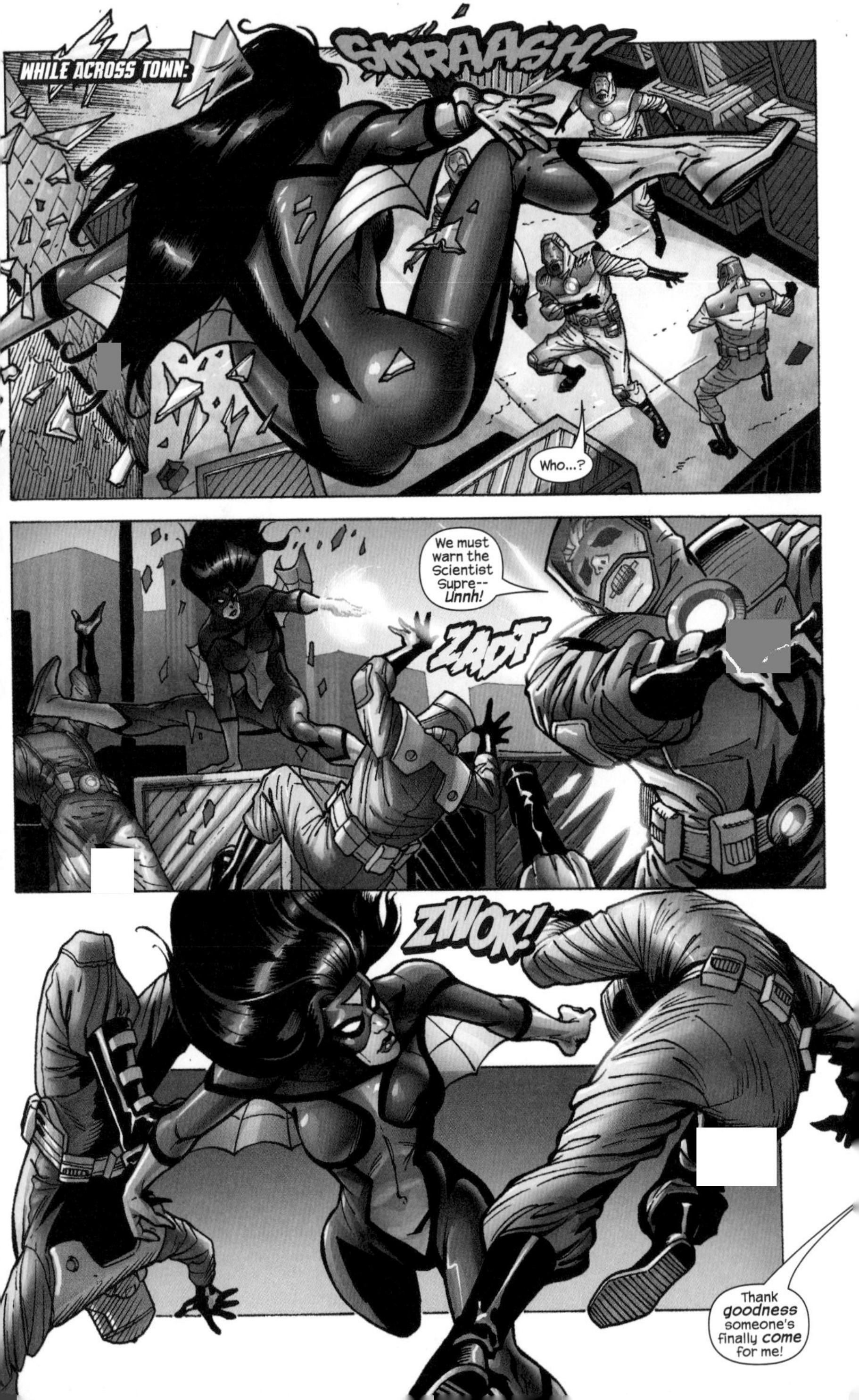
WHILE ACROSS TOWN:
SKRAASH!
Who...?
We must warn the Scientist Supre-- *Unnh!*
ZADT
ZWOK!
Thank *goodness* someone's finally *come* for me!

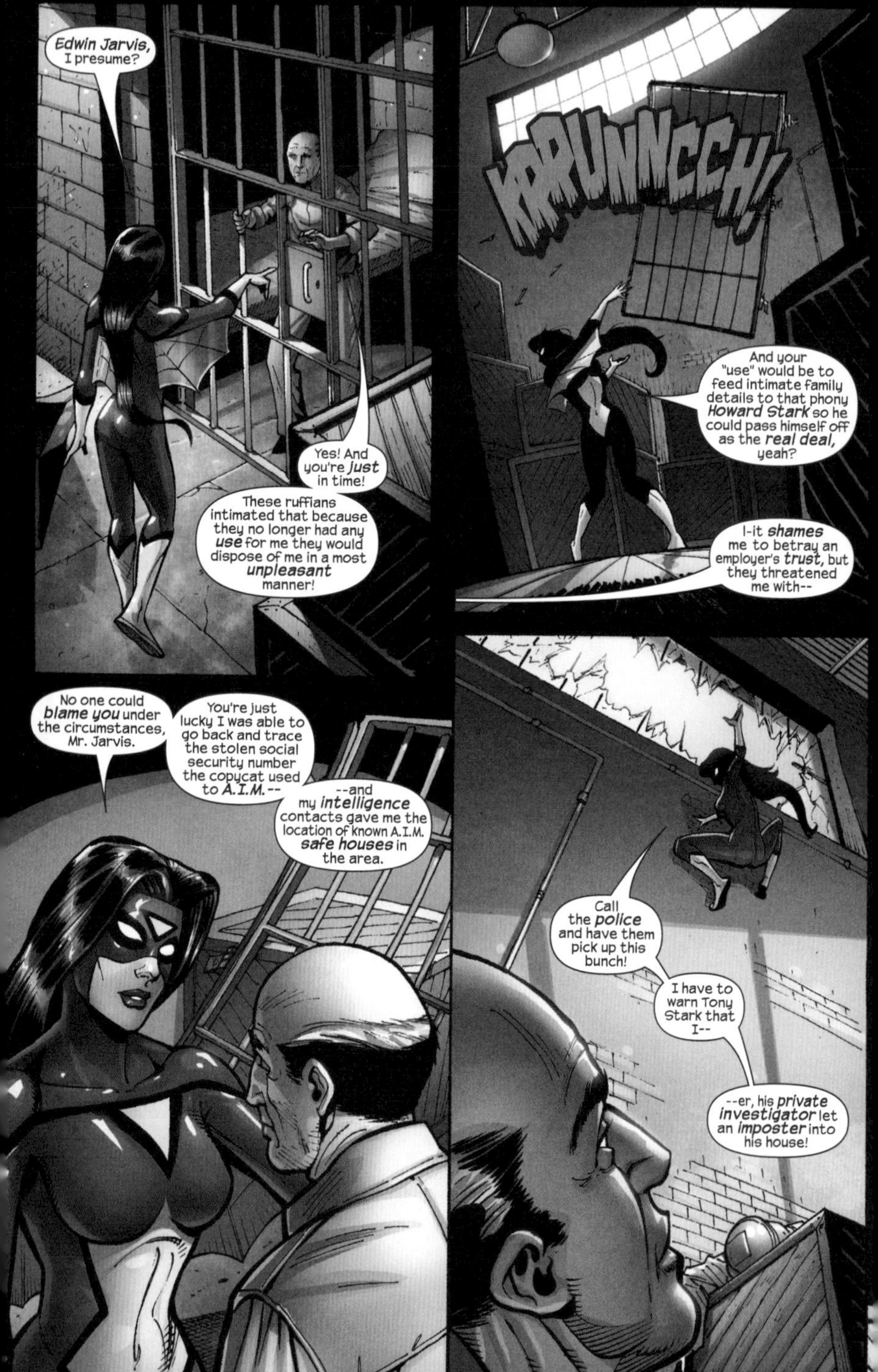

Edwin Jarvis, I presume?
Yes! And you're just in time!
These ruffians intimated that because they no longer had any use for me they would dispose of me in a most unpleasant manner!
KRRUNNCCH!
And your "use" would be to feed intimate family details to that phony Howard Stark so he could pass himself off as the real deal, yeah?
I-it shames me to betray an employer's trust, but they threatened me with--
No one could blame you under the circumstances, Mr. Jarvis.
You're just lucky I was able to go back and trace the stolen social security number the copycat used to A.I.M.--
--and my intelligence contacts gave me the location of known A.I.M. safe houses in the area.
Call the police and have them pick up this bunch!
I have to warn Tony Stark that I--
--er, his private investigator let an imposter into his house!

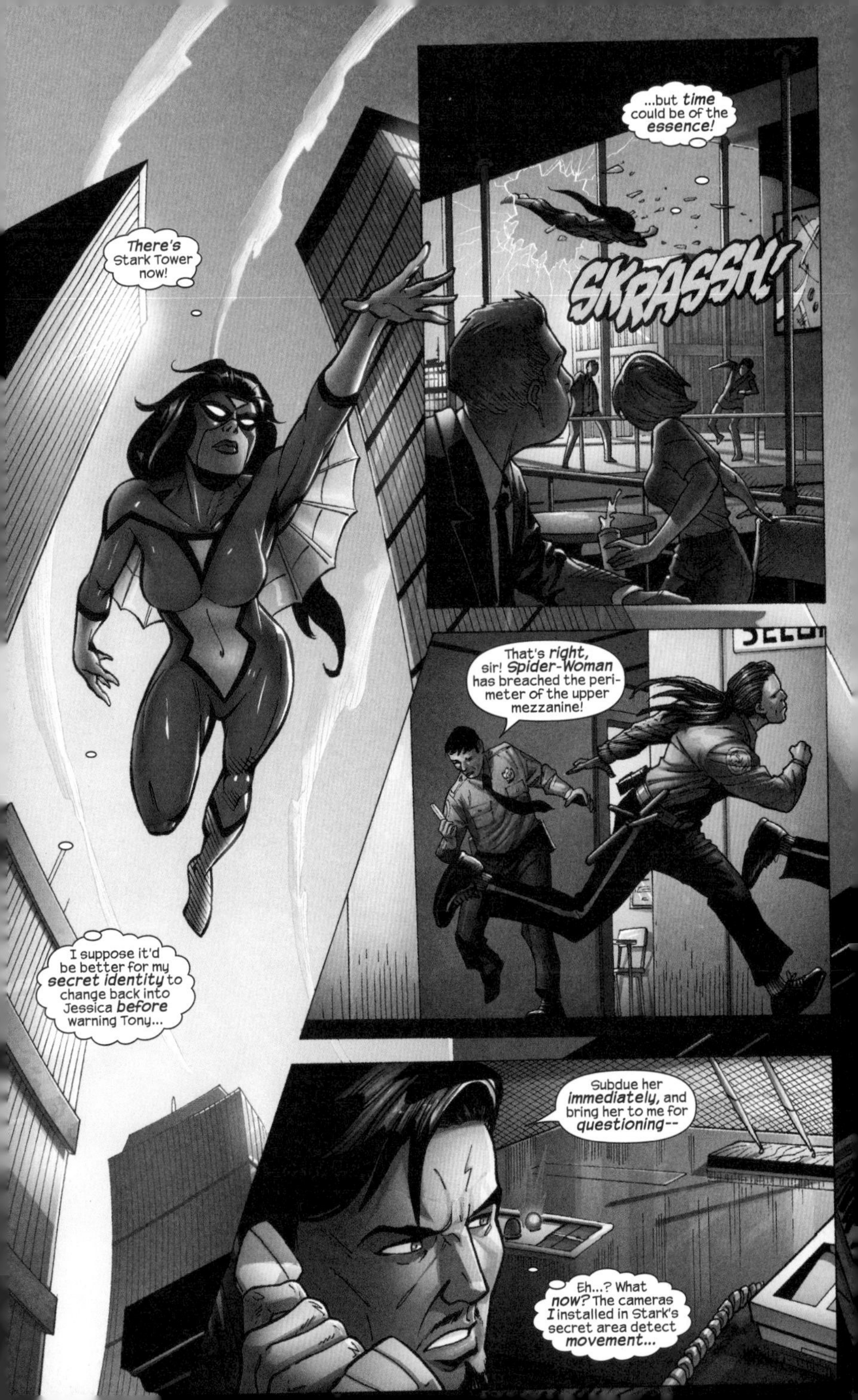

There's Stark Tower now!
I suppose it'd be better for my secret identity to change back into Jessica before warning Tony...
...but time could be of the essence!
SKRASSH!
That's right, sir! Spider-Woman has breached the perimeter of the upper mezzanine!
Subdue her immediately, and bring her to me for questioning--
Eh...? What now? The cameras I installed in Stark's secret area detect movement...

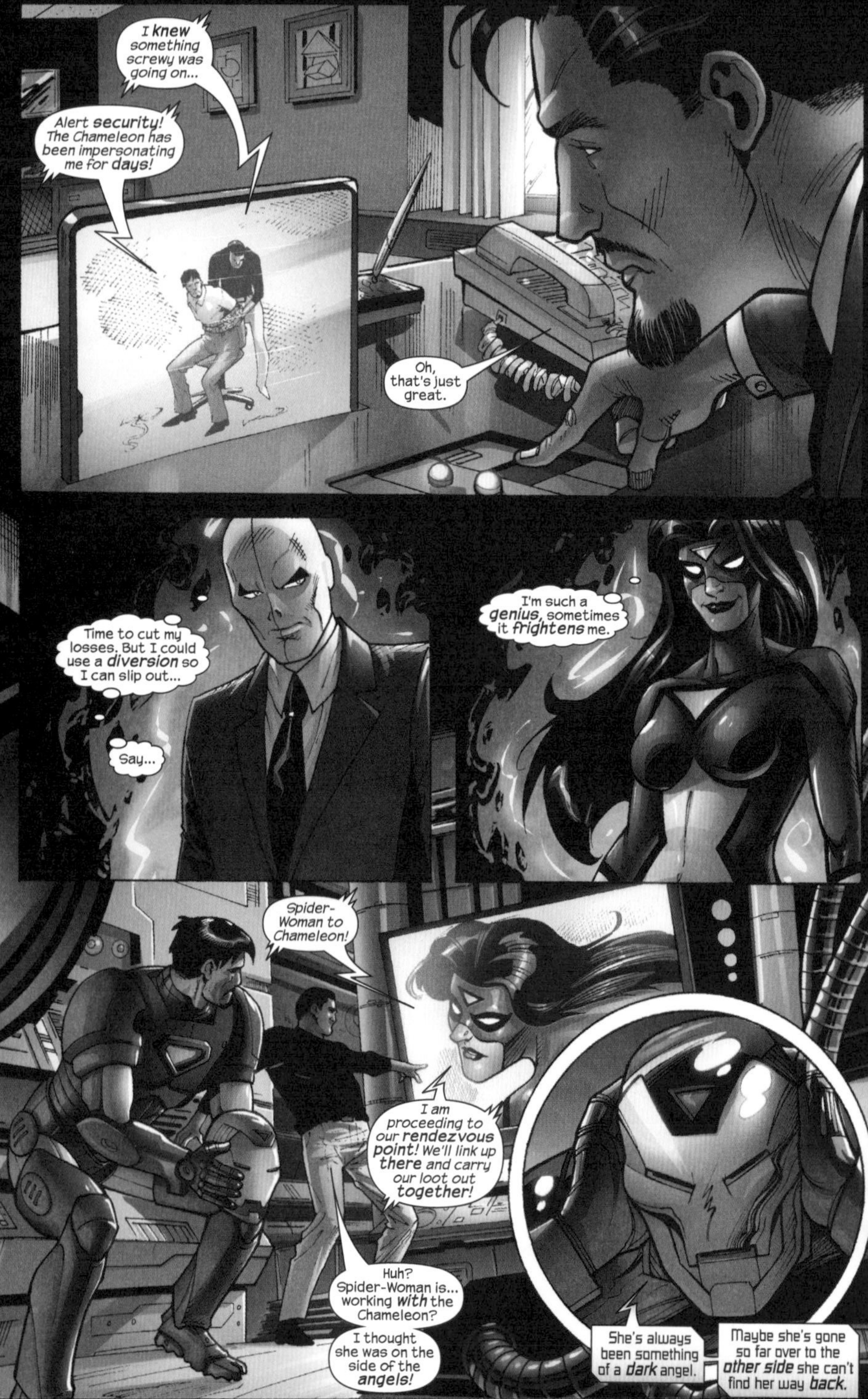
I knew something screwy was going on...
Alert security! The Chameleon has been impersonating me for days!
Oh, that's just great.
Time to cut my losses. But I could use a diversion so I can slip out...
Say...
I'm such a genius, sometimes it frightens me.
Spider-Woman to Chameleon!
I am proceeding to our rendezvous point! We'll link up there and carry our loot out together!
Huh? Spider-Woman is... working with the Chameleon?
I thought she was on the side of the angels!
She's always been something of a dark angel.
Maybe she's gone so far over to the other side she can't find her way back.

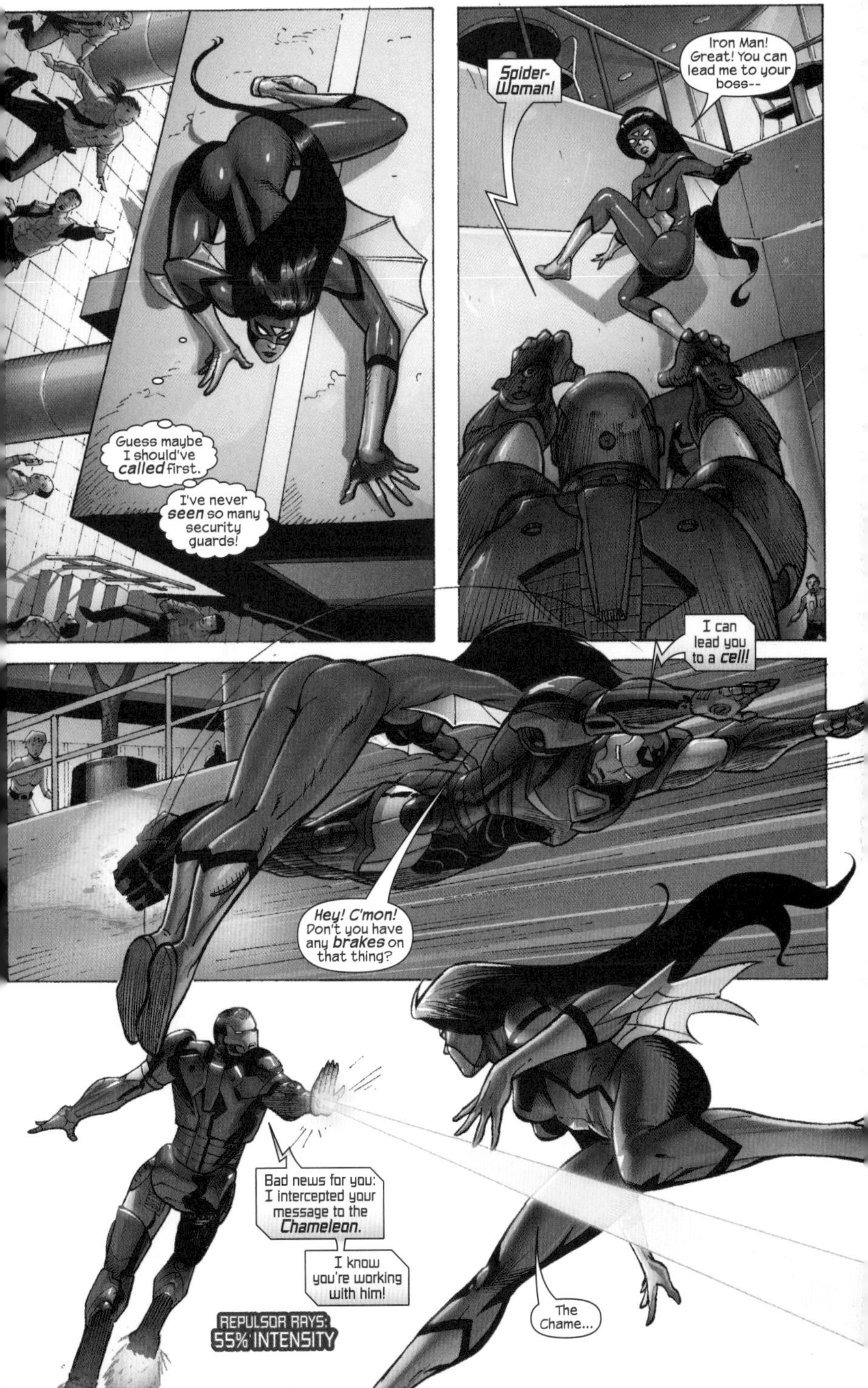

Guess maybe I should've called first.
I've never seen so many security guards!
Spider-Woman!
Iron Man! Great! You can lead me to your boss--
I can lead you to a cell!
Hey! C'mon! Don't you have any brakes on that thing?
Bad news for you: I intercepted your message to the Chameleon.
I know you're working with him!
REPULSOR RAYS: 55% INTENSITY
The Chame...

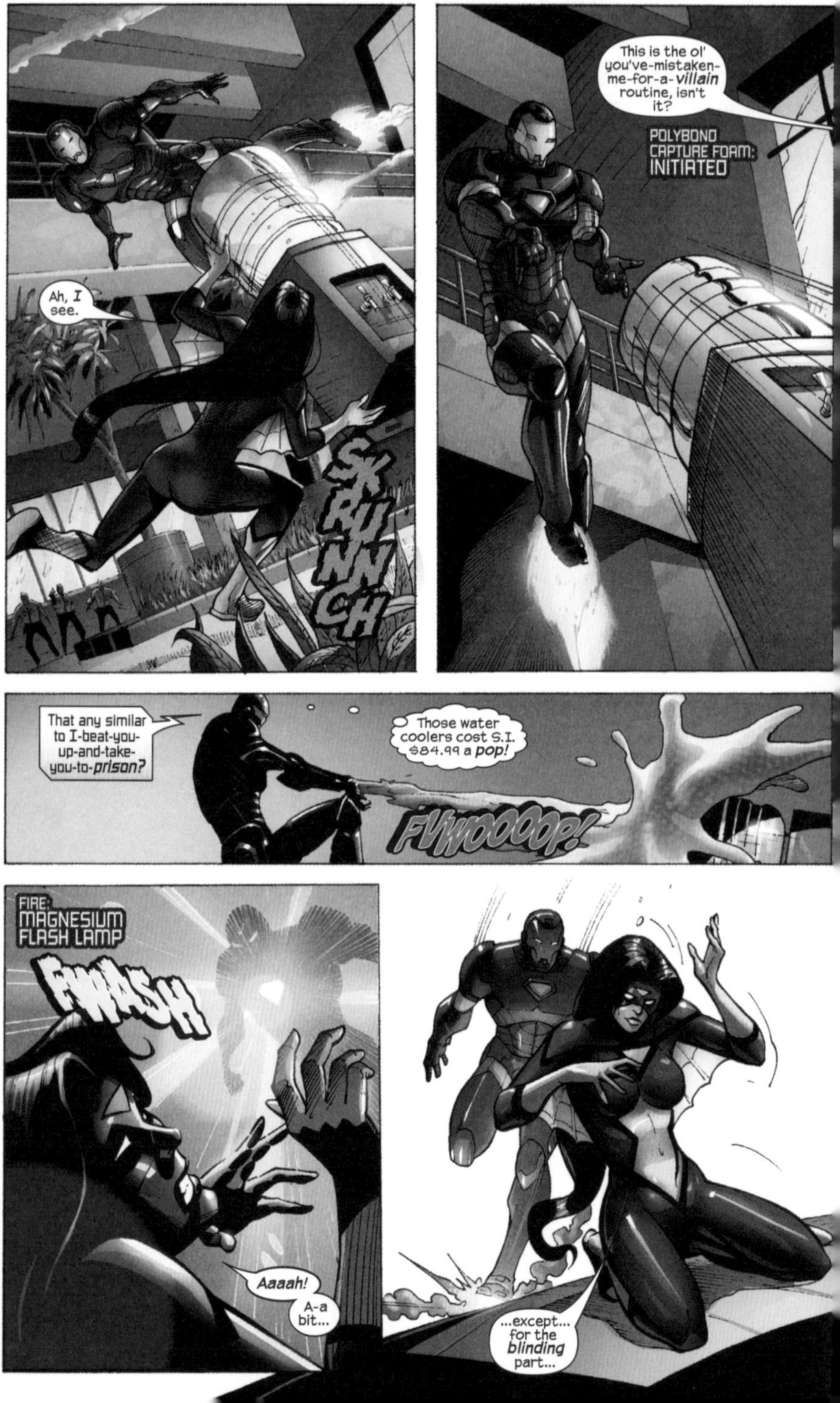
Ah, I see.
SKRUNNCH
This is the ol' you've-mistaken-me-for-a-villain routine, isn't it?
POLYBOND CAPTURE FOAM: INITIATED
That any similar to I-beat-you-up-and-take-you-to-prison?
Those water coolers cost S.I. $84.99 a pop!
FVWOOOOP!
FIRE: MAGNESIUM FLASH LAMP
FWASH
Aaaah!
A-a bit...
...except... for the blinding part...

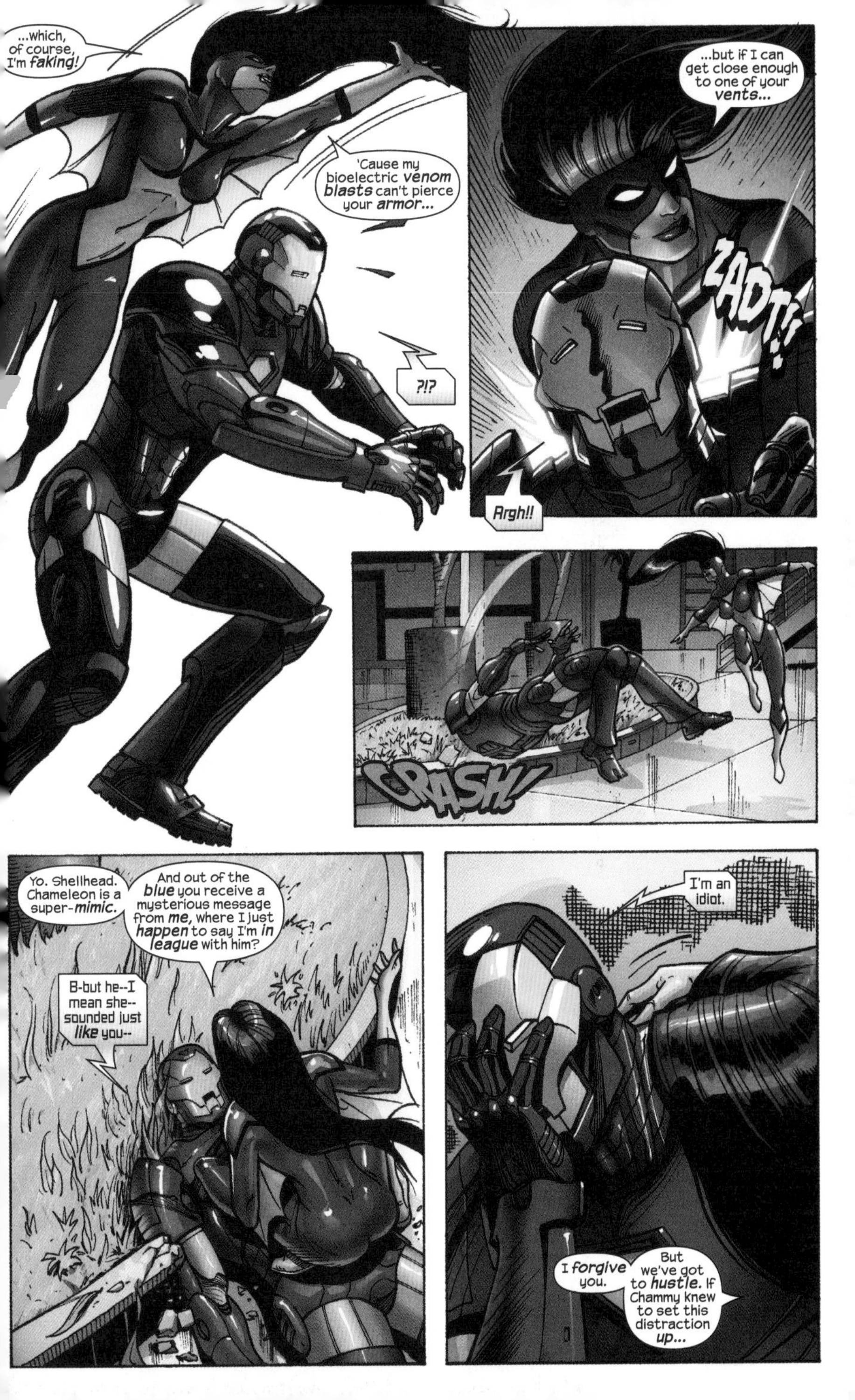
...which, of course, I'm faking!
'Cause my bioelectric venom blasts can't pierce your armor...
?!?
...but if I can get close enough to one of your vents...
ZADT!!
Argh!!
CRASH!
Yo. Shellhead. Chameleon is a super-mimic.
And out of the blue you receive a mysterious message from me, where I just happen to say I'm in league with him?
B-but he--I mean she--sounded just like you--
I'm an idiot.
I forgive you.
But we've got to hustle. If Chammy knew to set this distraction up...

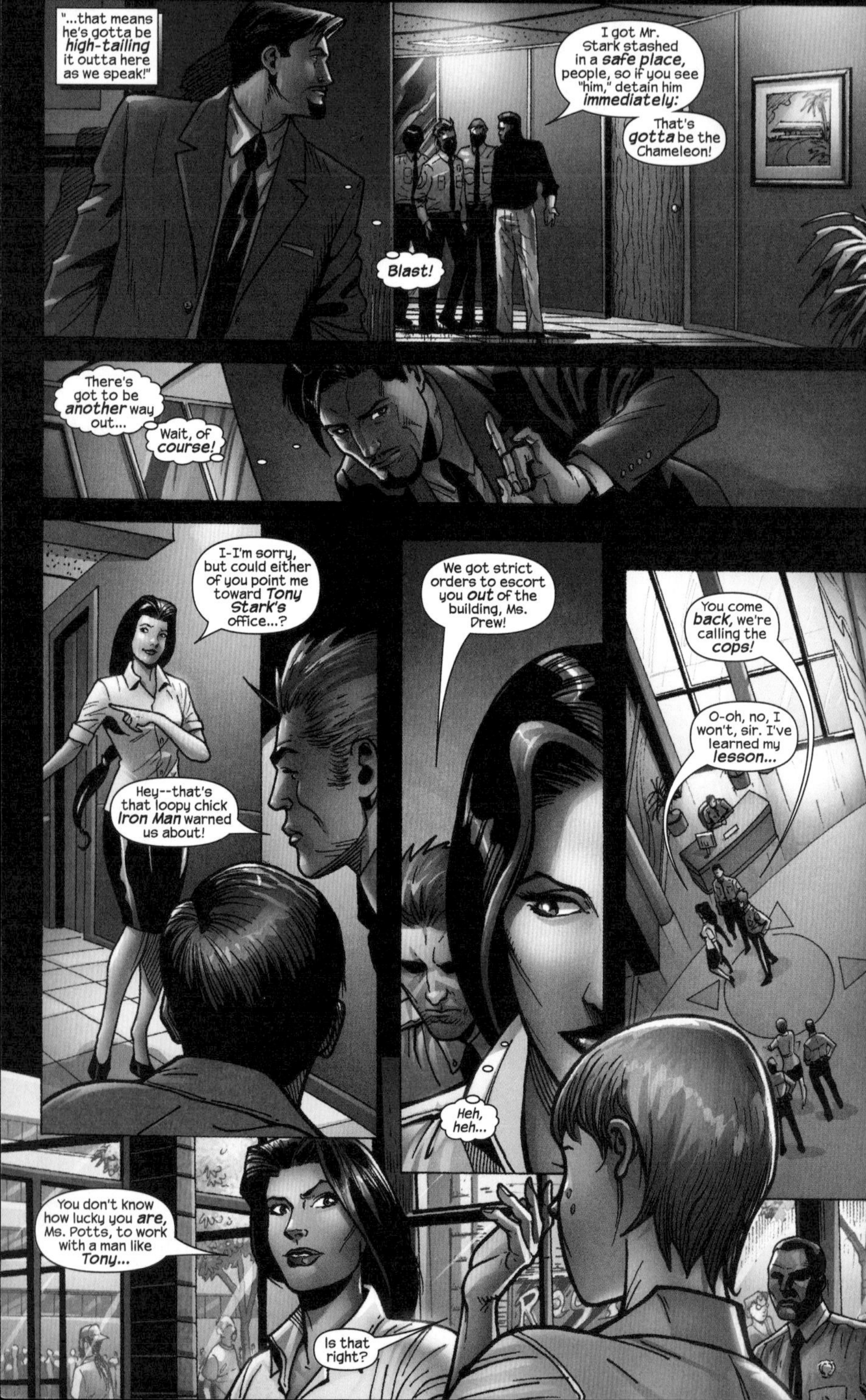

"...that means he's gotta be high-tailing it outta here as we speak!"
I got Mr. Stark stashed in a safe place, people, so if you see "him," detain him immediately:
That's gotta be the Chameleon!
Blast!
There's got to be another way out...
Wait, of course!
I-I'm sorry, but could either of you point me toward Tony Stark's office...?
Hey--that's that loopy chick Iron Man warned us about!
We got strict orders to escort you out of the building, Ms. Drew!
Heh, heh...
You come back, we're calling the cops!
O-oh, no, I won't, sir. I've learned my lesson...
You don't know how lucky you are, Ms. Potts, to work with a man like Tony...
Is that right?

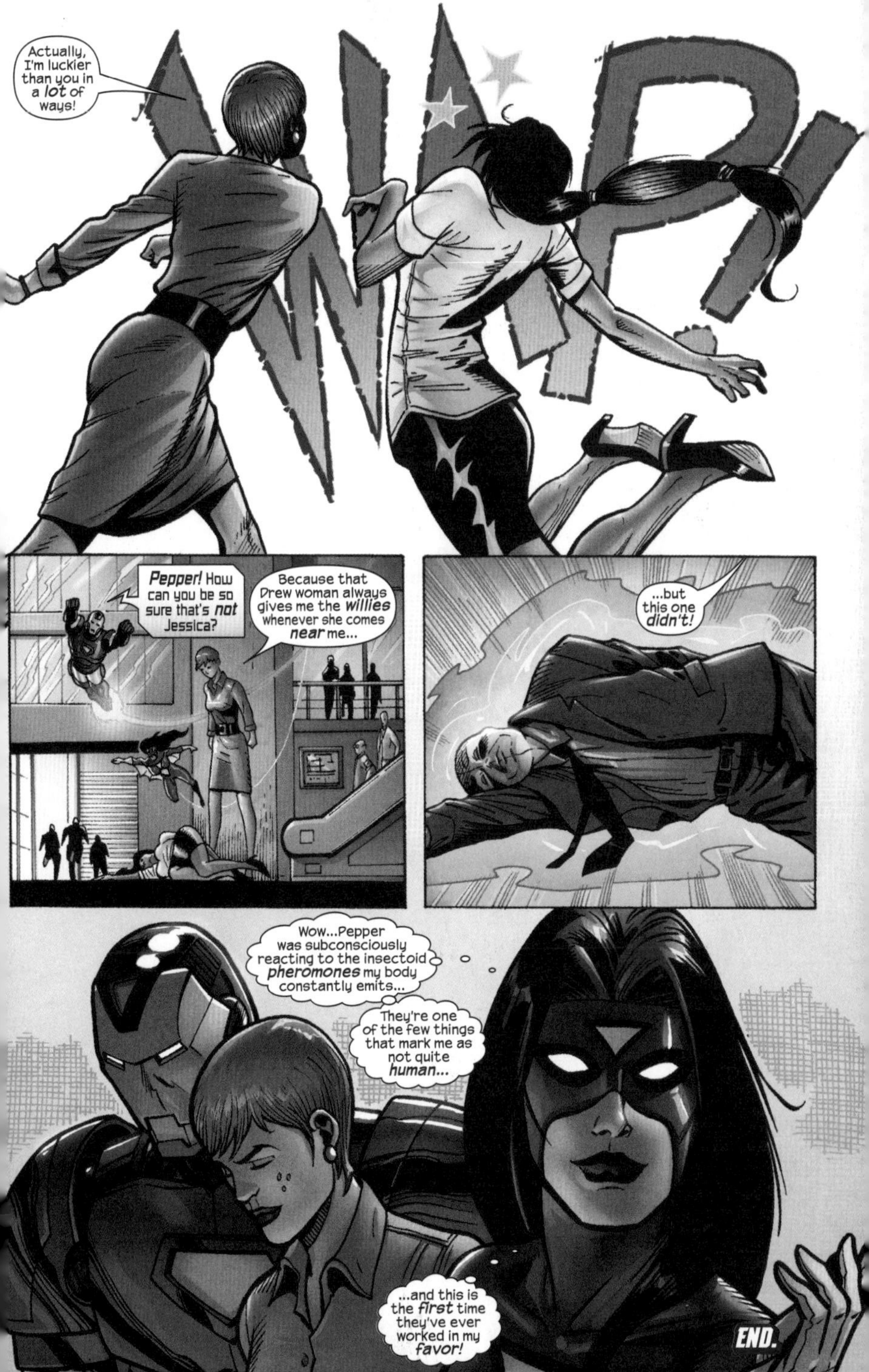

Actually, I'm luckier than you in a *lot* of ways!
Pepper! How can you be so sure that's *not* Jessica?
Because that Drew woman always gives me the *willies* whenever she comes *near* me...
...but this one *didn't!*
Wow...Pepper was subconsciously reacting to the insectoid *pheromones* my body constantly emits...
They're one of the few things that mark me as not quite *human*...
...and this is the *first* time they've ever worked in my *favor!*
END.

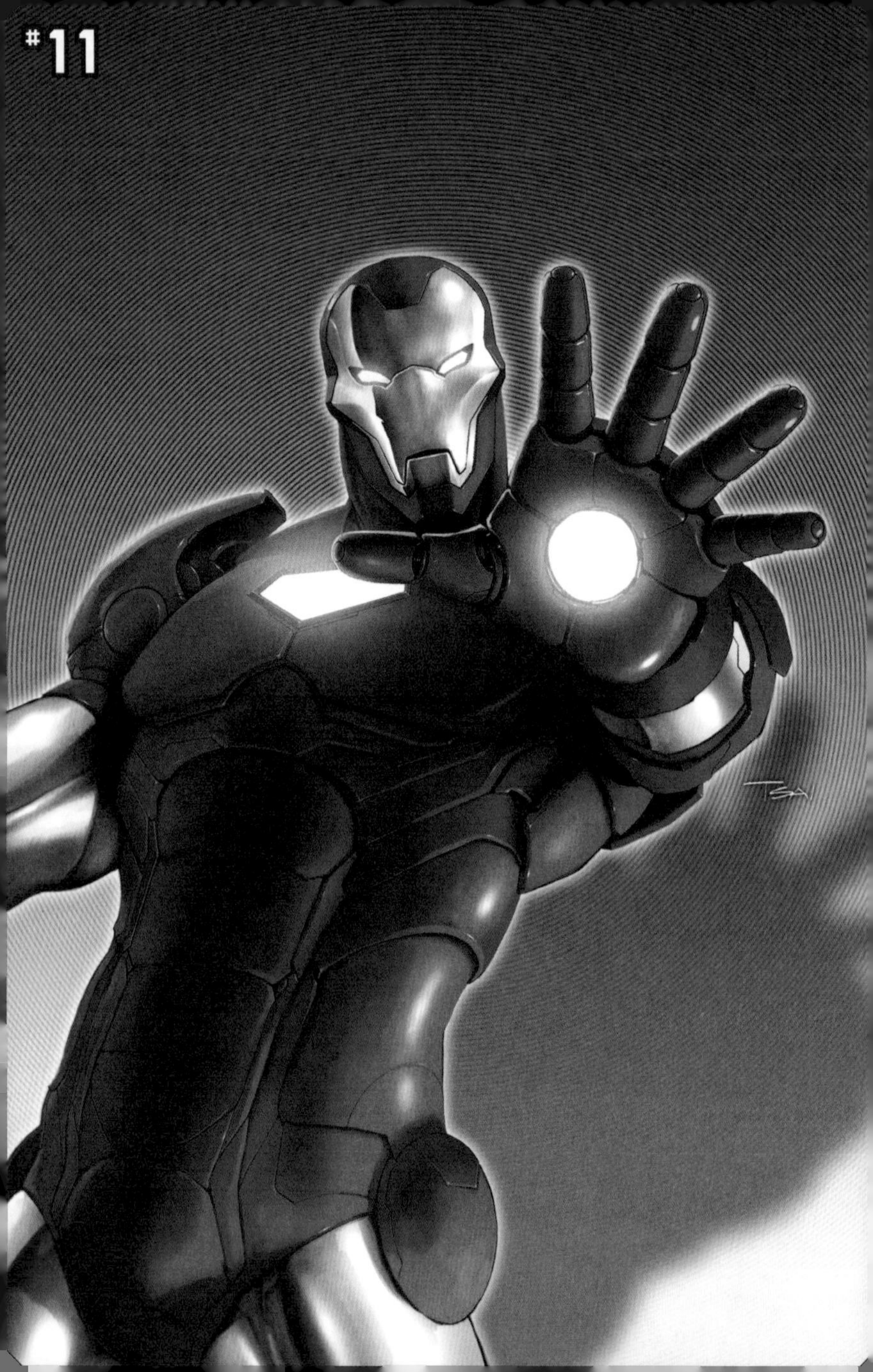
#11

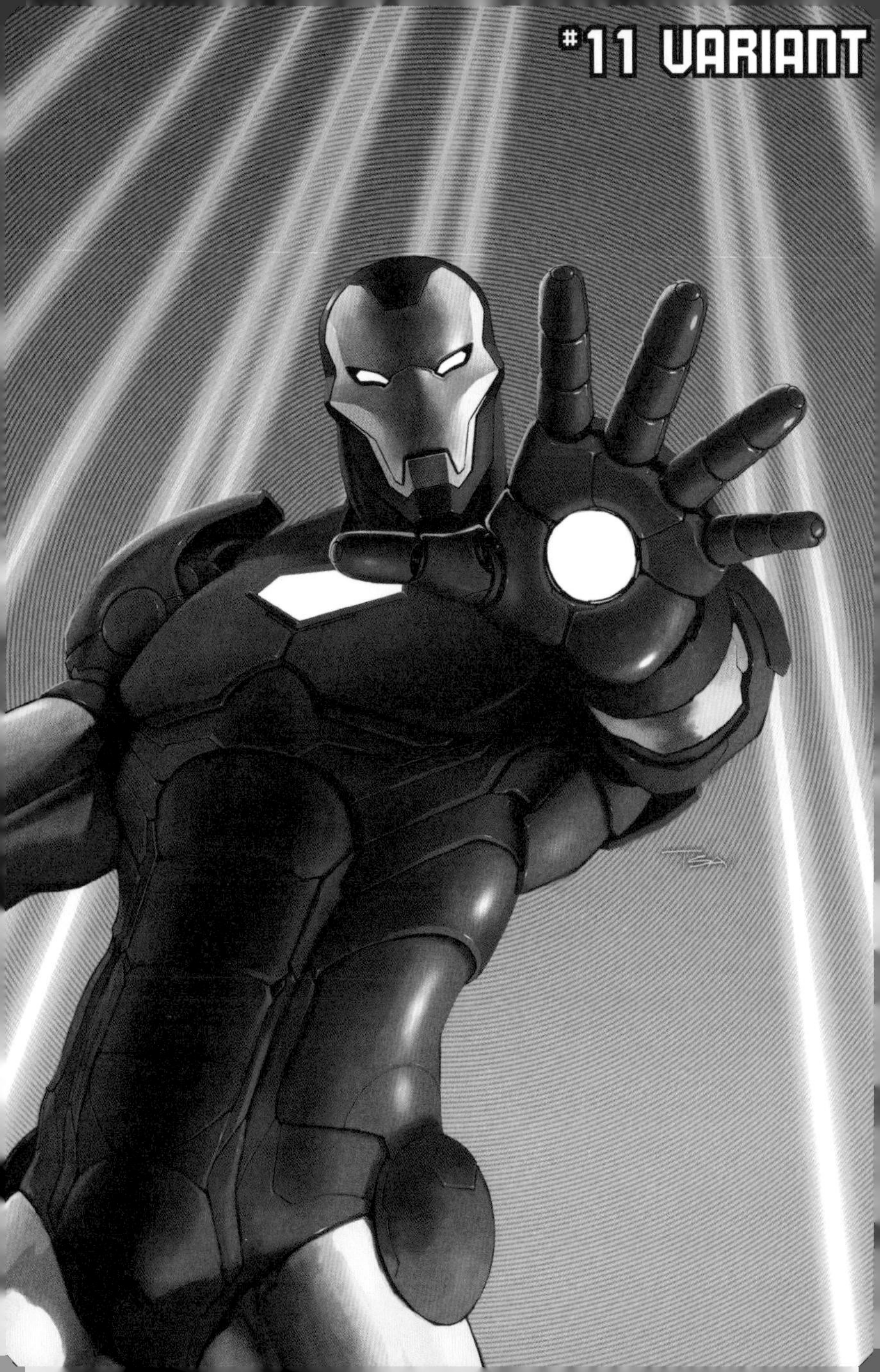
#11 VARIANT

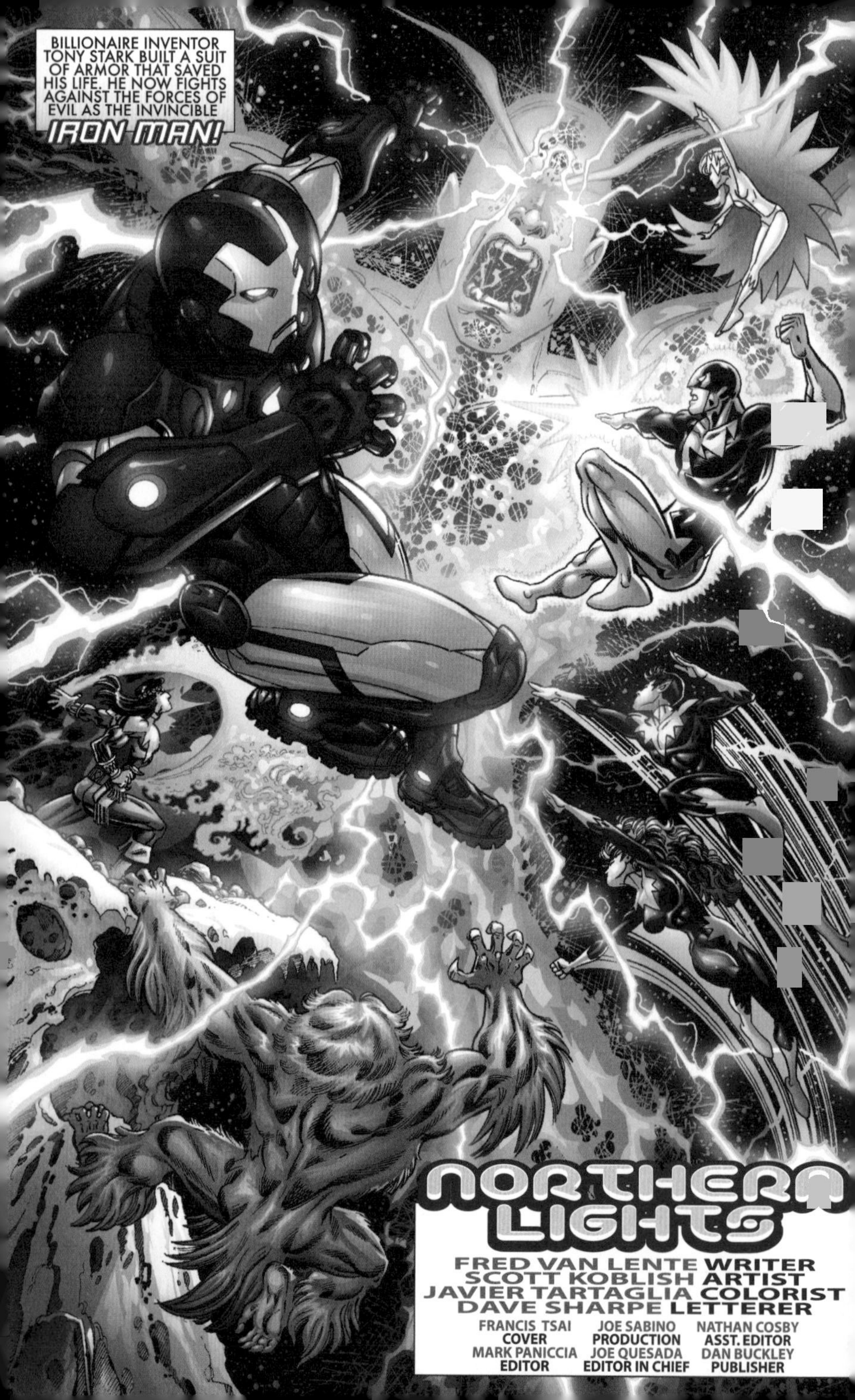
BILLIONAIRE INVENTOR TONY STARK BUILT A SUIT OF ARMOR THAT SAVED HIS LIFE. HE NOW FIGHTS AGAINST THE FORCES OF EVIL AS THE INVINCIBLE IRON MAN!
NORTHERN LIGHTS
FRED VAN LENTE WRITER
SCOTT KOBLISH ARTIST
JAVIER TARTAGLIA COLORIST
DAVE SHARPE LETTERER
FRANCIS TSAI COVER
JOE SABINO PRODUCTION
NATHAN COSBY ASST. EDITOR
MARK PANICCIA EDITOR
JOE QUESADA EDITOR IN CHIEF
DAN BUCKLEY PUBLISHER

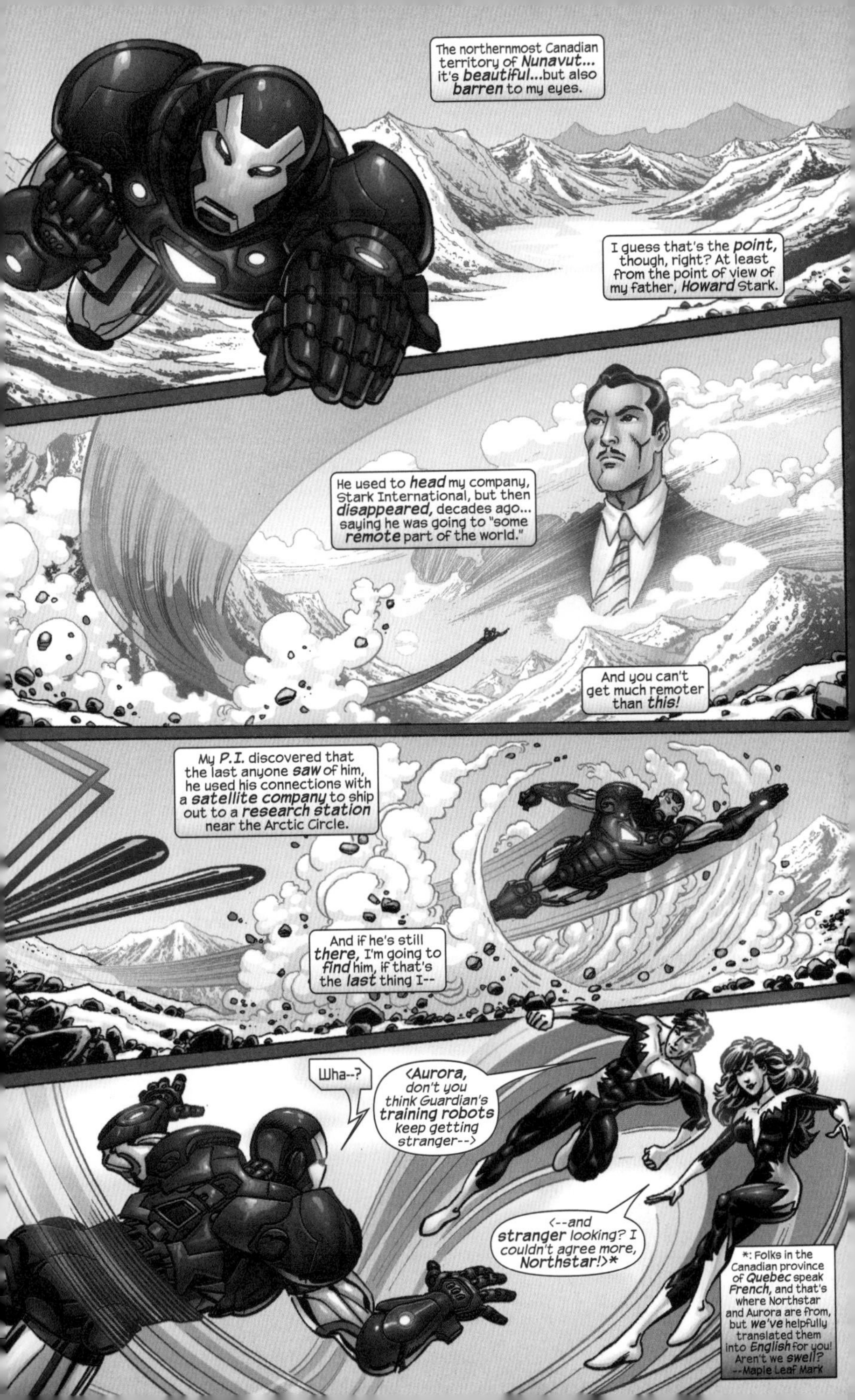
The northernmost Canadian territory of Nunavut... it's beautiful...but also barren to my eyes.
I guess that's the point, though, right? At least from the point of view of my father, Howard Stark.
He used to head my company, Stark International, but then disappeared, decades ago... saying he was going to "some remote part of the world."
And you can't get much remoter than this!
My P.I. discovered that the last anyone saw of him, he used his connections with a satellite company to ship out to a research station near the Arctic Circle.
And if he's still there, I'm going to find him, if that's the last thing I--
Wha--?
<Aurora, don't you think Guardian's training robots keep getting stranger-->
<--and stranger looking? I couldn't agree more, Northstar!>*
*: Folks in the Canadian province of Quebec speak French, and that's where Northstar and Aurora are from, but we've helpfully translated them into English for you! Aren't we swell? --Maple Leaf Mark

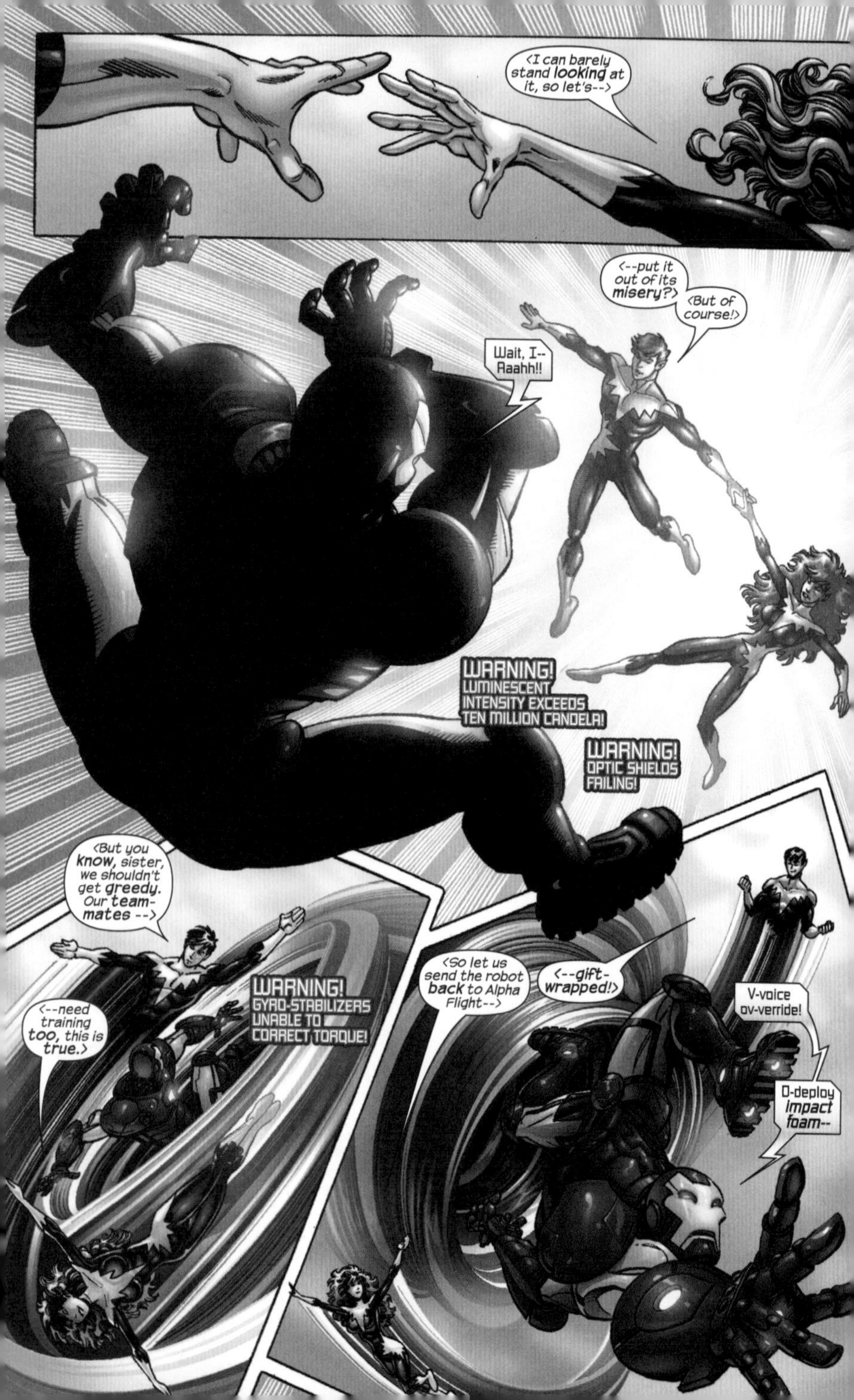

<I can barely stand looking at it, so let's-->
<--put it out of its misery?>
<But of course!>
Wait, I-- Aaahh!!
WARNING! LUMINESCENT INTENSITY EXCEEDS TEN MILLION CANDELA!
WARNING! OPTIC SHIELDS FAILING!
<But you know, sister, we shouldn't get greedy. Our teammates -->
<--need training too, this is true.>
WARNING! GYRO-STABILIZERS UNABLE TO CORRECT TORQUE!
<So let us send the robot back to Alpha Flight-->
<--gift-wrapped!>
V-voice ov-verride!
D-deploy impact foam--

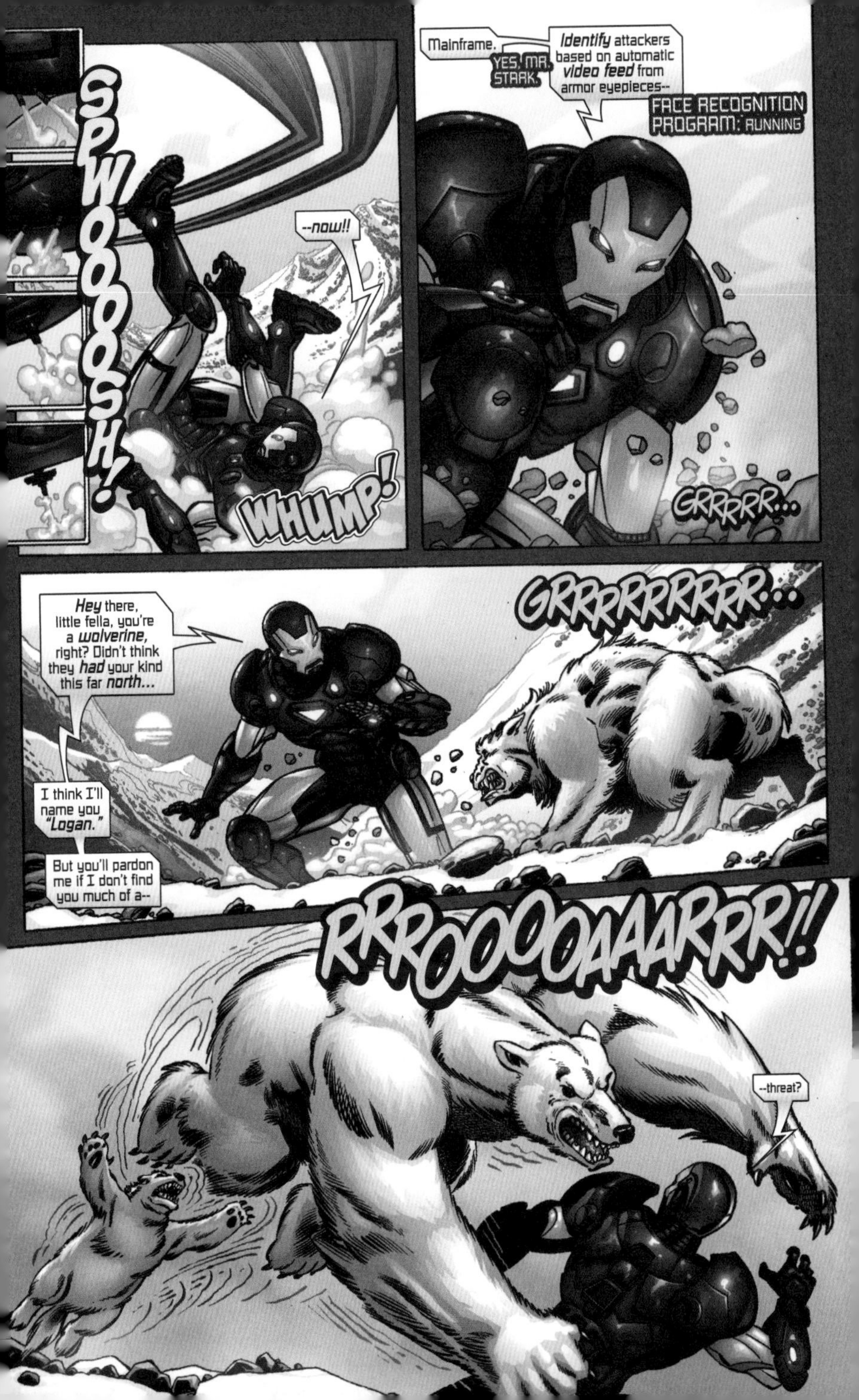
SPWOOOOOSH!
--now!!
WHUMP!
Mainframe.
YES, MR. STARK.
Identify attackers based on automatic video feed from armor eyepieces--
FACE RECOGNITION PROGRAM: RUNNING
GRRRRR...
GRRRRRRRRR...
Hey there, little fella, you're a wolverine, right? Didn't think they had your kind this far north...
I think I'll name you "Logan."
But you'll pardon me if I don't find you much of a--
RRROOOOAAARRR!!
--threat?

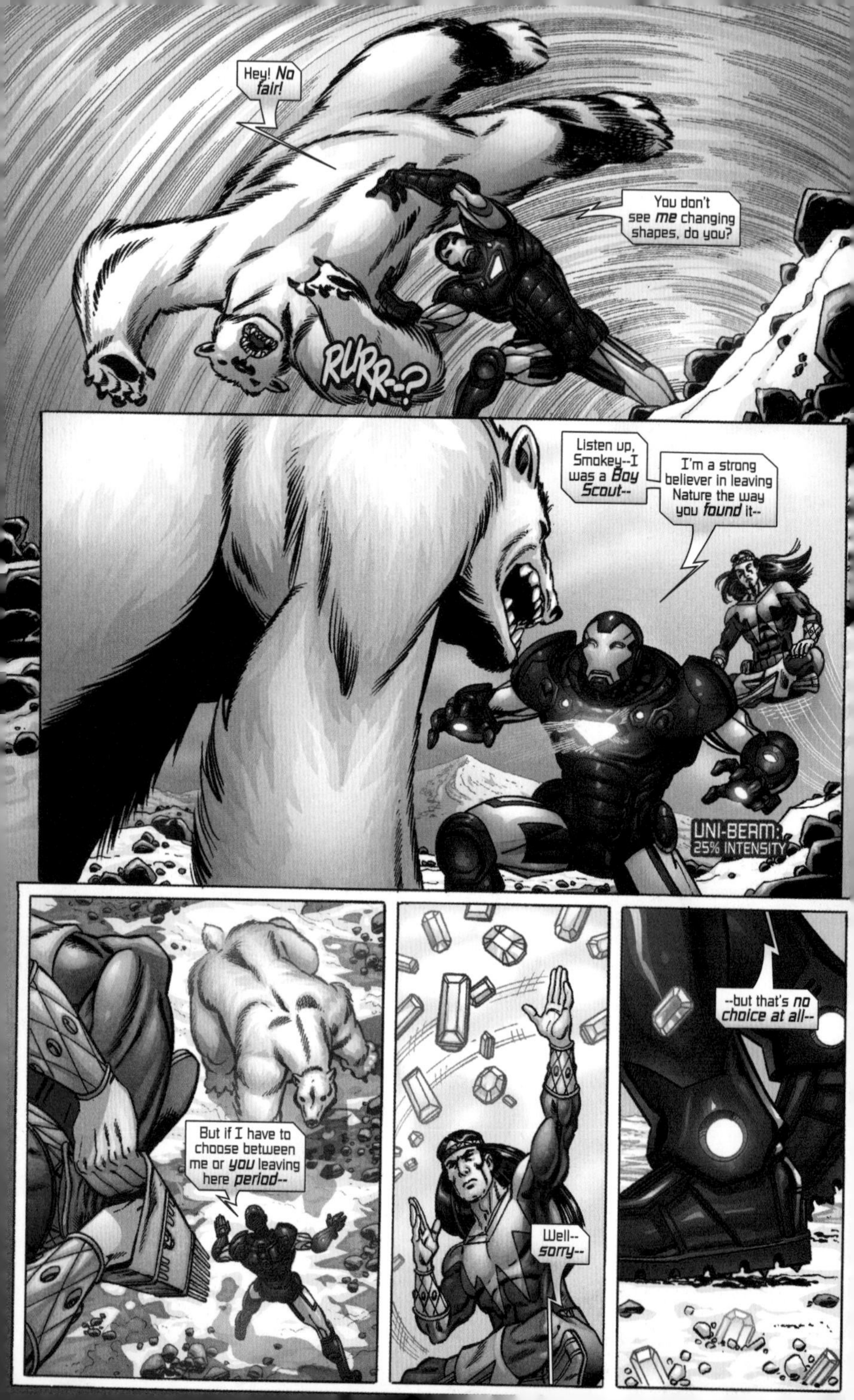
Hey! *No fair!*
You don't see *me* changing shapes, do you?
RURR--?
Listen up, Smokey--I was a *Boy Scout*--
I'm a strong believer in leaving Nature the way you *found* it--
UNI-BEAM: 25% INTENSITY
But if I have to choose between me or *you* leaving here *period*--
Well-- *sorry*--
--but that's *no choice at all*--

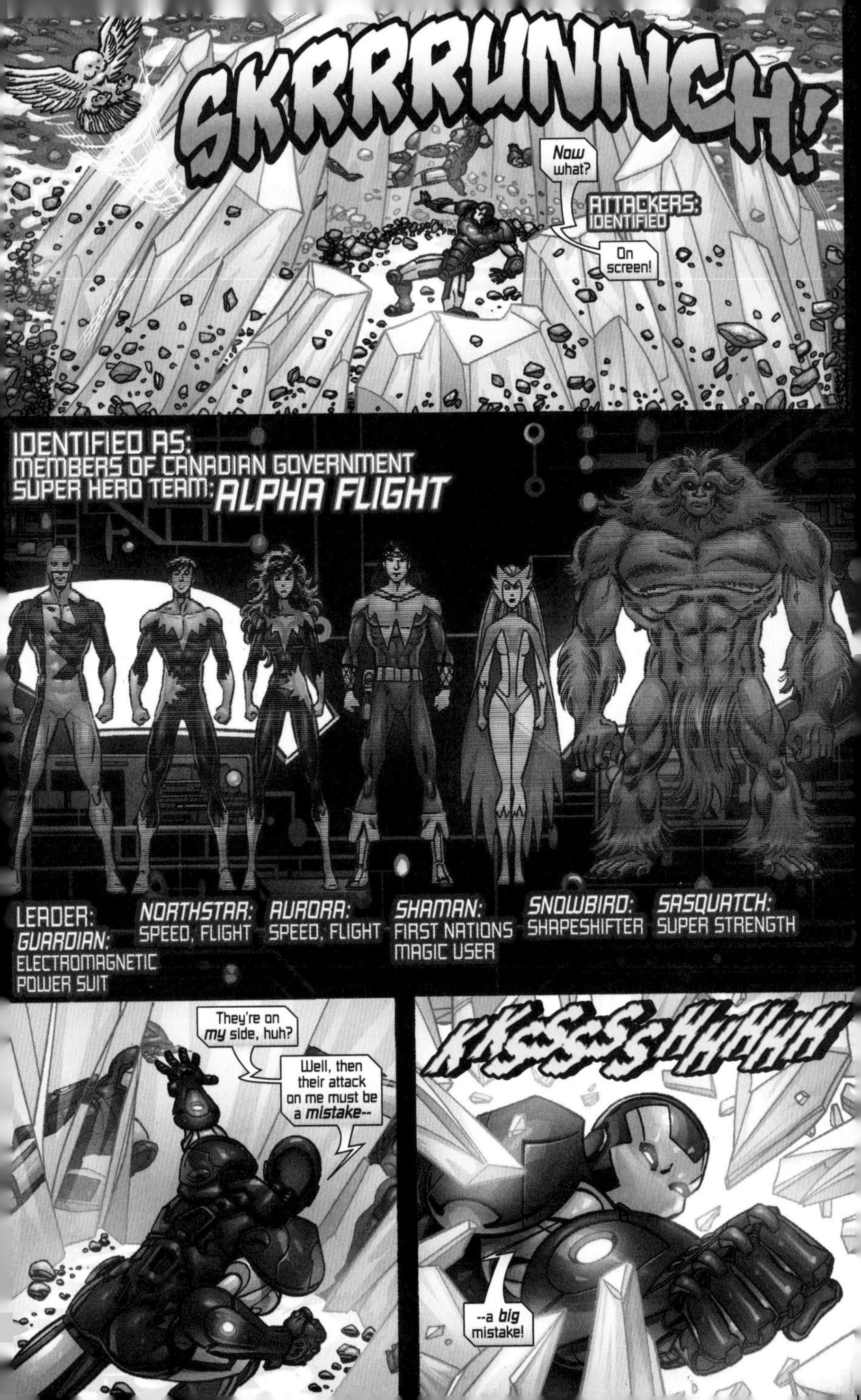
SKRRRUNNCH!
Now what?
ATTACKERS: IDENTIFIED
On screen!
IDENTIFIED AS:
MEMBERS OF CANADIAN GOVERNMENT
SUPER HERO TEAM: ALPHA FLIGHT
LEADER: GUARDIAN: ELECTROMAGNETIC POWER SUIT
NORTHSTAR: SPEED, FLIGHT
AURORA: SPEED, FLIGHT
SHAMAN: FIRST NATIONS MAGIC USER
SNOWBIRD: SHAPESHIFTER
SASQUATCH: SUPER STRENGTH
They're on *my* side, huh?
Well, then their attack on me must be a *mistake*--
KKSSSSHHHHH
--a *big* mistake!

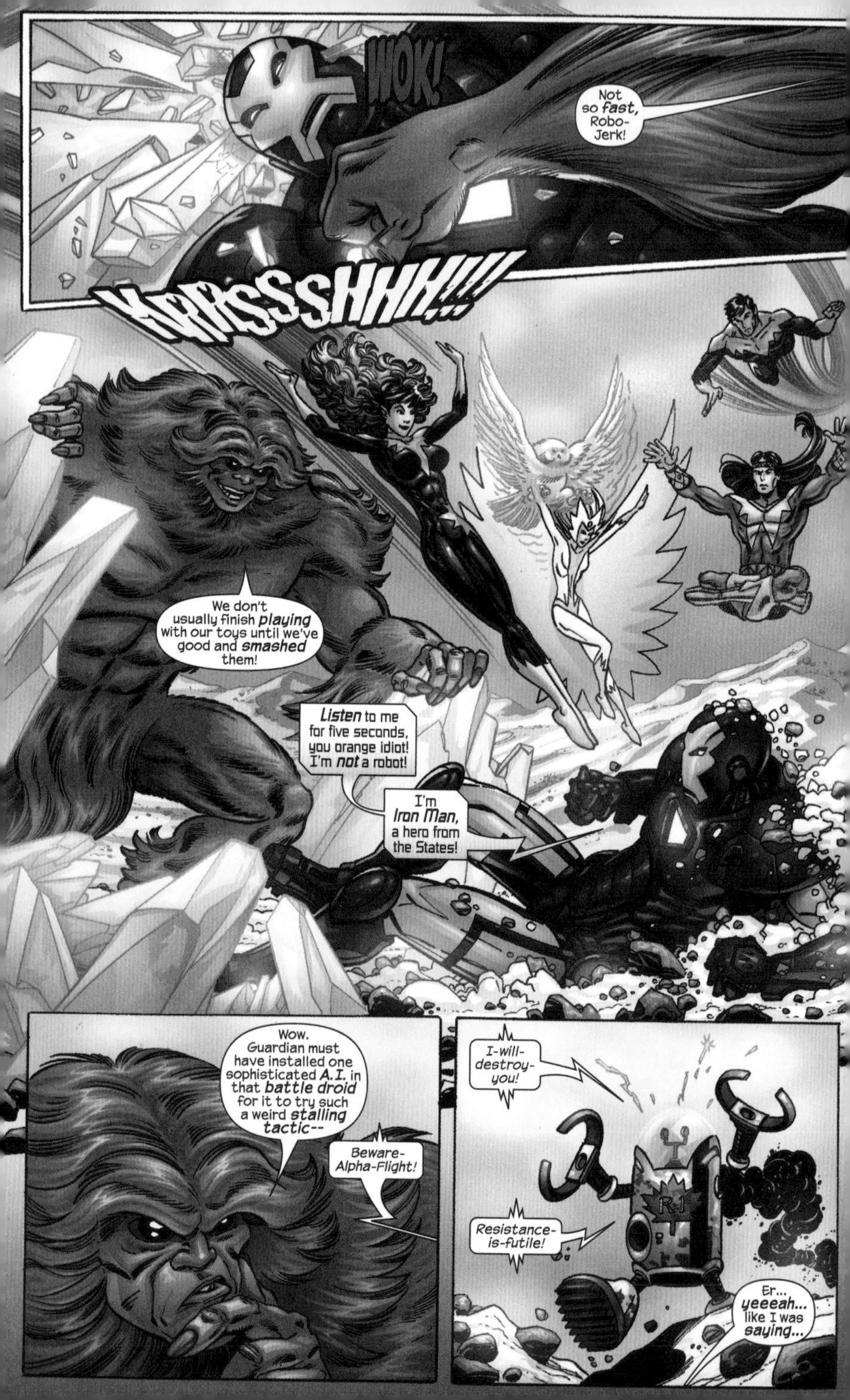
WOK!
Not so fast, Robo-Jerk!
We don't usually finish playing with our toys until we've good and smashed them!
Listen to me for five seconds, you orange idiot! I'm not a robot!
I'm Iron Man, a hero from the States!
Wow. Guardian must have installed one sophisticated A.I. in that battle droid for it to try such a weird stalling tactic--
Beware-Alpha-Flight!
I-will-destroy-you!
Resistance-is-futile!
R-1
Er... yeeeah... like I was saying...

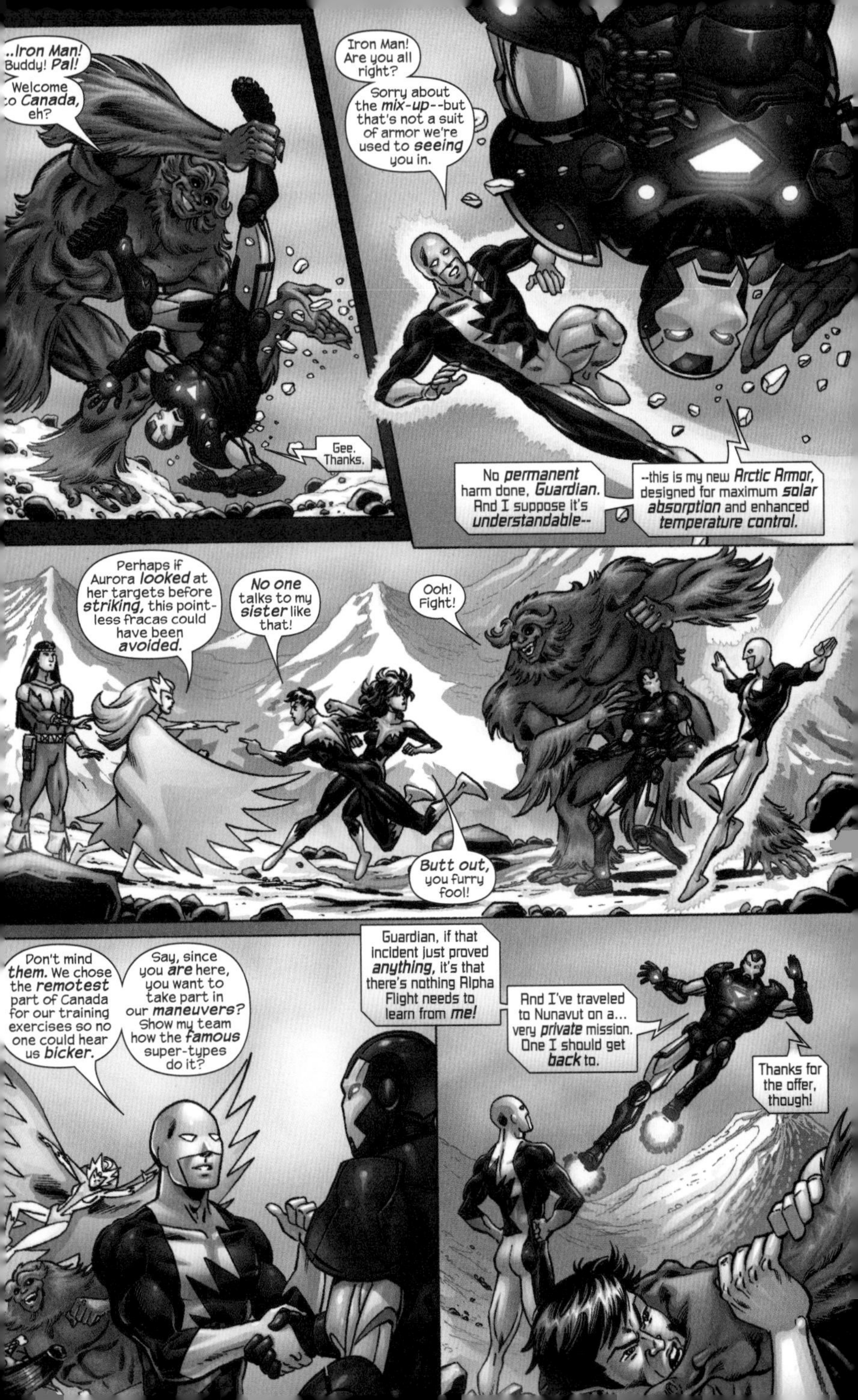
..Iron Man! Buddy! Pal!
Welcome to Canada, eh?
Gee. Thanks.
Iron Man! Are you all right?
Sorry about the mix-up--but that's not a suit of armor we're used to seeing you in.
No permanent harm done, Guardian. And I suppose it's understandable--
--this is my new Arctic Armor, designed for maximum solar absorption and enhanced temperature control.
Perhaps if Aurora looked at her targets before striking, this pointless fracas could have been avoided.
No one talks to my sister like that!
Ooh! Fight!
Butt out, you furry fool!
Don't mind them. We chose the remotest part of Canada for our training exercises so no one could hear us bicker.
Say, since you are here, you want to take part in our maneuvers? Show my team how the famous super-types do it?
Guardian, if that incident just proved anything, it's that there's nothing Alpha Flight needs to learn from me!
And I've traveled to Nunavut on a... very private mission. One I should get back to.
Thanks for the offer, though!

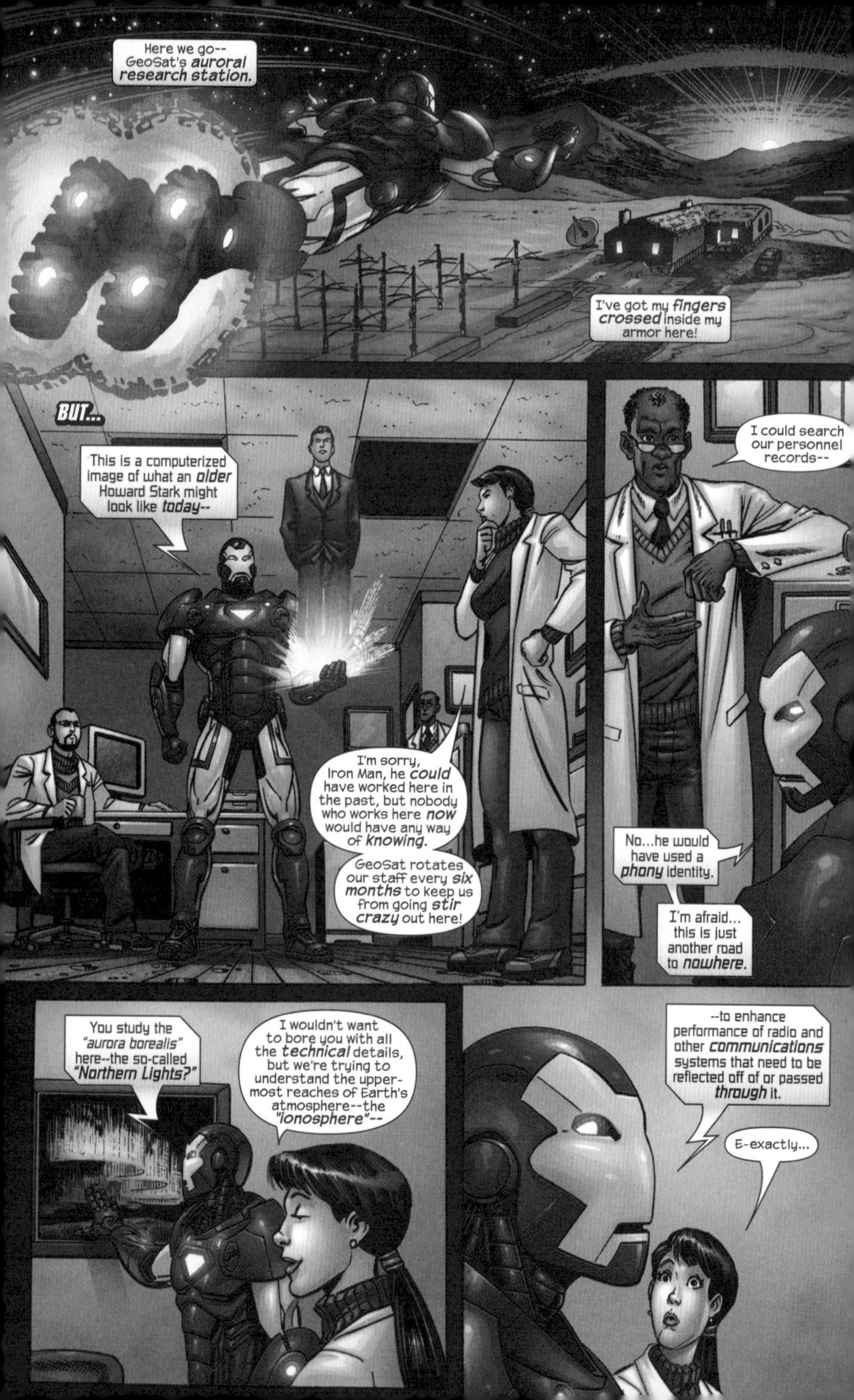

Here we go--
GeoSat's auroral research station.
I've got my fingers crossed inside my armor here!
BUT...
This is a computerized image of what an older Howard Stark might look like today--
I'm sorry, Iron Man, he could have worked here in the past, but nobody who works here now would have any way of knowing.
GeoSat rotates our staff every six months to keep us from going stir crazy out here!
I could search our personnel records--
No...he would have used a phony identity.
I'm afraid... this is just another road to nowhere.
You study the "aurora borealis" here--the so-called "Northern Lights?"
I wouldn't want to bore you with all the technical details, but we're trying to understand the uppermost reaches of Earth's atmosphere--the "ionosphere"--
--to enhance performance of radio and other communications systems that need to be reflected off of or passed through it.
E-exactly...

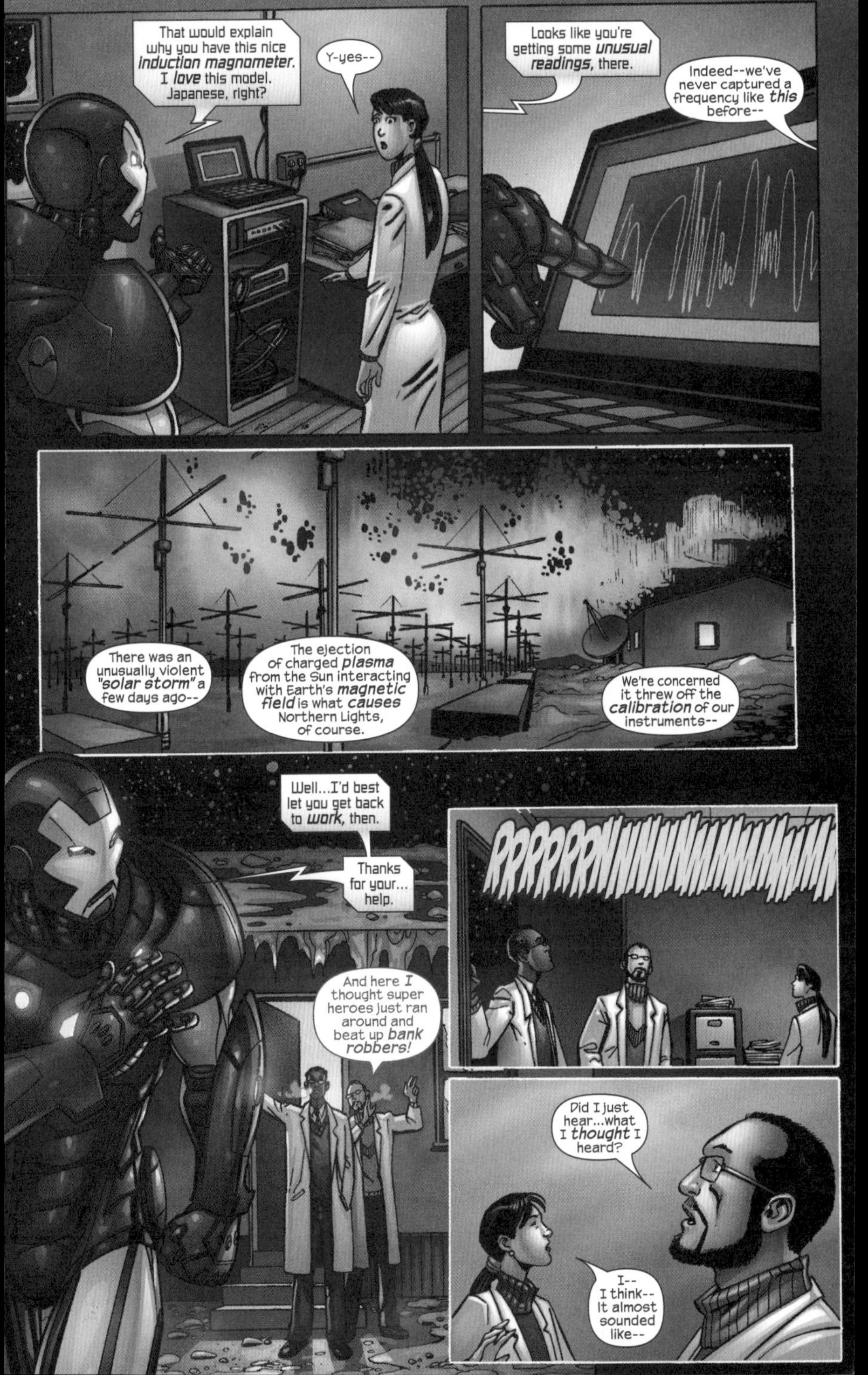
That would explain why you have this nice *induction magnometer*. I *love* this model. Japanese, right?
Y-yes--
Looks like you're getting some *unusual readings*, there.
Indeed--we've never captured a frequency like *this* before--
There was an unusually violent *"solar storm"* a few days ago--
The ejection of charged *plasma* from the Sun interacting with Earth's *magnetic field* is what *causes* Northern Lights, of course.
We're concerned it threw off the *calibration* of our instruments--
Well...I'd best let you get back to *work*, then.
Thanks for your... help.
And here *I* thought super heroes just ran around and beat up *bank robbers!*
RRRRRRNNNNNMMMMMMM
Did I just hear...what I *thought* I heard?
I-- I think-- It almost sounded like--

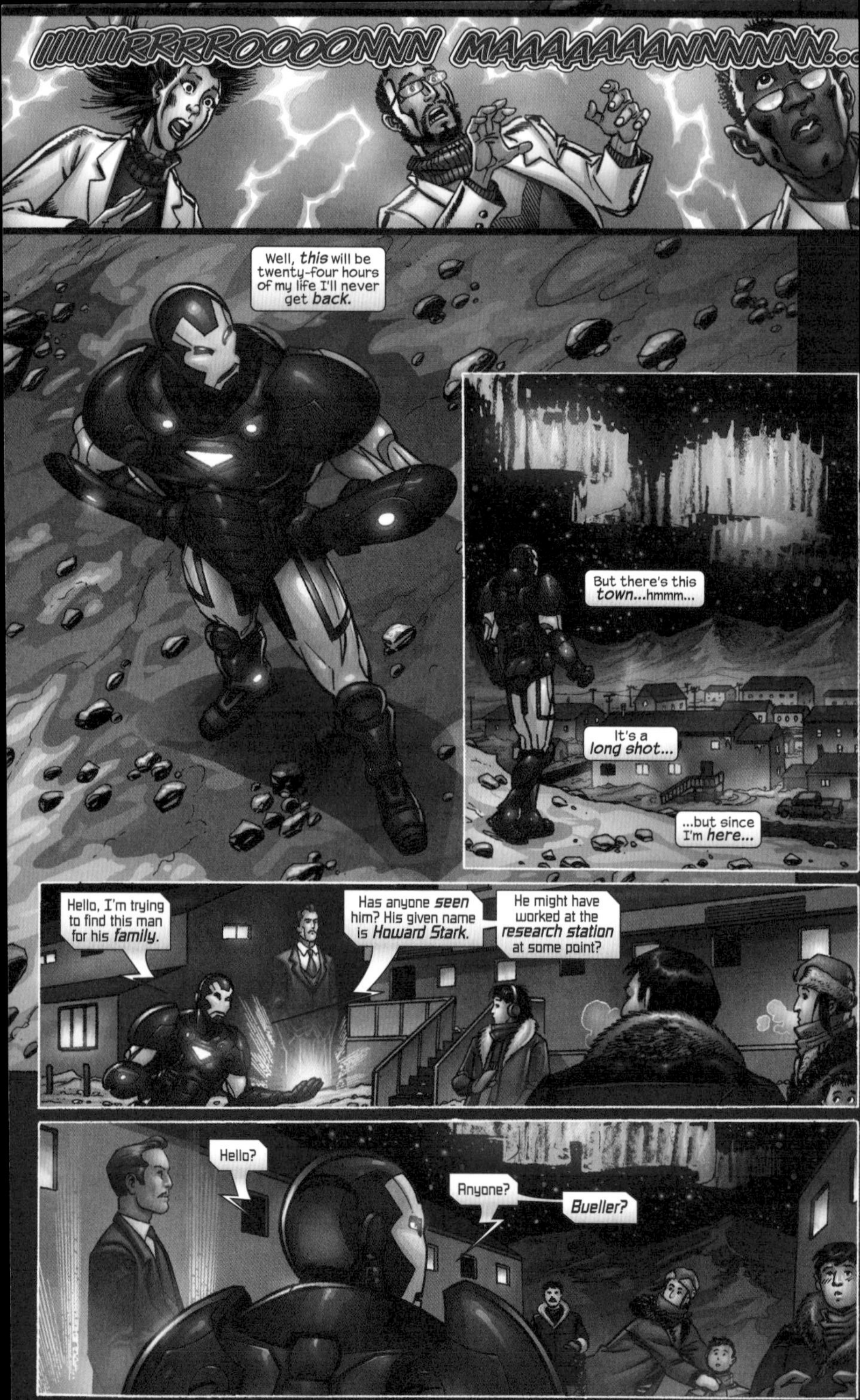
IIIIIIIRRRRROOOOONNN MAAAAAAANNNNNN...
Well, this will be twenty-four hours of my life I'll never get back.
But there's this town...hmmm...
It's a long shot...
...but since I'm here...
Hello, I'm trying to find this man for his family.
Has anyone seen him? His given name is Howard Stark.
He might have worked at the research station at some point?
Hello?
Anyone?
Bueller?

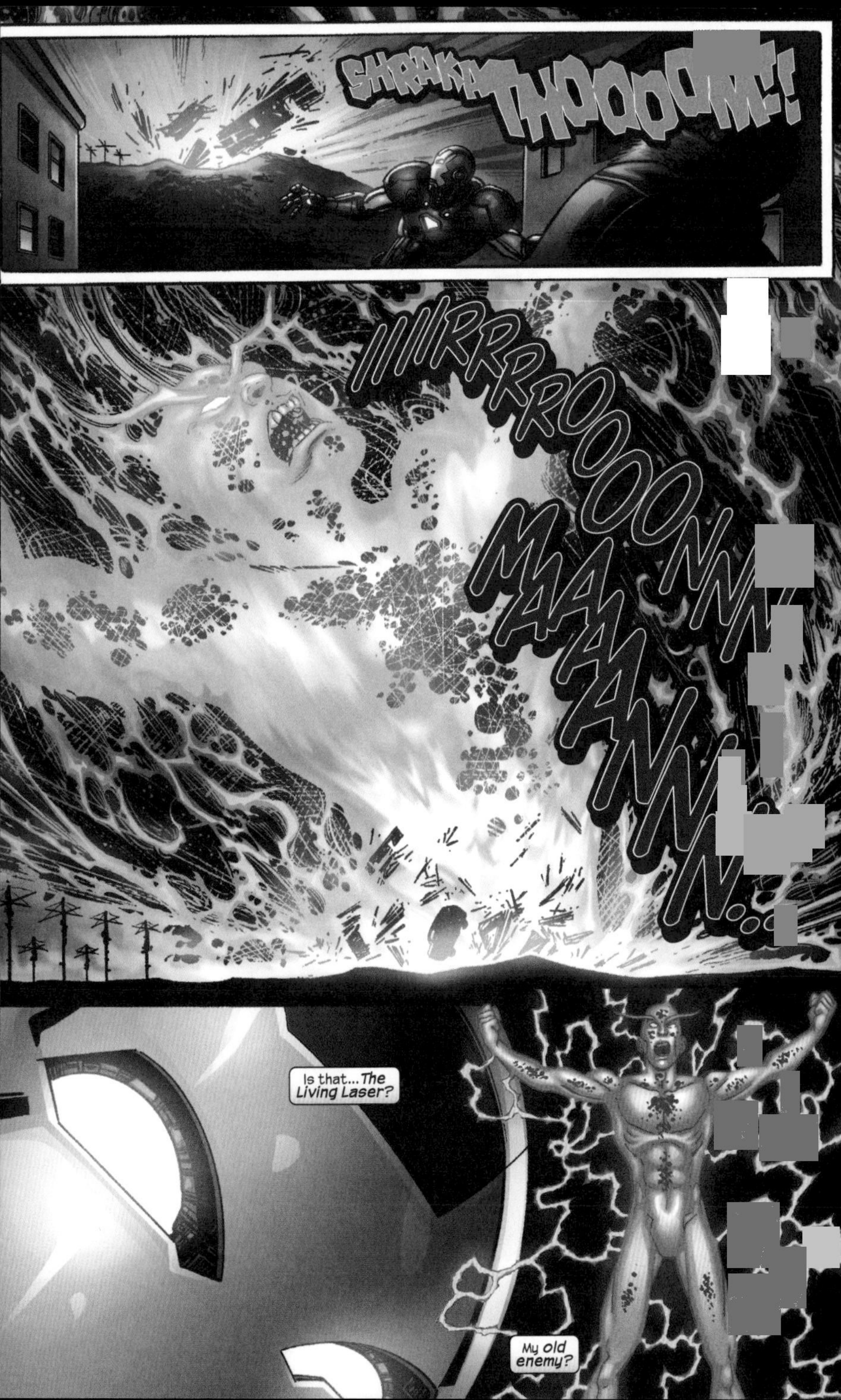

SHRAKATHOOOOOM!
IIIIRRRROOOOONNN
MAAAANNNN...
Is that... The Living Laser?
My old enemy?

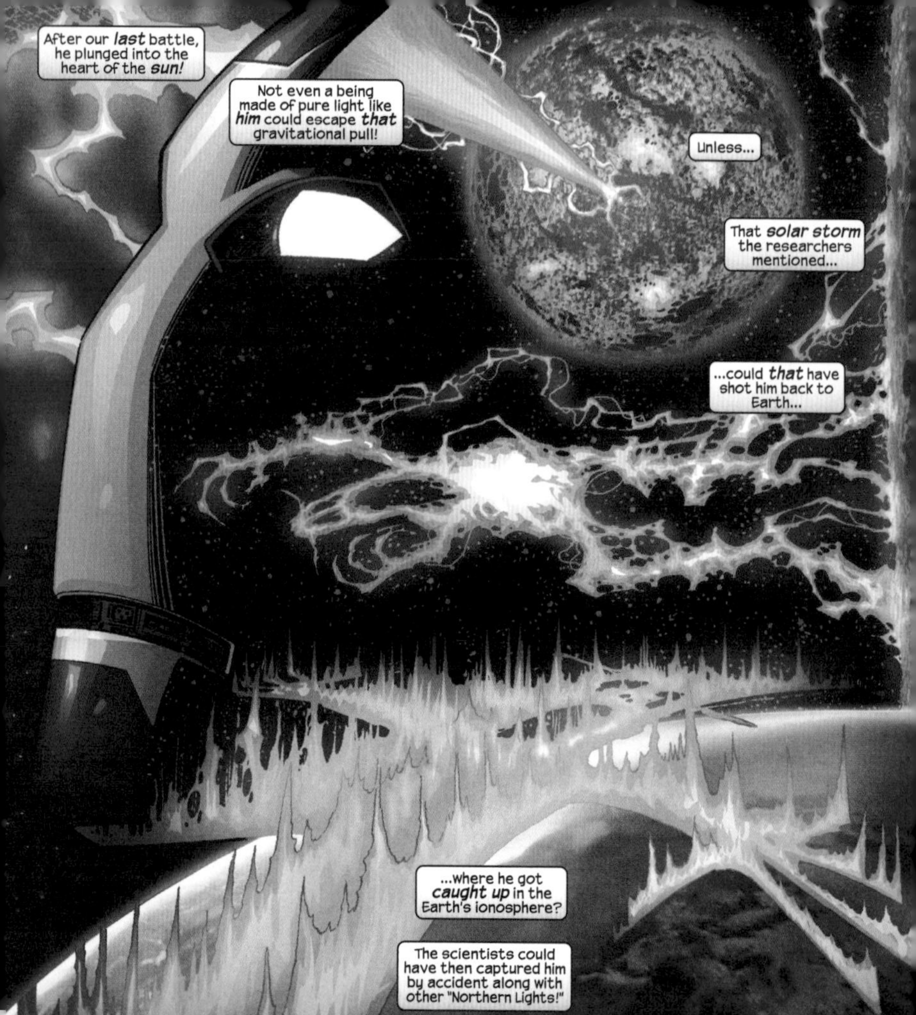
After our *last* battle, he plunged into the heart of the *sun!*
Not even a being made of pure light like *him* could escape *that* gravitational pull!
Unless...
That *solar storm* the researchers mentioned...
...could *that* have shot him back to Earth...
...where he got *caught up* in the Earth's ionosphere?
The scientists could have then captured him by accident along with other "Northern Lights!"

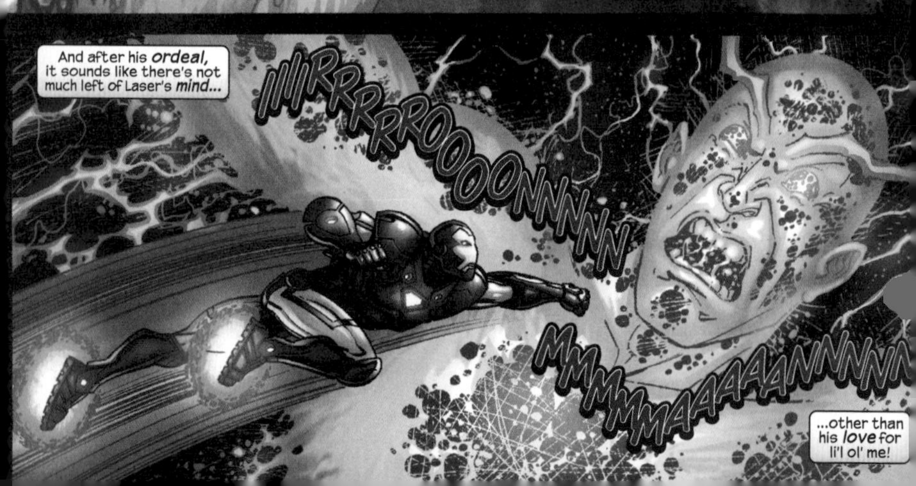
And after his *ordeal,* it sounds like there's not much left of Laser's *mind...*
IIIIRRRRRROOOOONNNNNN
MMMMMAAAAAANNNNNN
...other than his *love* for li'l ol' me!

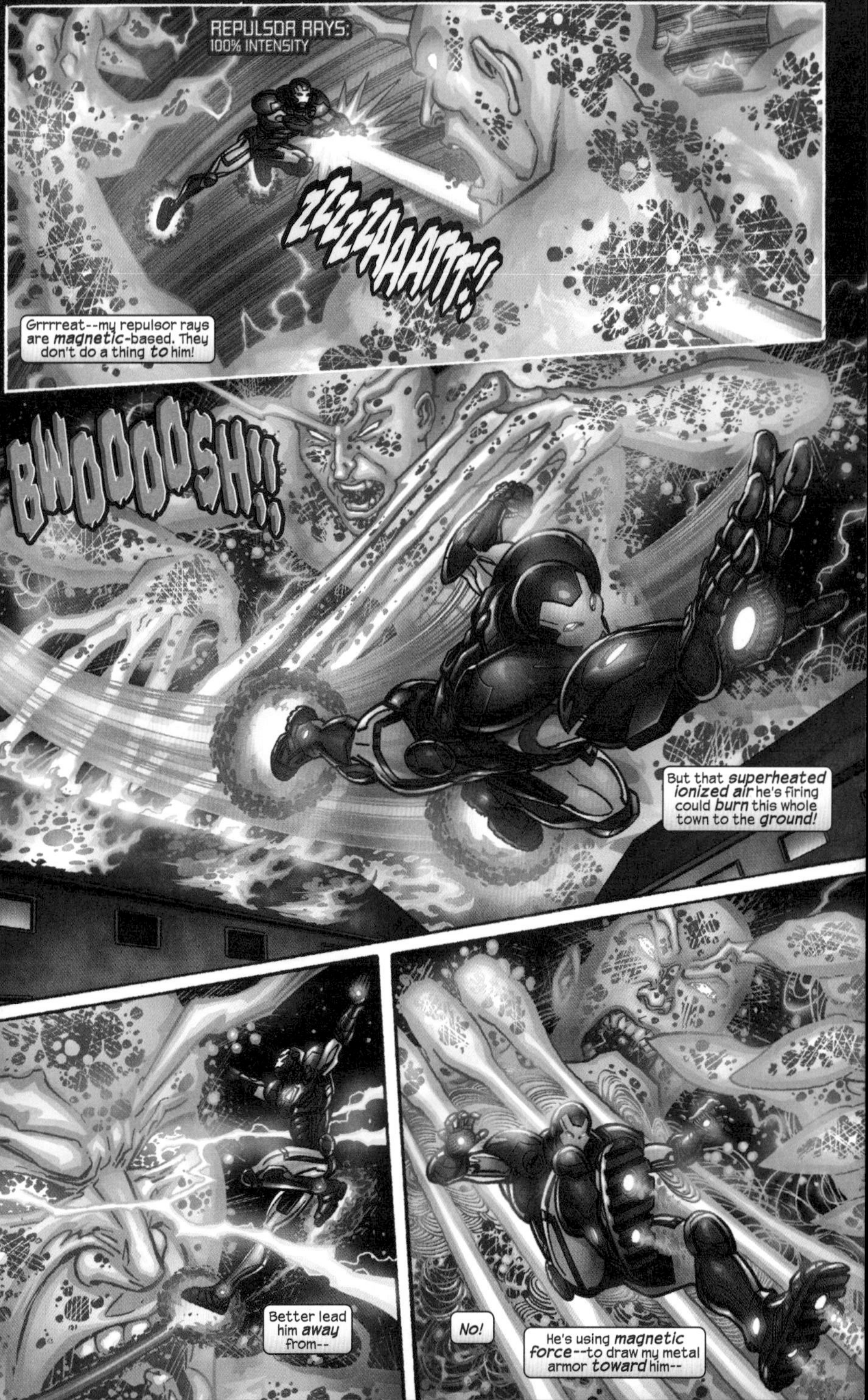
REPULSOR RAYS:
100% INTENSITY
ZZZZZAAATTT!!
Grrrreat--my repulsor rays are magnetic-based. They don't do a thing to him!
BWOOOOSH!!
But that superheated ionized air he's firing could burn this whole town to the ground!
Better lead him away from--
No!
He's using magnetic force--to draw my metal armor toward him--

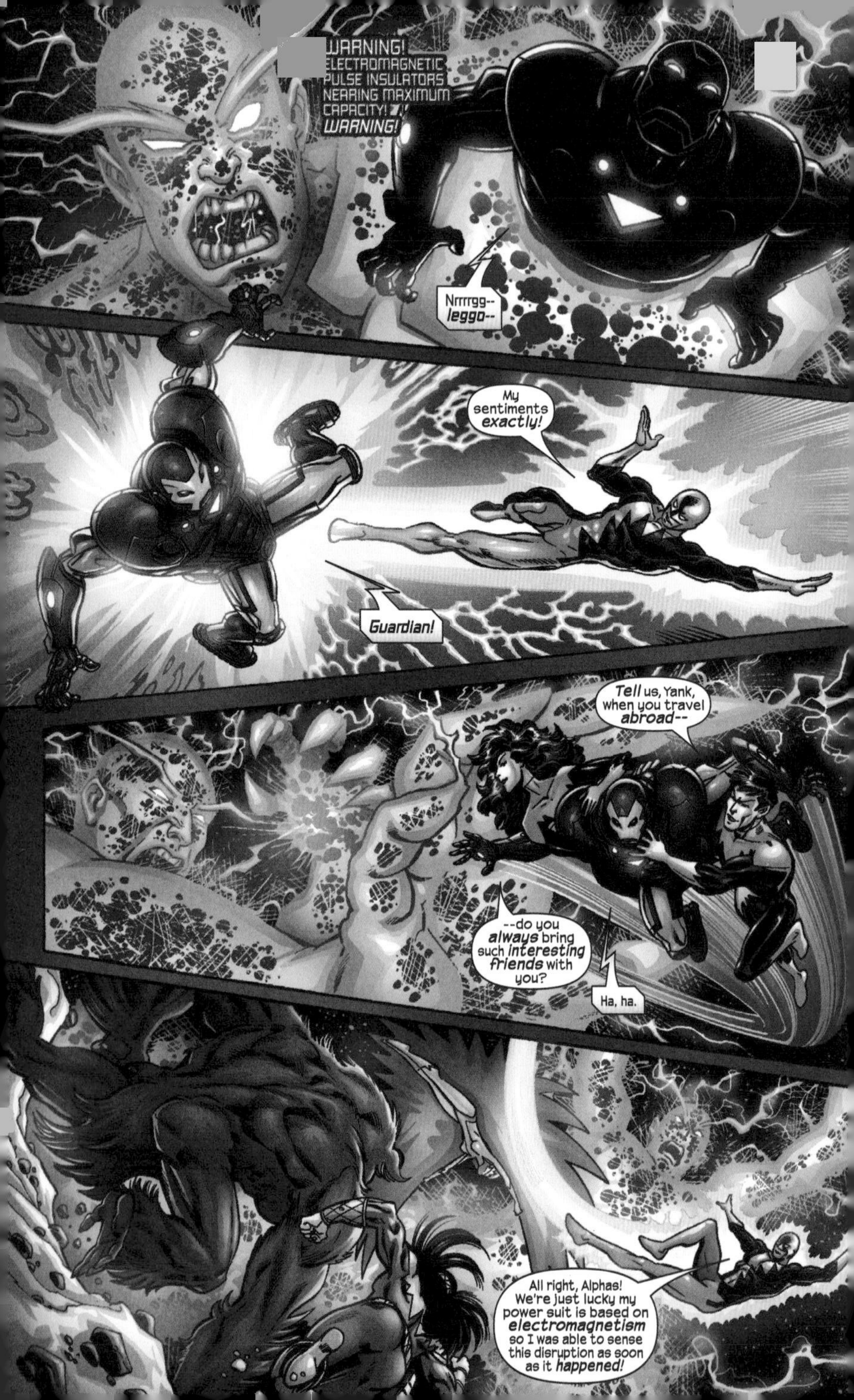
WARNING! ELECTROMAGNETIC PULSE INSULATORS NEARING MAXIMUM CAPACITY! WARNING!
Nrrrrgg-- leggo--
My sentiments exactly!
Guardian!
Tell us, Yank, when you travel abroad--
--do you always bring such interesting friends with you?
Ha, ha.
All right, Alphas! We're just lucky my power suit is based on electromagnetism so I was able to sense this disruption as soon as it happened!

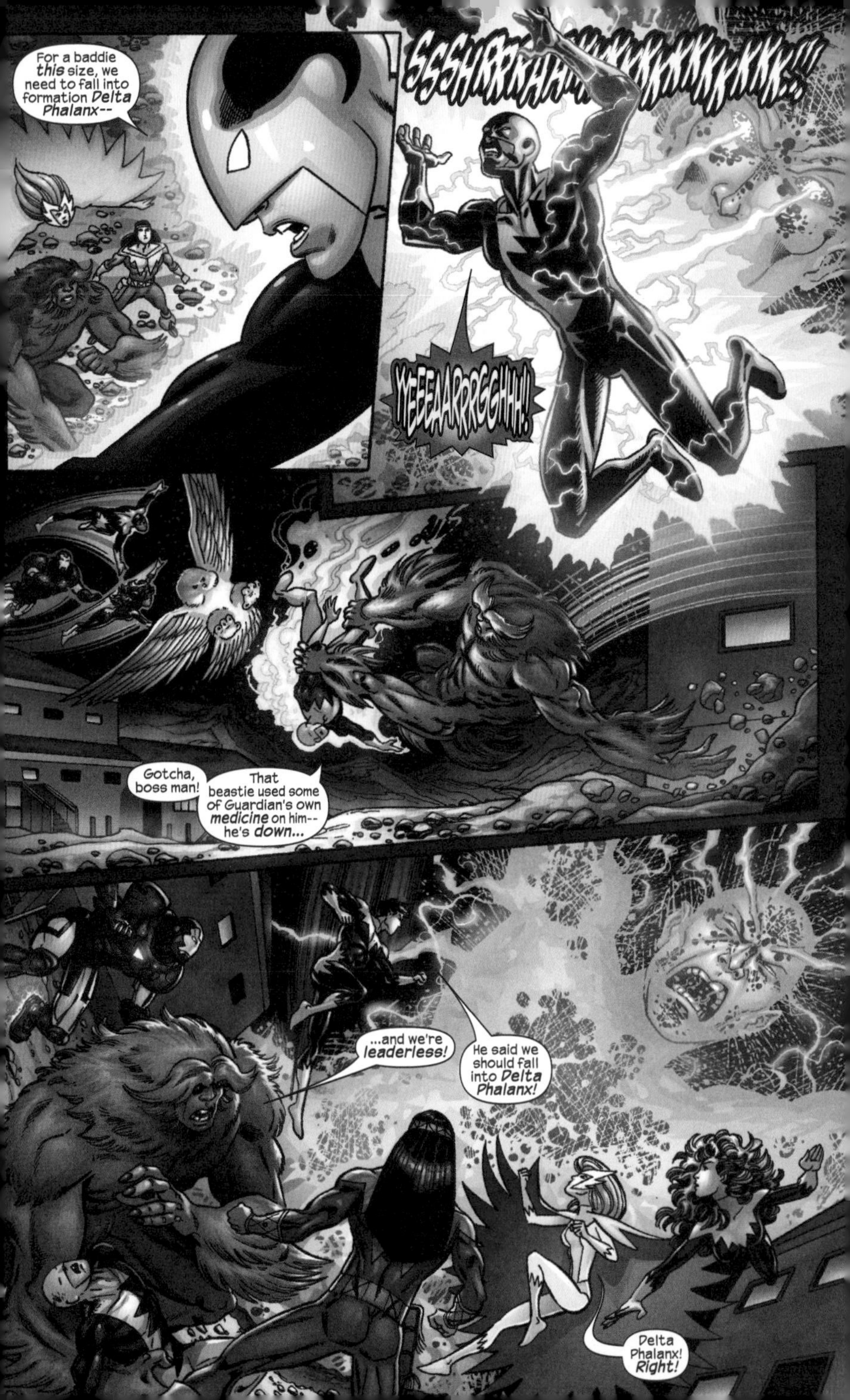
For a baddie *this* size, we need to fall into formation *Delta Phalanx*--
YYEEEAARRRGGHH!
Gotcha, boss man!
That beastie used some of Guardian's own *medicine* on him-- he's *down*...
...and we're *leaderless!*
He said we should fall into *Delta Phalanx!*
Delta Phalanx! *Right!*

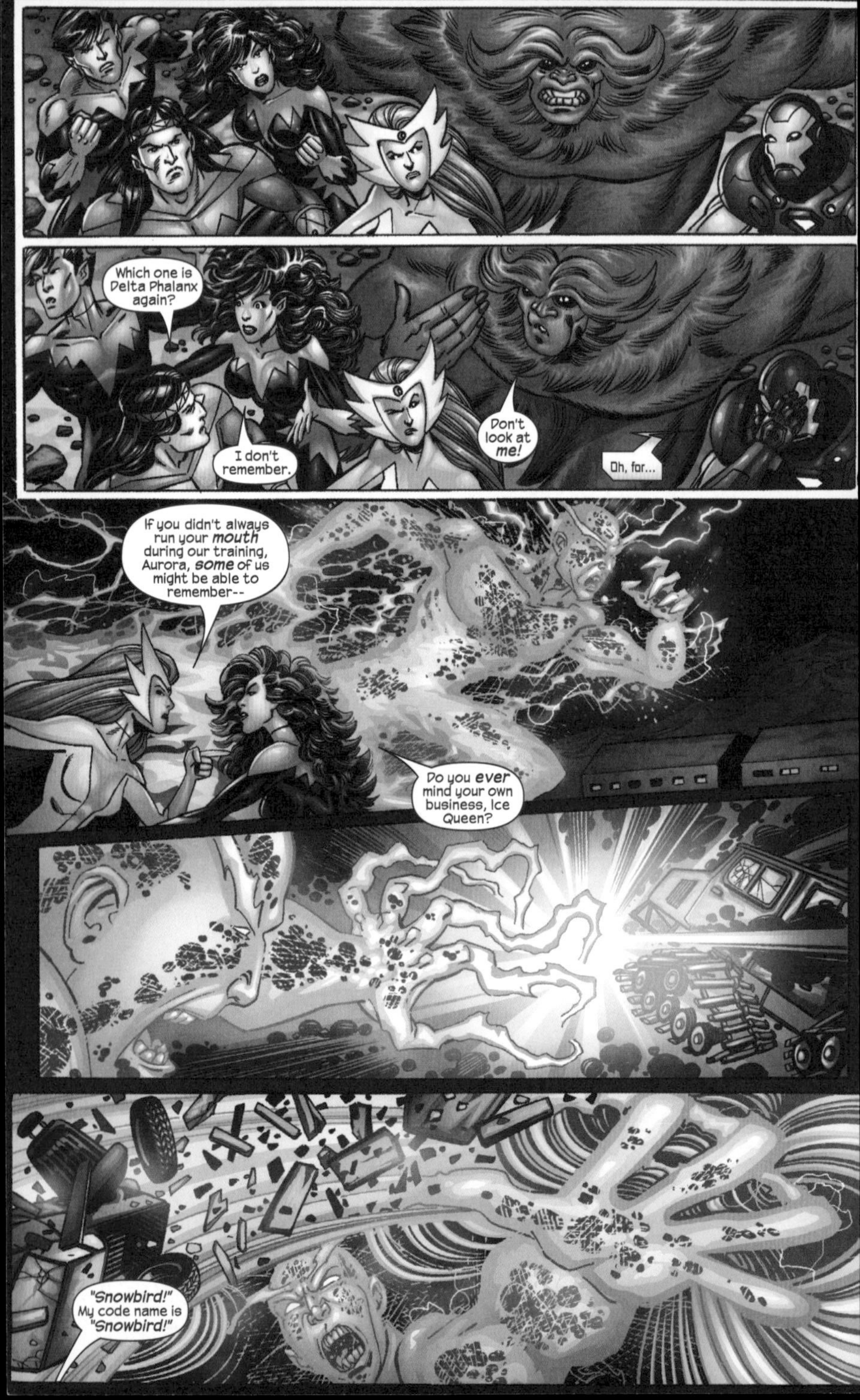
Which one is Delta Phalanx again?
I don't remember.
Don't look at me!
Oh, for...
If you didn't always run your mouth during our training, Aurora, some of us might be able to remember--
Do you ever mind your own business, Ice Queen?
"Snowbird!" My code name is "Snowbird!"

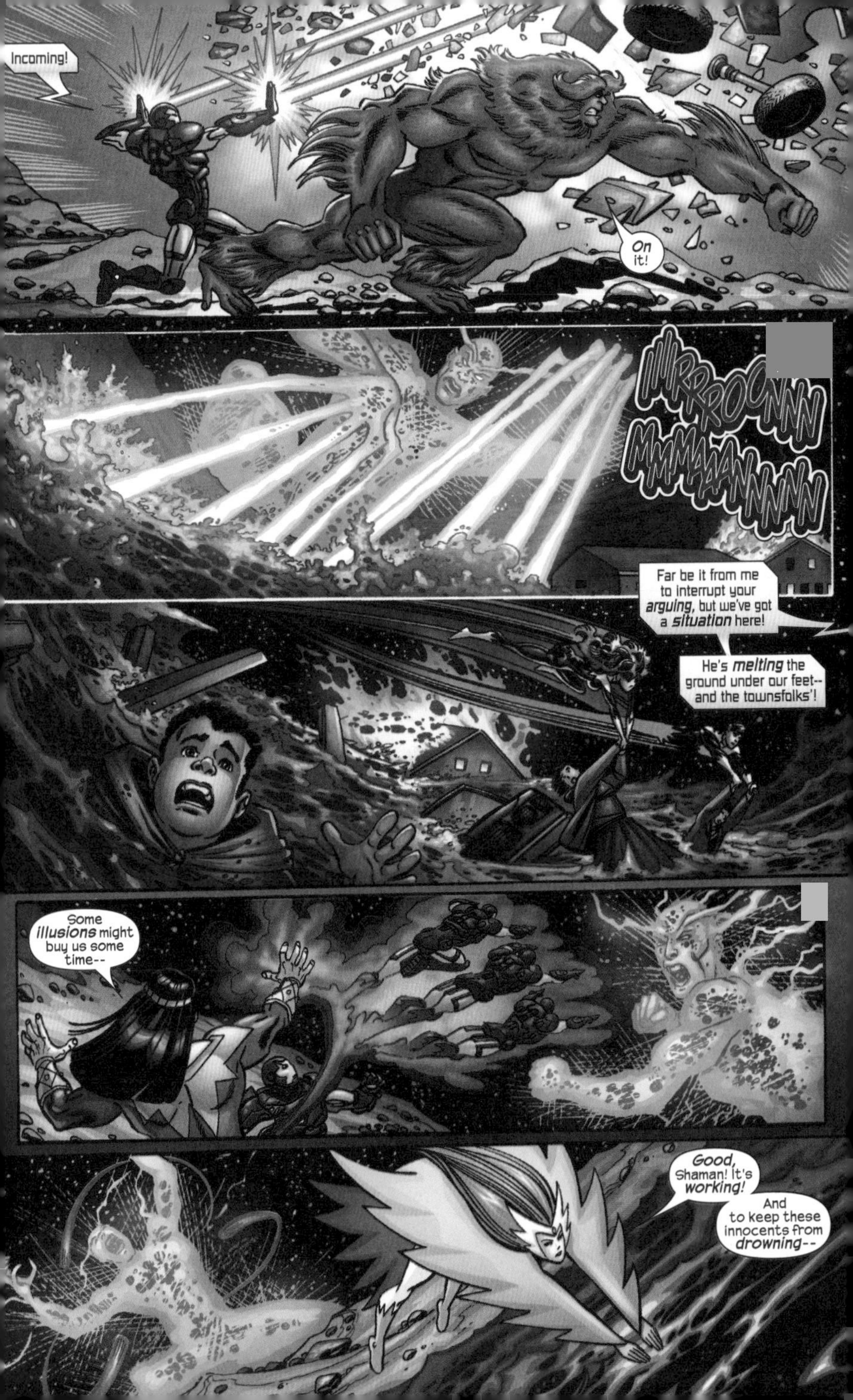
Incoming!
On it!
IIIRRROOONNN MMMAAANNNNN
Far be it from me to interrupt your *arguing*, but we've got a *situation* here!
He's *melting* the ground under our feet-- and the townsfolks'!
Some *illusions* might buy us some time--
Good, Shaman! It's *working!*
And to keep these innocents from *drowning*--

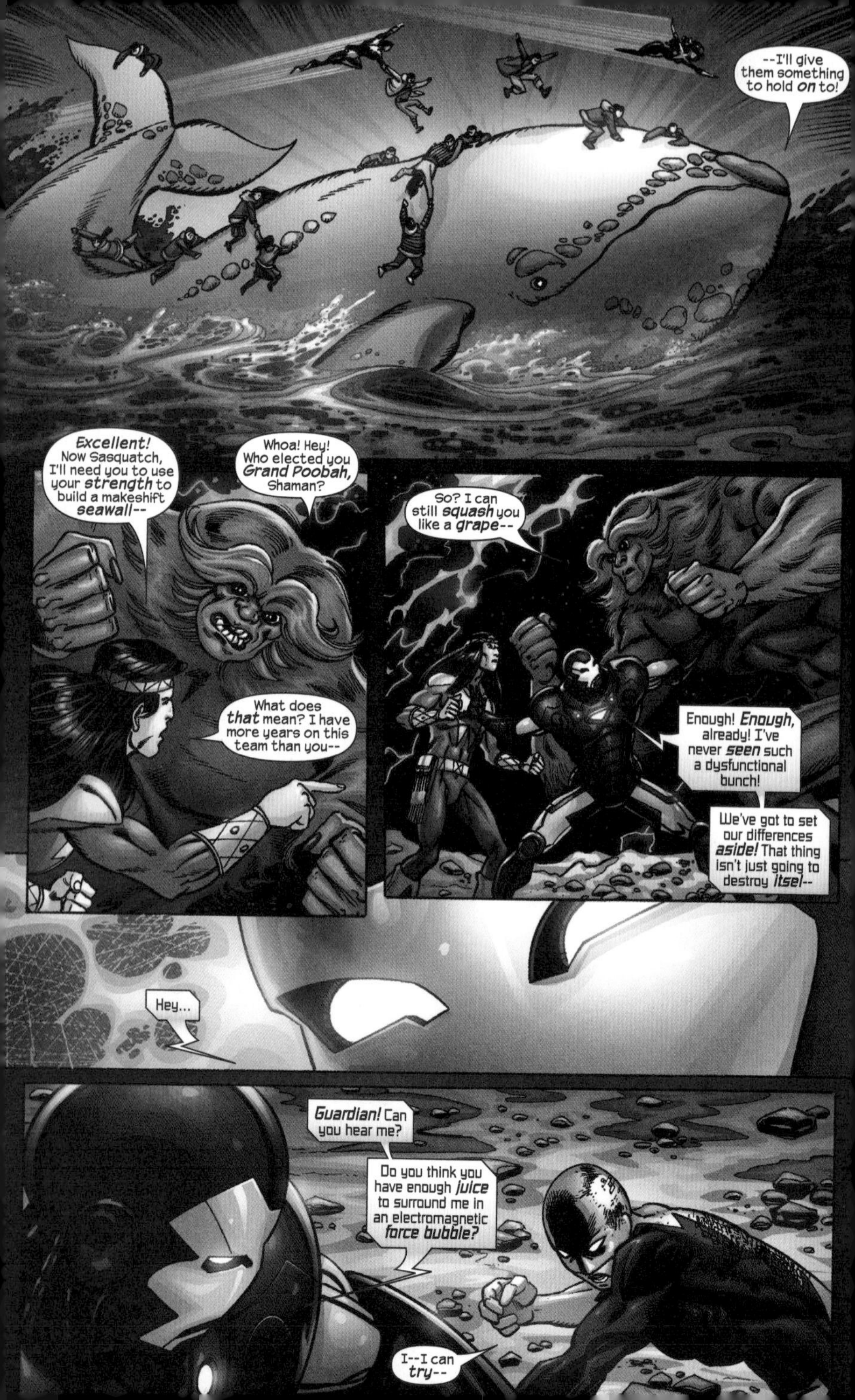
--I'll give them something to hold *on* to!
Excellent! Now Sasquatch, I'll need you to use your *strength* to build a makeshift *seawall*--
Whoa! Hey! Who elected you *Grand Poobah,* Shaman?
What does *that* mean? I have more years on this team than you--
So? I can still *squash* you like a *grape*--
Enough! *Enough,* already! I've never *seen* such a dysfunctional bunch!
We've got to set our differences *aside!* That thing isn't just going to destroy *itsel*--
Hey...
Guardian! Can you hear me?
Do you think you have enough *juice* to surround me in an electromagnetic *force bubble?*
I--I can *try*--

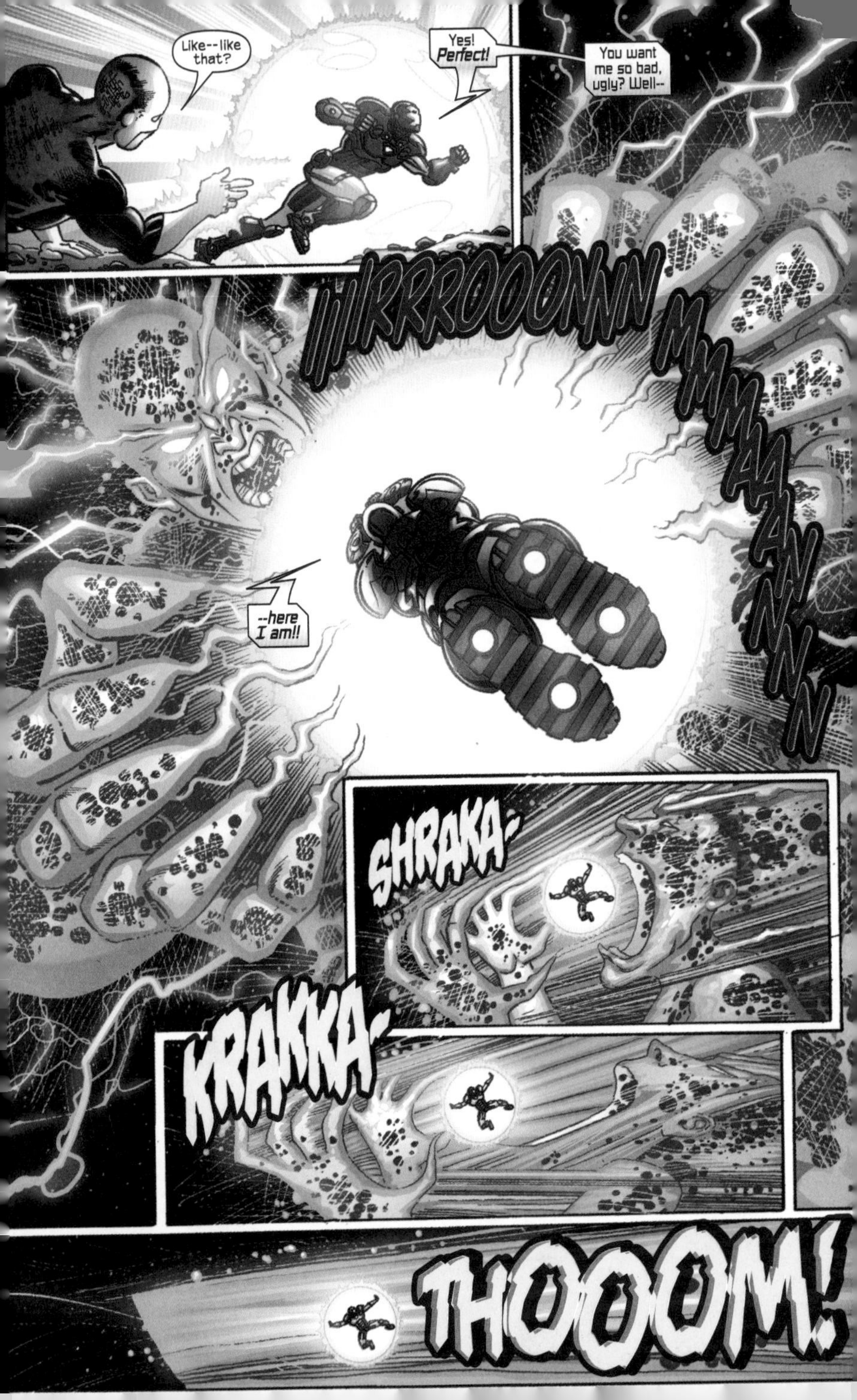

Like--like that?
Yes! Perfect!
You want me so bad, ugly? Well--
WHRRROOONNN
MMMAAANNNNN
--here I am!!
SHRAKA-
KRAKKA-
THOOOM!

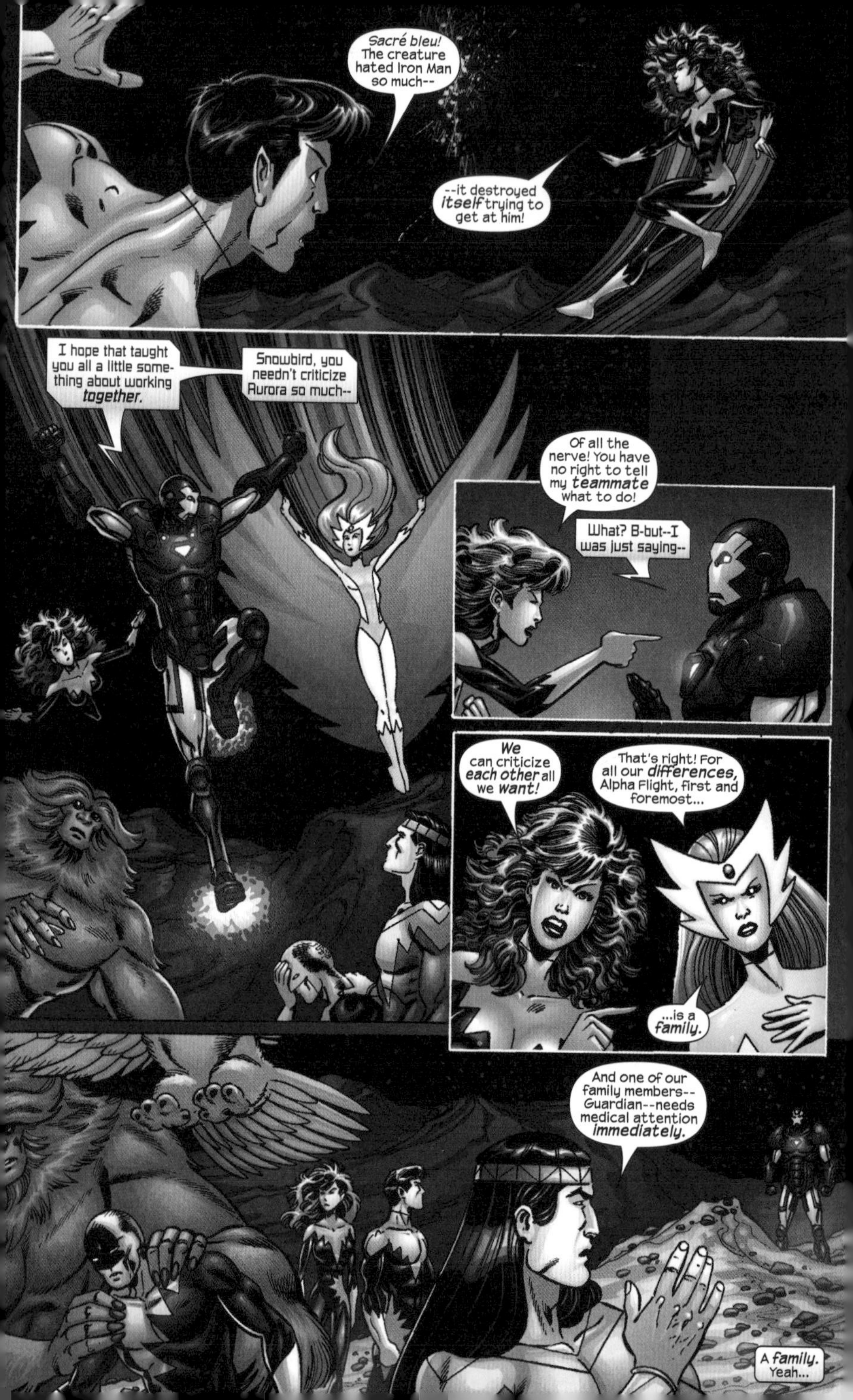
Sacré bleu! The creature hated Iron Man so much--
--it destroyed *itself* trying to get at him!
I hope that taught you all a little something about working *together.*
Snowbird, you needn't criticize Aurora so much--
Of all the nerve! You have no right to tell my *teammate* what to do!
What? B-but--I was just saying--
We can criticize *each other* all we *want!*
That's right! For all our *differences,* Alpha Flight, first and foremost...
...is a *family.*
And one of our family members--Guardian--needs medical attention *immediately.*
A *family.* Yeah...

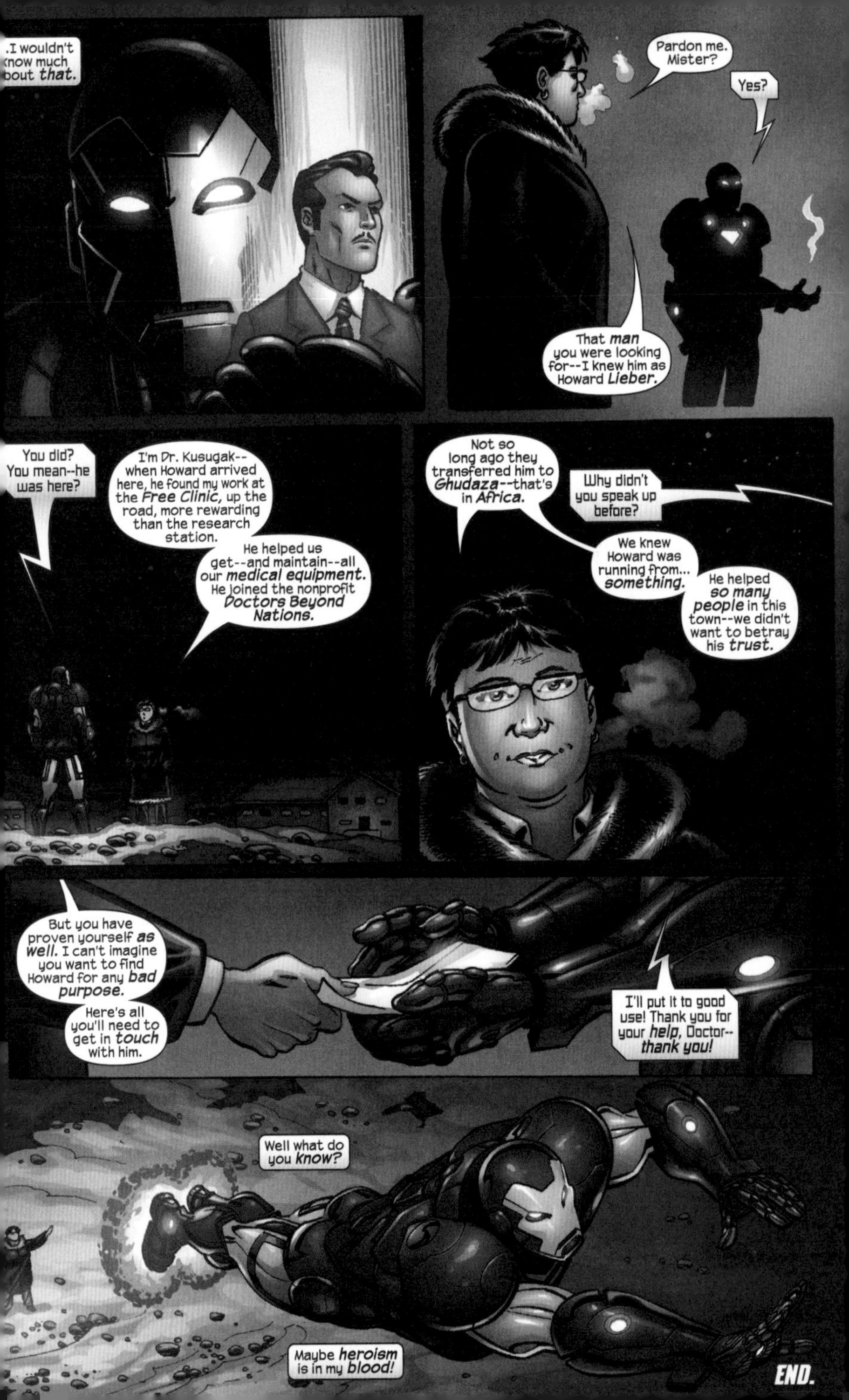

.I wouldn't
know much
bout that.
Pardon me.
Mister?
Yes?
That man
you were looking
for--I knew him as
Howard Lieber.
You did?
You mean--he
was here?
I'm Dr. Kusugak--
when Howard arrived
here, he found my work at
the Free Clinic, up the
road, more rewarding
than the research
station.
He helped us
get--and maintain--all
our medical equipment.
He joined the nonprofit
Doctors Beyond
Nations.
Not so
long ago they
transferred him to
Ghudaza--that's
in Africa.
Why didn't
you speak up
before?
We knew
Howard was
running from...
something.
He helped
so many
people in this
town--we didn't
want to betray
his trust.
But you have
proven yourself as
well. I can't imagine
you want to find
Howard for any bad
purpose.
Here's all
you'll need to
get in touch
with him.
I'll put it to good
use! Thank you for
your help, Doctor--
thank you!
Well what do
you know?
Maybe heroism
is in my blood!
END.

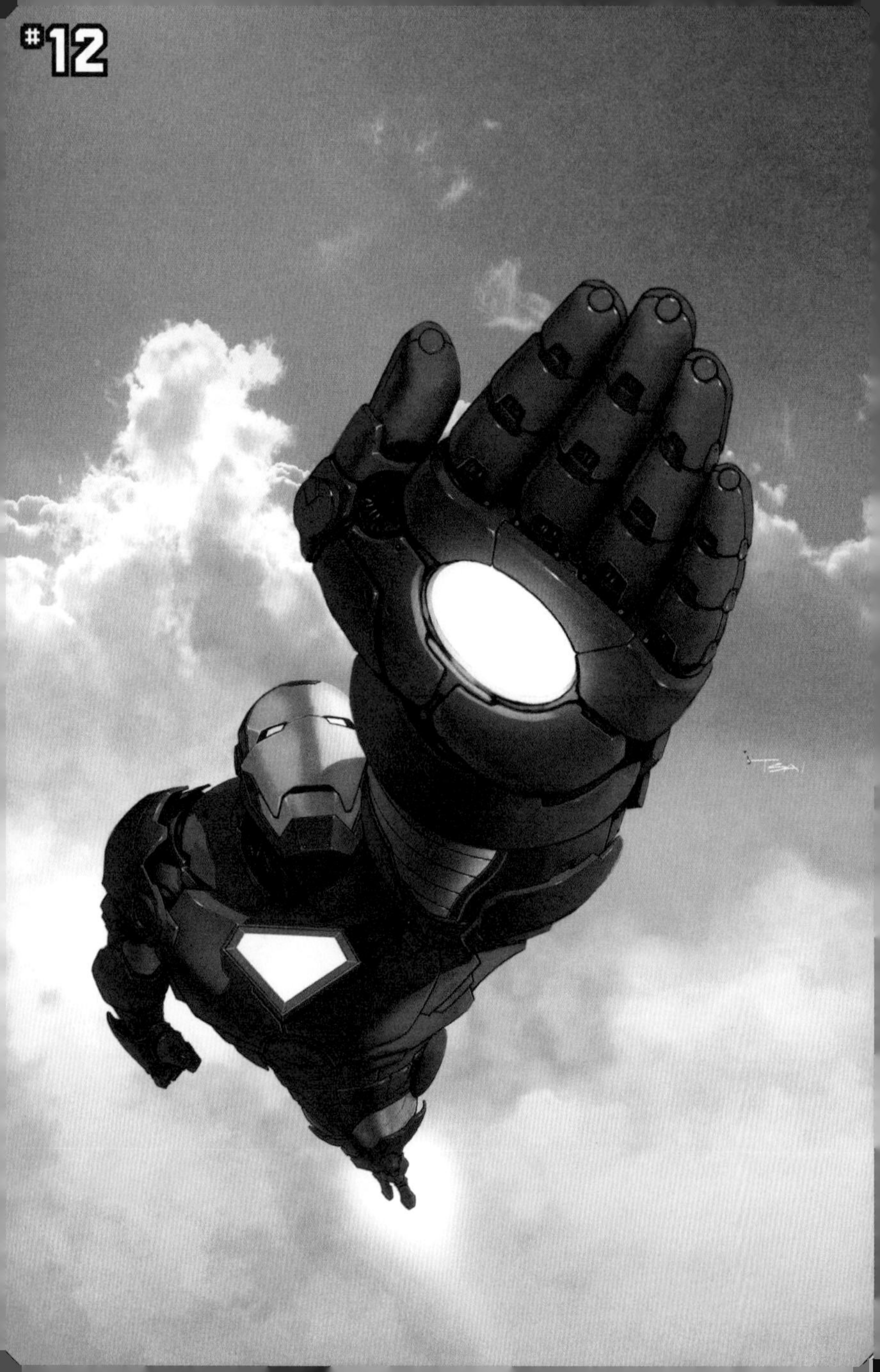
#12

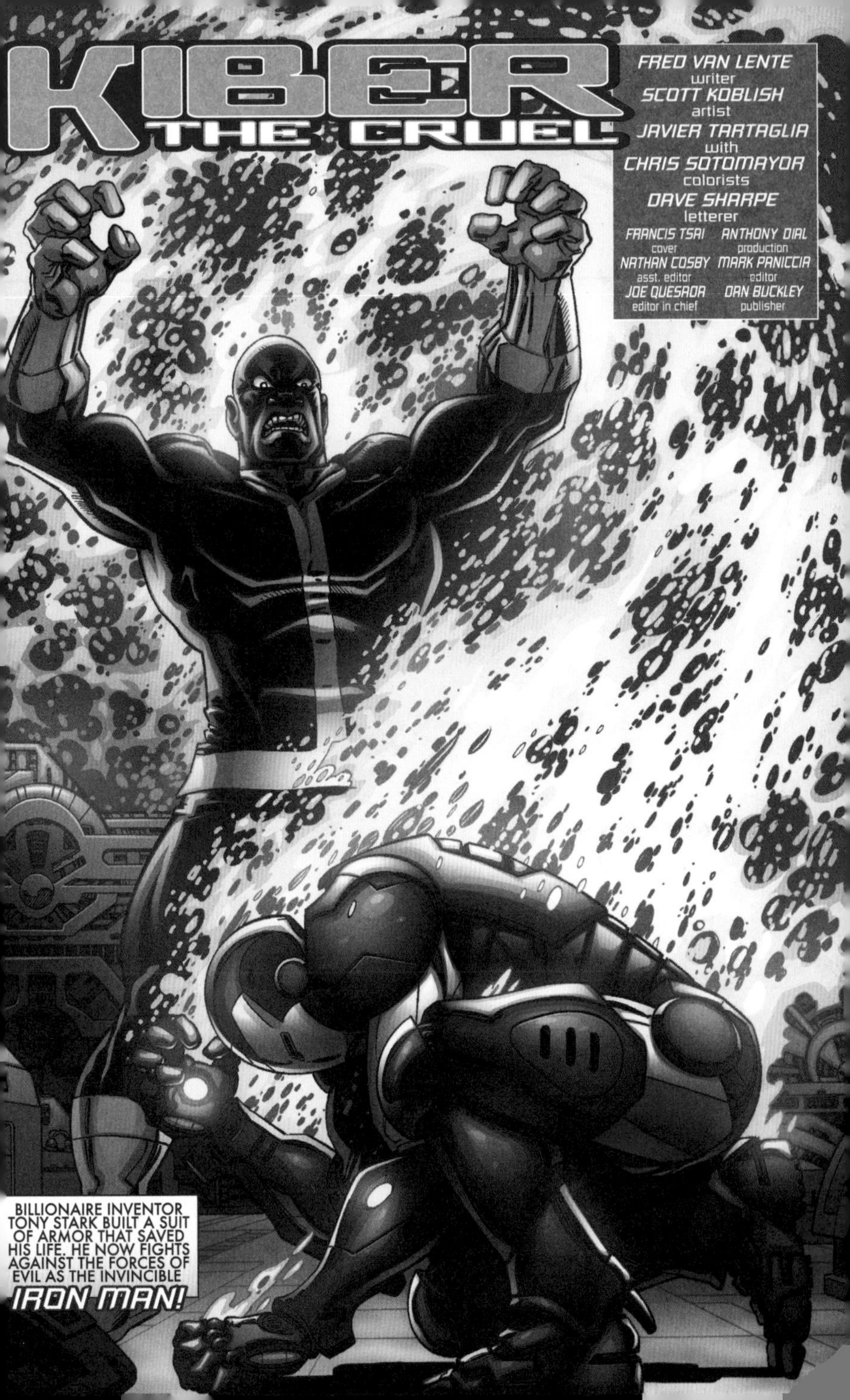
KIBER THE CRUEL
FRED VAN LENTE writer
SCOTT KOBLISH artist
JAVIER TARTAGLIA with CHRIS SOTOMAYOR colorists
DAVE SHARPE letterer
FRANCIS TSAI cover
ANTHONY DIAL production
NATHAN COSBY asst. editor
MARK PANICCIA editor
JOE QUESADA editor in chief
DAN BUCKLEY publisher
BILLIONAIRE INVENTOR TONY STARK BUILT A SUIT OF ARMOR THAT SAVED HIS LIFE. HE NOW FIGHTS AGAINST THE FORCES OF EVIL AS THE INVINCIBLE IRON MAN!

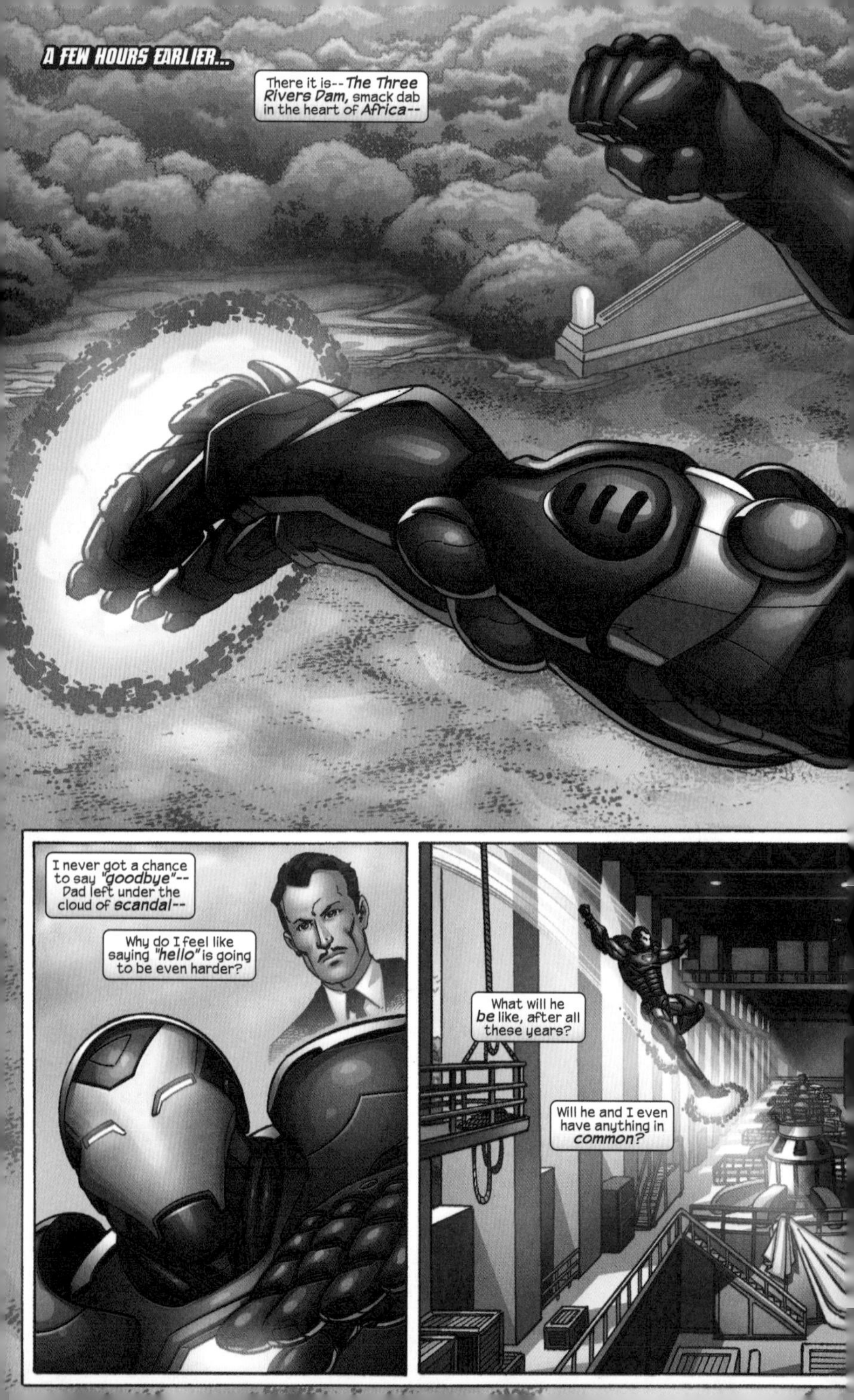
A FEW HOURS EARLIER...
There it is--*The Three Rivers Dam,* smack dab in the heart of *Africa*--
I never got a chance to say *"goodbye"*--Dad left under the cloud of *scandal*--
Why do I feel like saying *"hello"* is going to be even harder?
What will he *be* like, after all these years?
Will he and I even have anything in *common?*

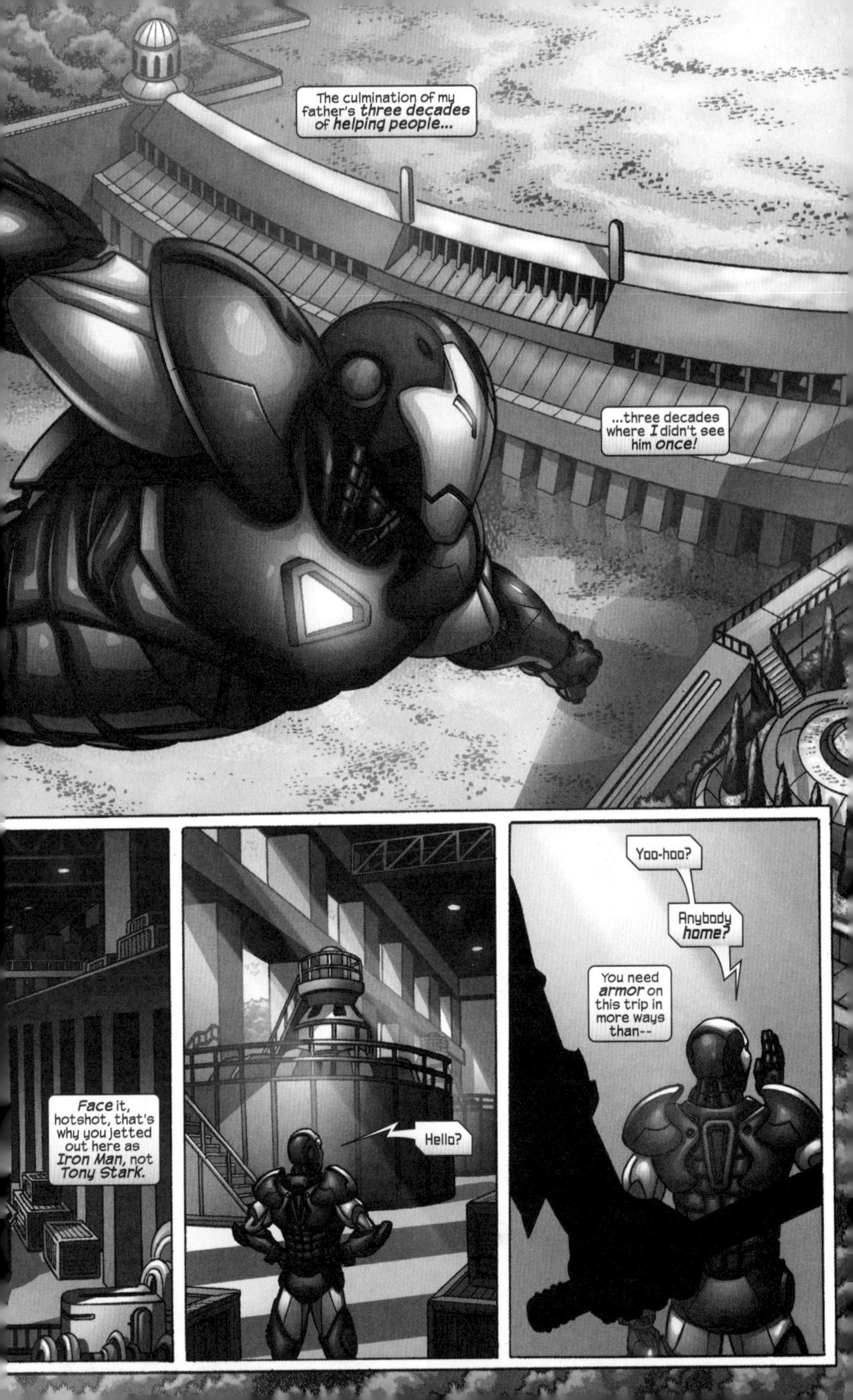
The culmination of my father's *three decades* of *helping people...*
...three decades where *I* didn't see him *once!*
Face it, hotshot, that's why you jetted out here as *Iron Man*, not *Tony Stark.*
Hello?
Yoo-hoo?
Anybody *home?*
You need *armor* on this trip in more ways than--

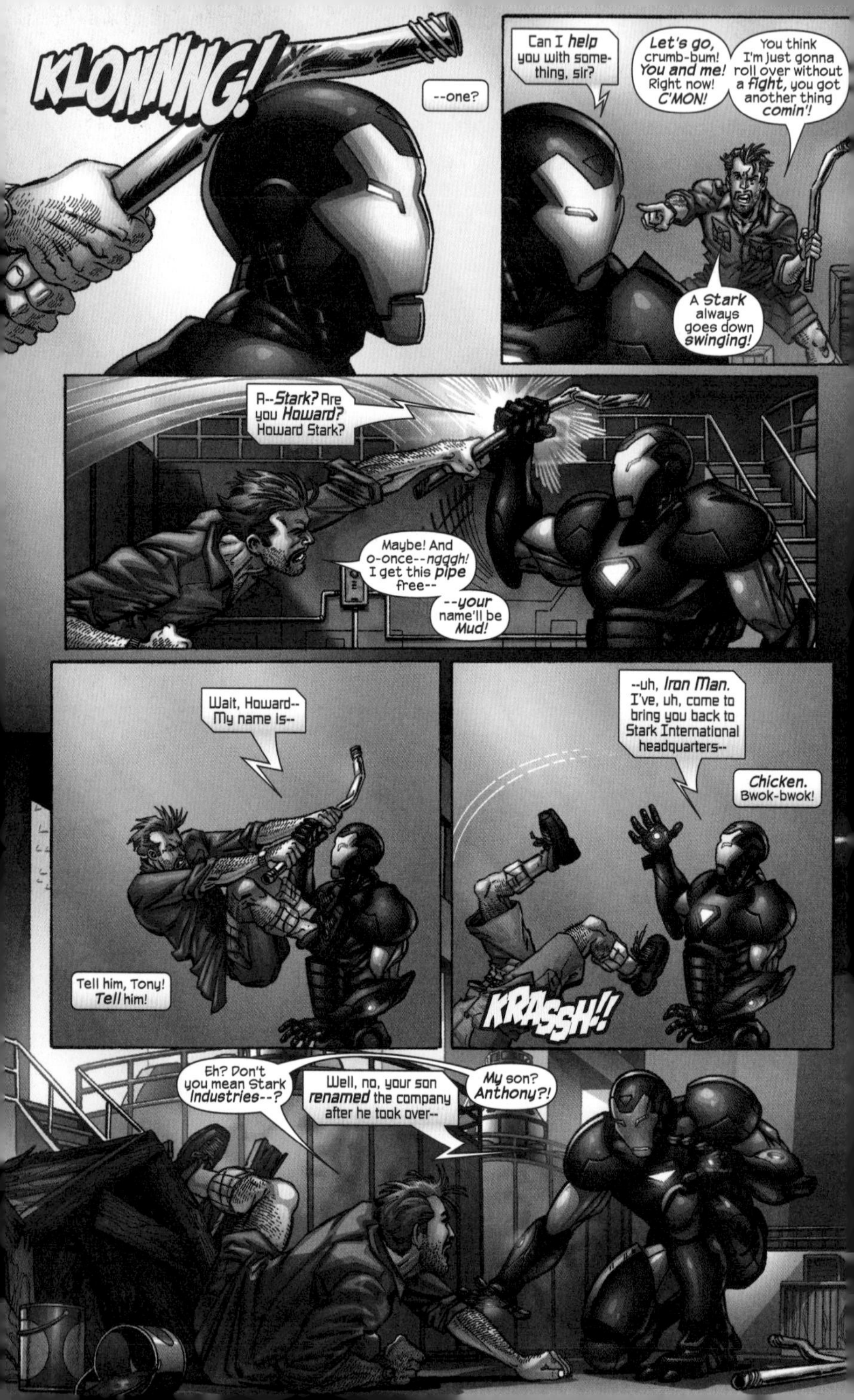
KLONNNG!
--one?
Can I help you with some-thing, sir?
Let's go, crumb-bum! You and me! Right now! C'MON!
You think I'm just gonna roll over without a fight, you got another thing comin'!
A Stark always goes down swinging!
A--Stark? Are you Howard? Howard Stark?
Maybe! And o-once--ngggh! I get this pipe free--
--your name'll be Mud!
Wait, Howard-- My name is--
Tell him, Tony! Tell him!
--uh, Iron Man. I've, uh, come to bring you back to Stark International headquarters--
Chicken. Bwok-bwok!
KRASSH!!
Eh? Don't you mean Stark Industries--?
Well, no, your son renamed the company after he took over--
My son? Anthony?!

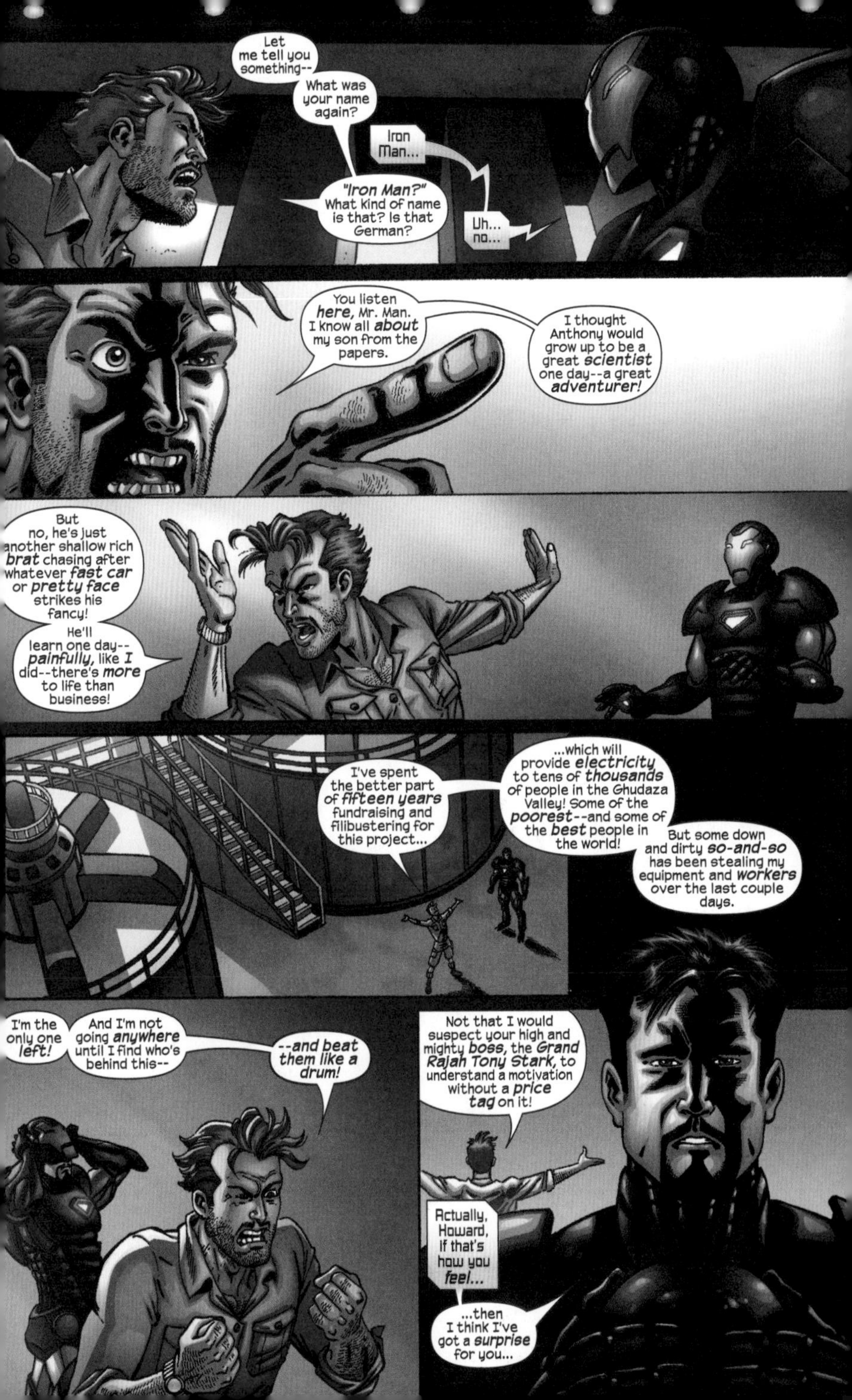

Let me tell you something--
What was your name again?
Iron Man...
"Iron Man?" What kind of name is that? Is that German?
Uh... no...
You listen here, Mr. Man. I know all about my son from the papers.
I thought Anthony would grow up to be a great scientist one day--a great adventurer!
But no, he's just another shallow rich brat chasing after whatever fast car or pretty face strikes his fancy!
He'll learn one day--painfully, like I did--there's more to life than business!
I've spent the better part of fifteen years fundraising and filibustering for this project...
...which will provide electricity to tens of thousands of people in the Ghudaza Valley! Some of the poorest--and some of the best people in the world!
But some down and dirty so-and-so has been stealing my equipment and workers over the last couple days.
I'm the only one left!
And I'm not going anywhere until I find who's behind this--
--and beat them like a drum!
Not that I would suspect your high and mighty boss, the Grand Rajah Tony Stark, to understand a motivation without a price tag on it!
Actually, Howard, if that's how you feel...
...then I think I've got a surprise for you...

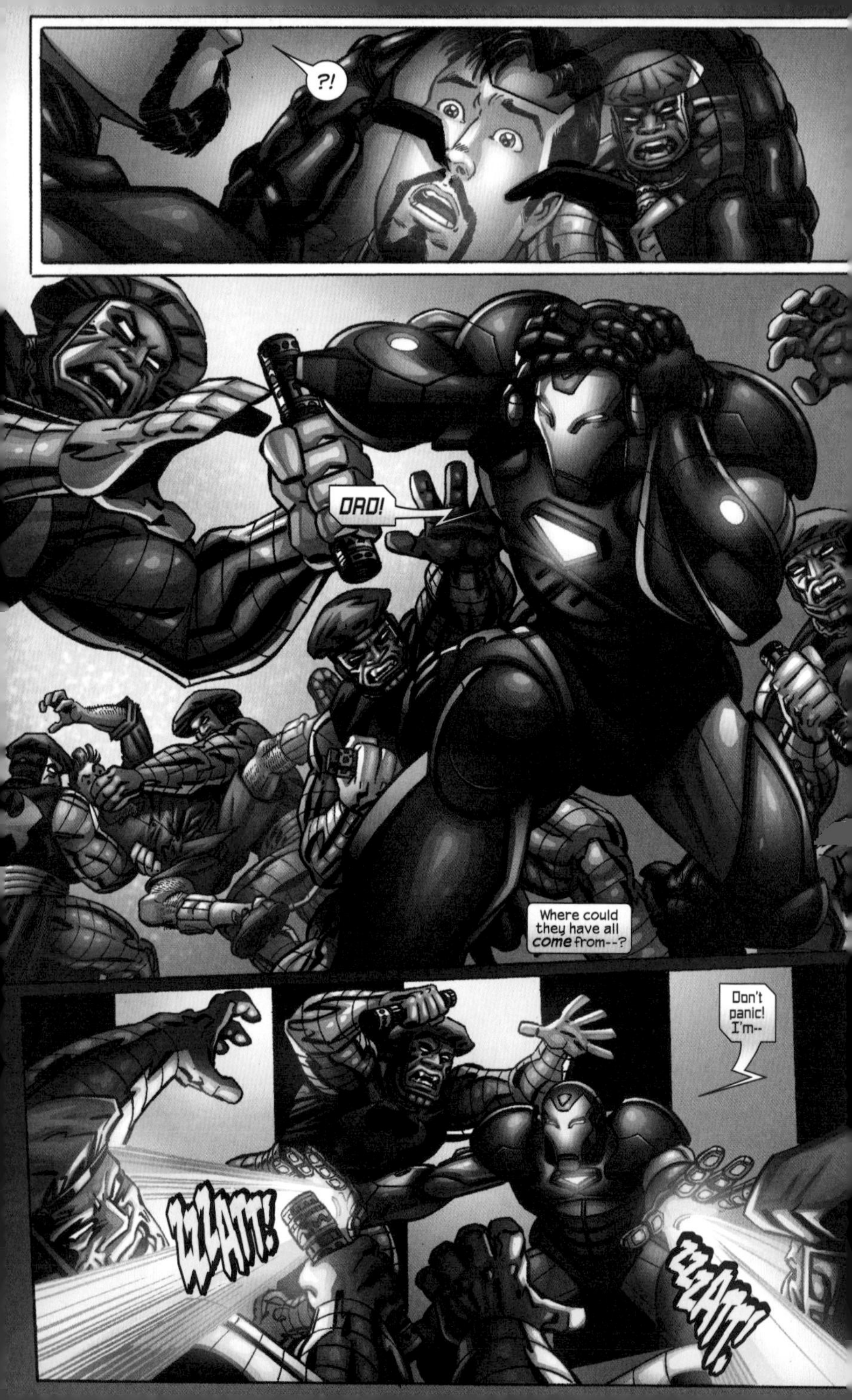
?!
DAD!
Where could they have all come from--?
Don't panic! I'm--
ZZLATT!
ZZZATT!

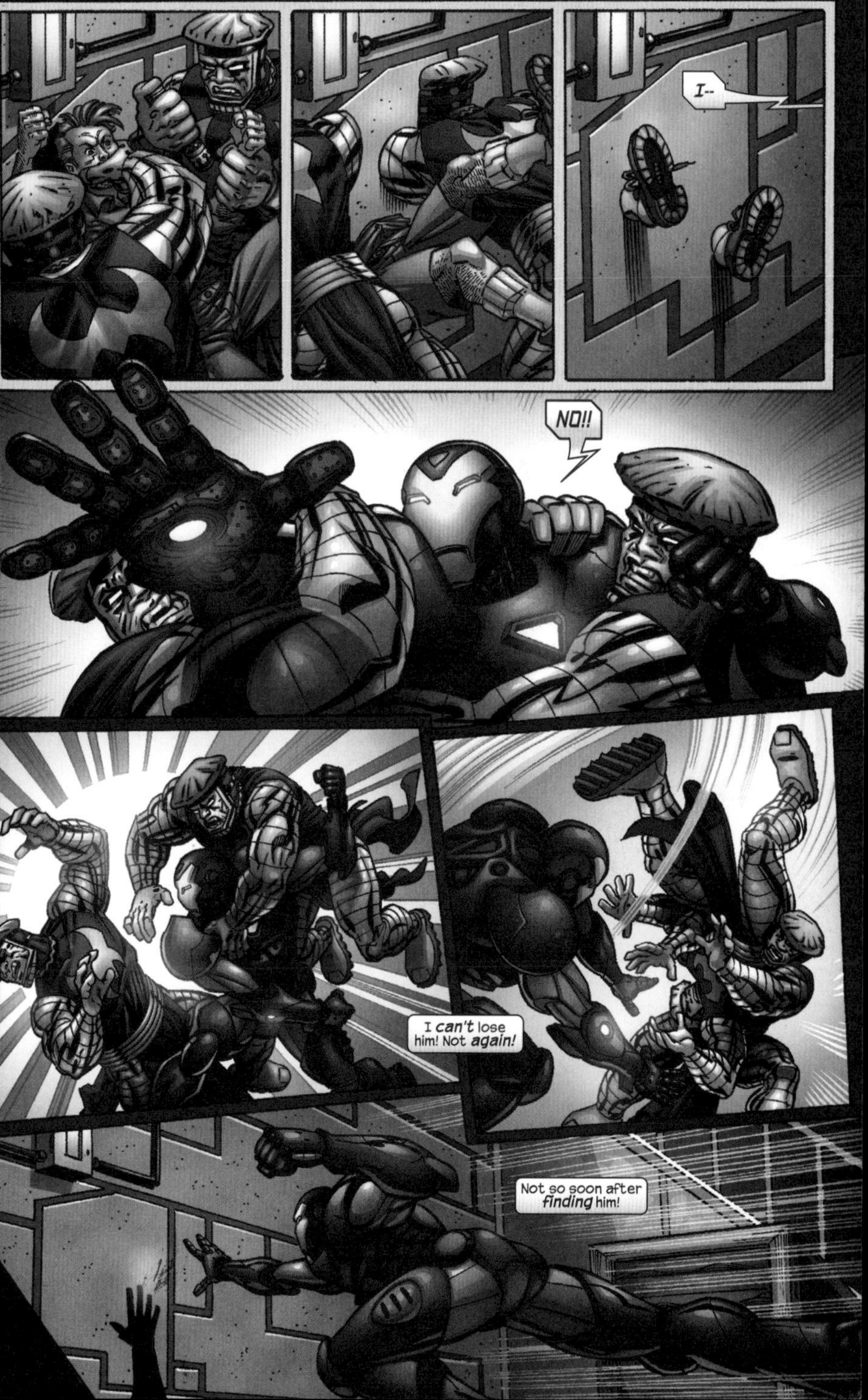
I--
NO!!
I can't lose him! Not again!
Not so soon after finding him!

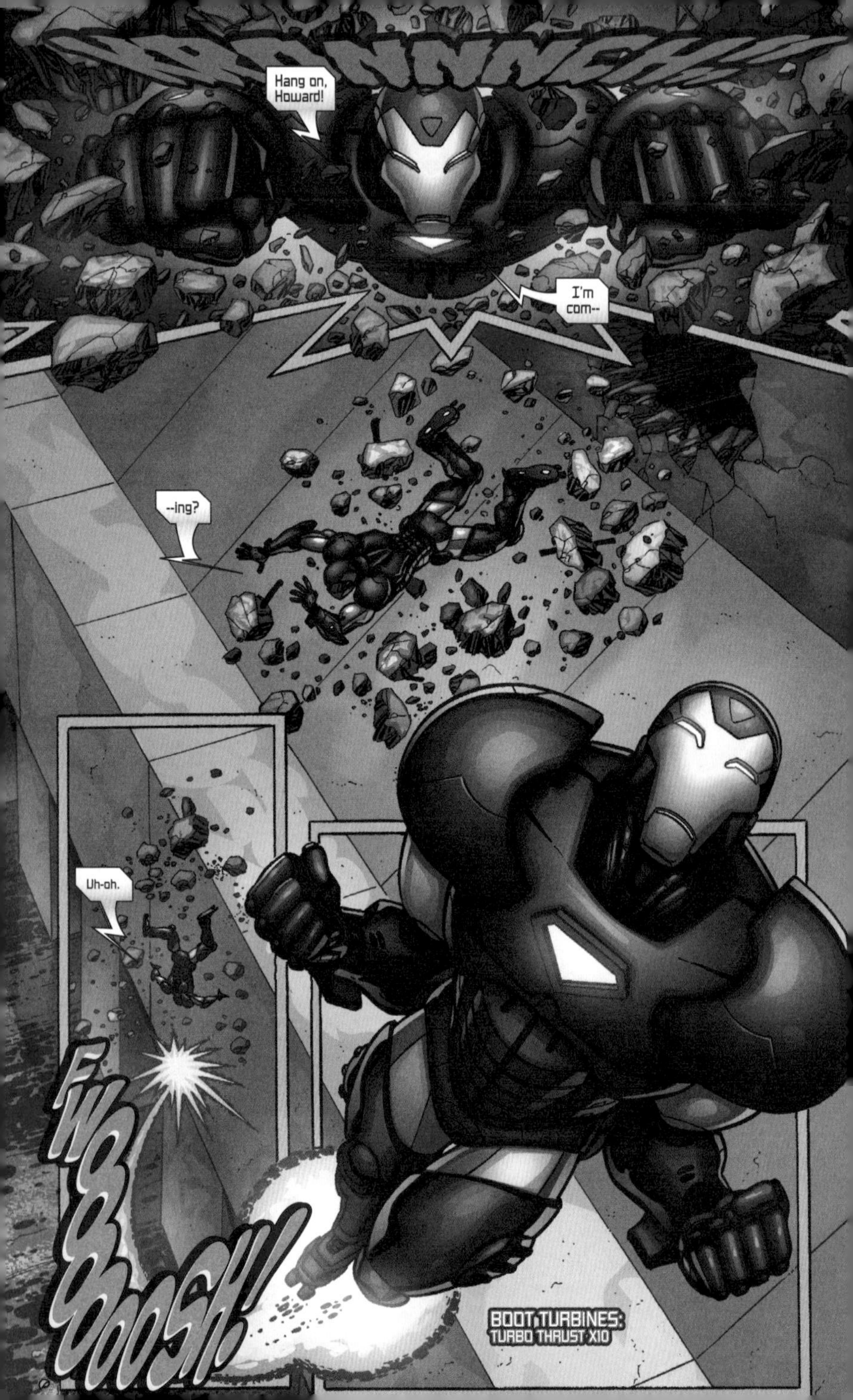
Hang on, Howard!
I'm com--
--ing?
Uh-oh.
BOOT TURBINES:
TURBO THRUST X10

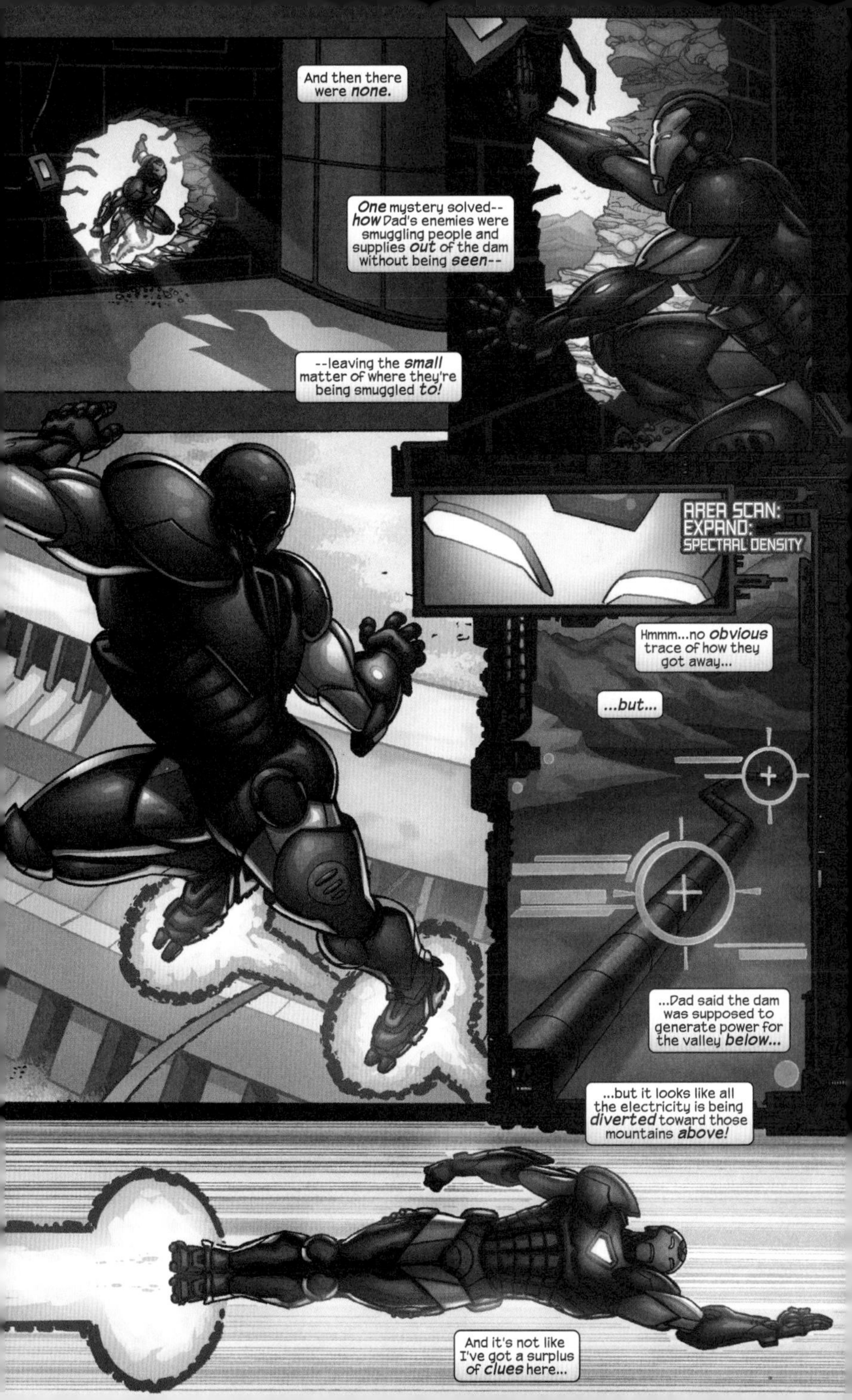
And then there were none.
One mystery solved--how Dad's enemies were smuggling people and supplies out of the dam without being seen--
--leaving the small matter of where they're being smuggled to!
AREA SCAN: EXPAND: SPECTRAL DENSITY
Hmmm...no obvious trace of how they got away...
...but...
...Dad said the dam was supposed to generate power for the valley below...
...but it looks like all the electricity is being diverted toward those mountains above!
And it's not like I've got a surplus of clues here...

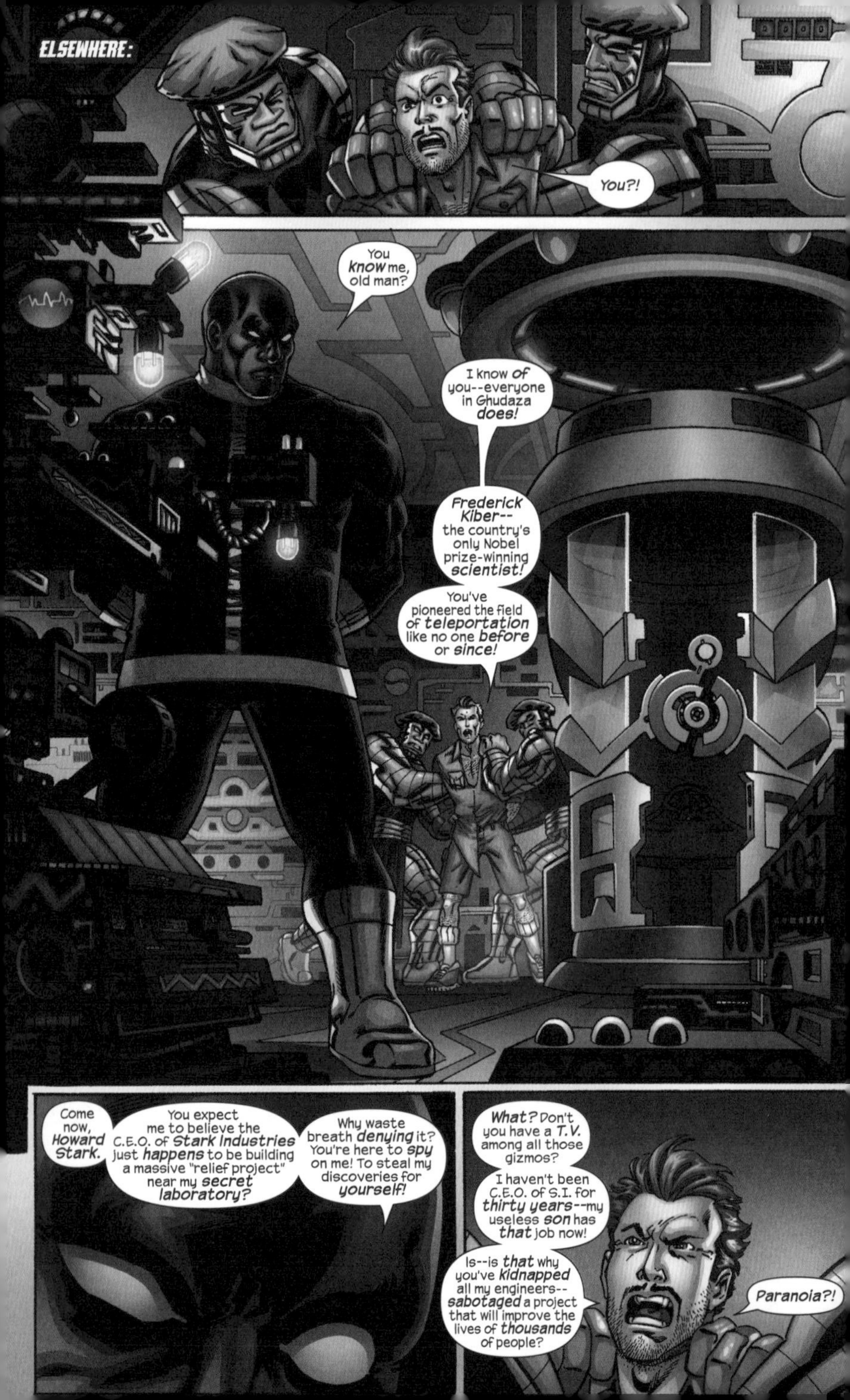
ELSEWHERE:
You?!
You know me, old man?
I know of you--everyone in Ghudaza does!
Frederick Kiber--the country's only Nobel prize-winning scientist!
You've pioneered the field of teleportation like no one before or since!
Come now, Howard Stark.
You expect me to believe the C.E.O. of Stark Industries just happens to be building a massive "relief project" near my secret laboratory?
Why waste breath denying it? You're here to spy on me! To steal my discoveries for yourself!
What? Don't you have a T.V. among all those gizmos?
I haven't been C.E.O. of S.I. for thirty years--my useless son has that job now!
Is--is that why you've kidnapped all my engineers--sabotaged a project that will improve the lives of thousands of people?
Paranoia?!

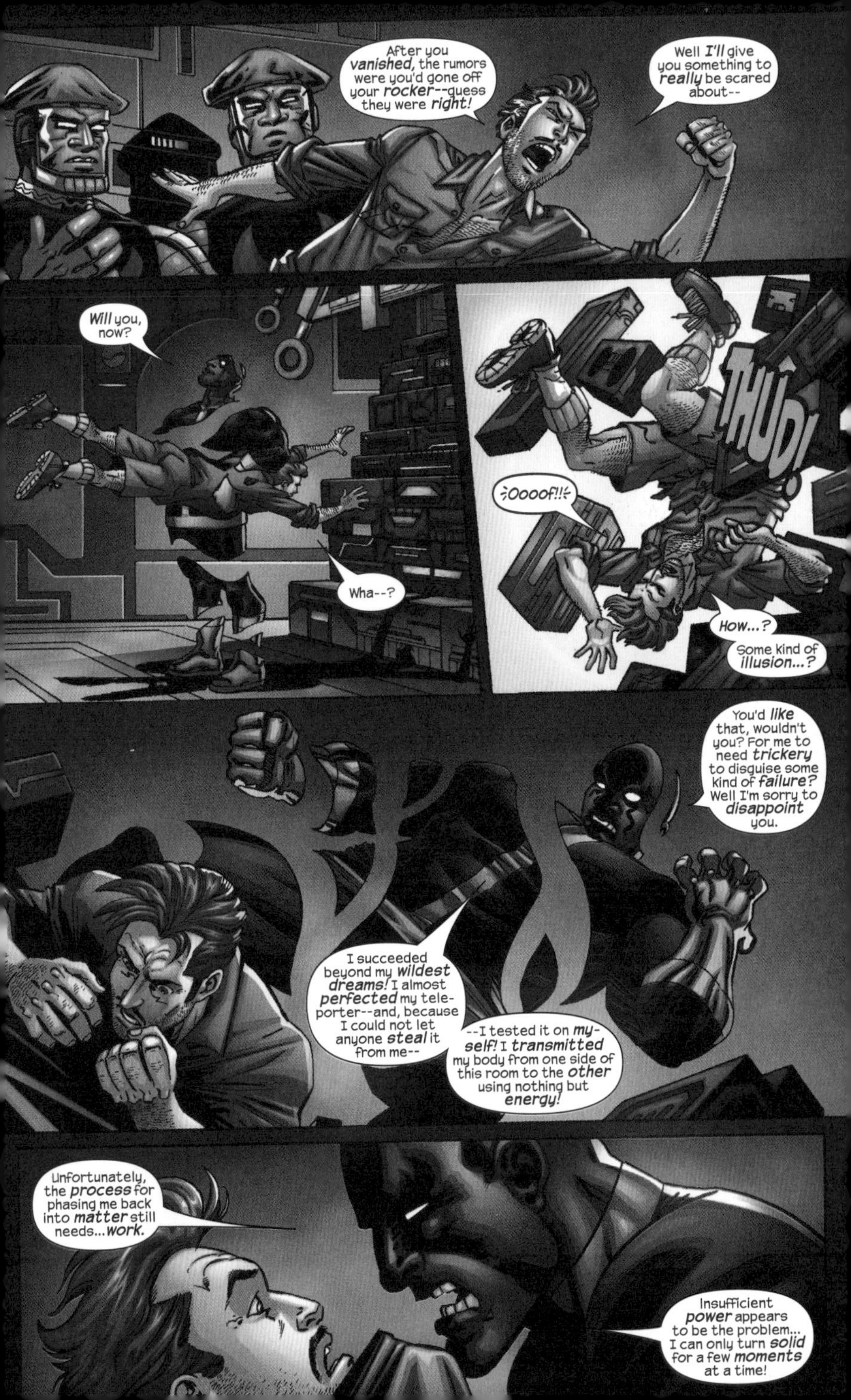
After you vanished, the rumors were you'd gone off your rocker--guess they were right!
Well I'll give you something to really be scared about--
Will you, now?
Wha--?
THUD!
Oooof!!
How...?
Some kind of illusion...?
You'd like that, wouldn't you? For me to need trickery to disguise some kind of failure? Well I'm sorry to disappoint you.
I succeeded beyond my wildest dreams! I almost perfected my teleporter--and, because I could not let anyone steal it from me--
--I tested it on myself! I transmitted my body from one side of this room to the other using nothing but energy!
Unfortunately, the process for phasing me back into matter still needs...work.
Insufficient power appears to be the problem... I can only turn solid for a few moments at a time!

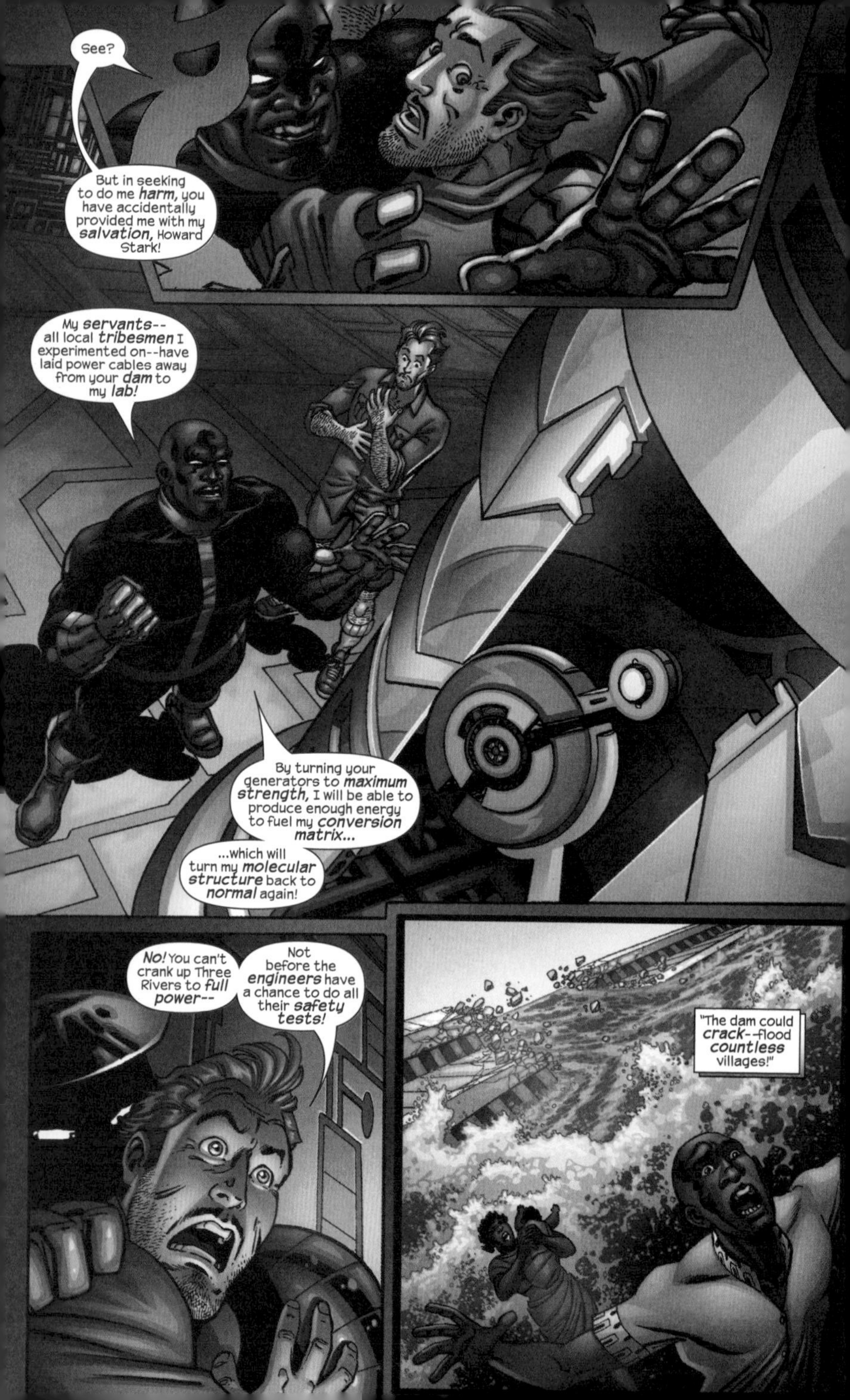
See?
But in seeking to do me harm, you have accidentally provided me with my salvation, Howard Stark!
My servants--all local tribesmen I experimented on--have laid power cables away from your dam to my lab!
By turning your generators to maximum strength, I will be able to produce enough energy to fuel my conversion matrix...
...which will turn my molecular structure back to normal again!
No! You can't crank up Three Rivers to full power--
Not before the engineers have a chance to do all their safety tests!
"The dam could crack--flood countless villages!"

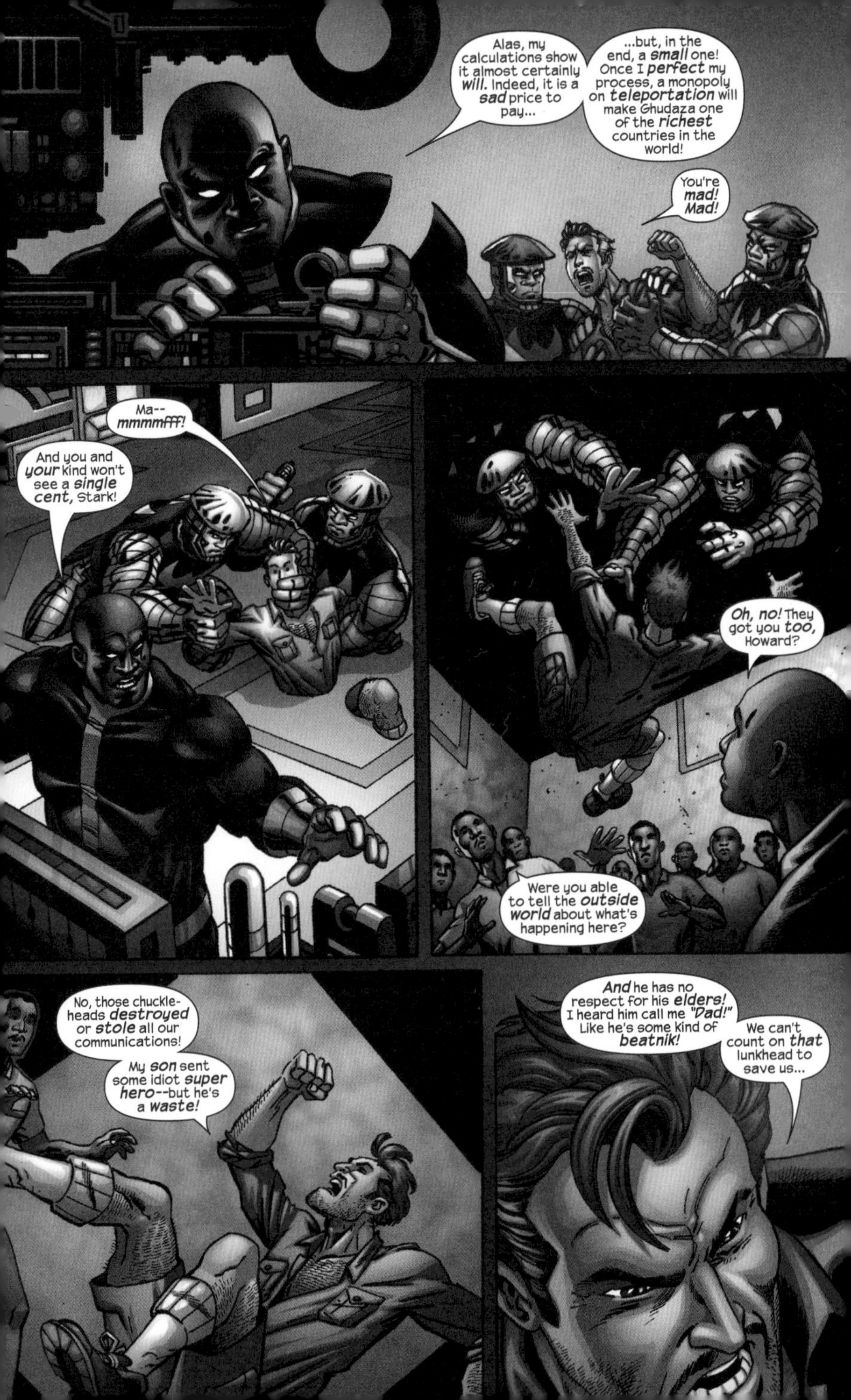

Alas, my calculations show it almost certainly will. Indeed, it is a sad price to pay...
...but, in the end, a small one! Once I perfect my process, a monopoly on teleportation will make Ghudaza one of the richest countries in the world!
You're mad! Mad!
Ma--mmmmfff!
And you and your kind won't see a single cent, Stark!
Oh, no! They got you too, Howard?
Were you able to tell the outside world about what's happening here?
No, those chuckle-heads destroyed or stole all our communications!
My son sent some idiot super hero--but he's a waste!
And he has no respect for his elders! I heard him call me "Dad!" Like he's some kind of beatnik!
We can't count on that lunkhead to save us...

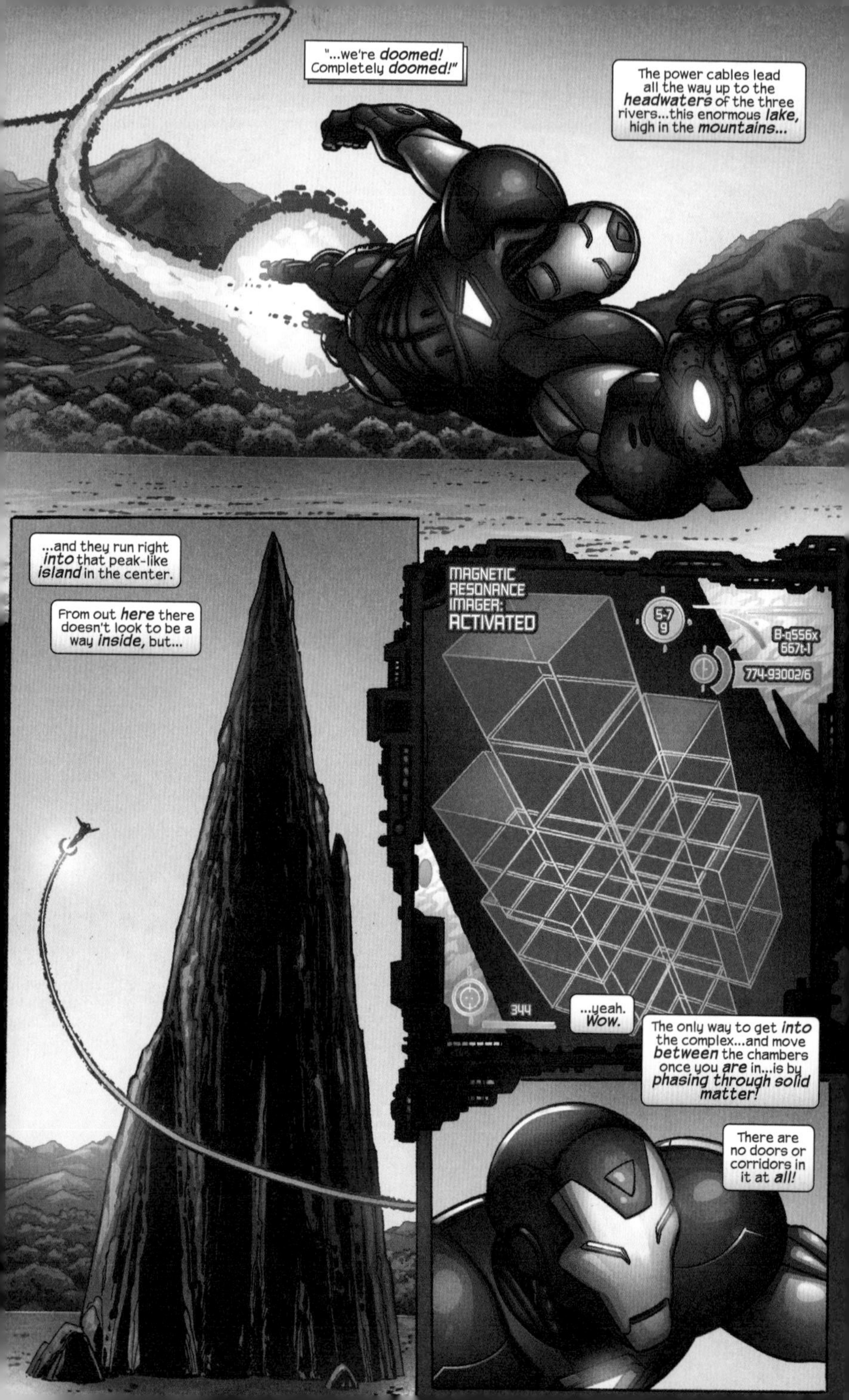
"...we're doomed! Completely doomed!"
The power cables lead all the way up to the headwaters of the three rivers...this enormous lake, high in the mountains...
...and they run right into that peak-like island in the center.
From out here there doesn't look to be a way inside, but...
MAGNETIC RESONANCE IMAGER: ACTIVATED
5-7 9
B-q556x 667t-1
774-93002/6
344
...yeah. Wow.
The only way to get into the complex...and move between the chambers once you are in...is by phasing through solid matter!
There are no doors or corridors in it at all!

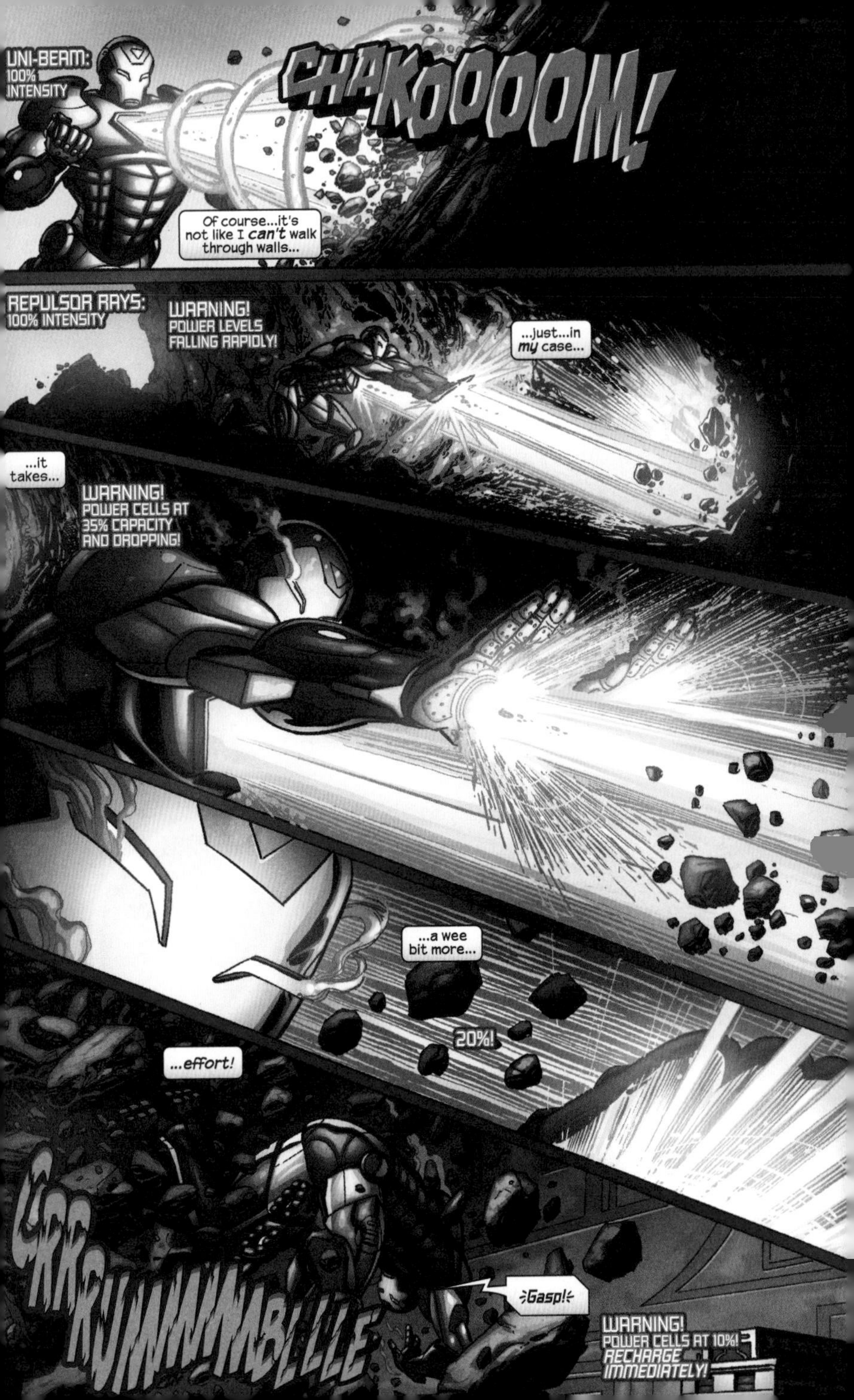
UNI-BEAM: 100% INTENSITY
CHAKOOOOM!
Of course...it's not like I *can't* walk through walls...
REPULSOR RAYS: 100% INTENSITY
WARNING! POWER LEVELS FALLING RAPIDLY!
...just...in *my* case...
...it takes...
WARNING! POWER CELLS AT 35% CAPACITY AND DROPPING!
...a wee bit more...
20%!
...effort!
GRRRUMMMBLLLE
Gasp!
WARNING! POWER CELLS AT 10%! *RECHARGE IMMEDIATELY!*

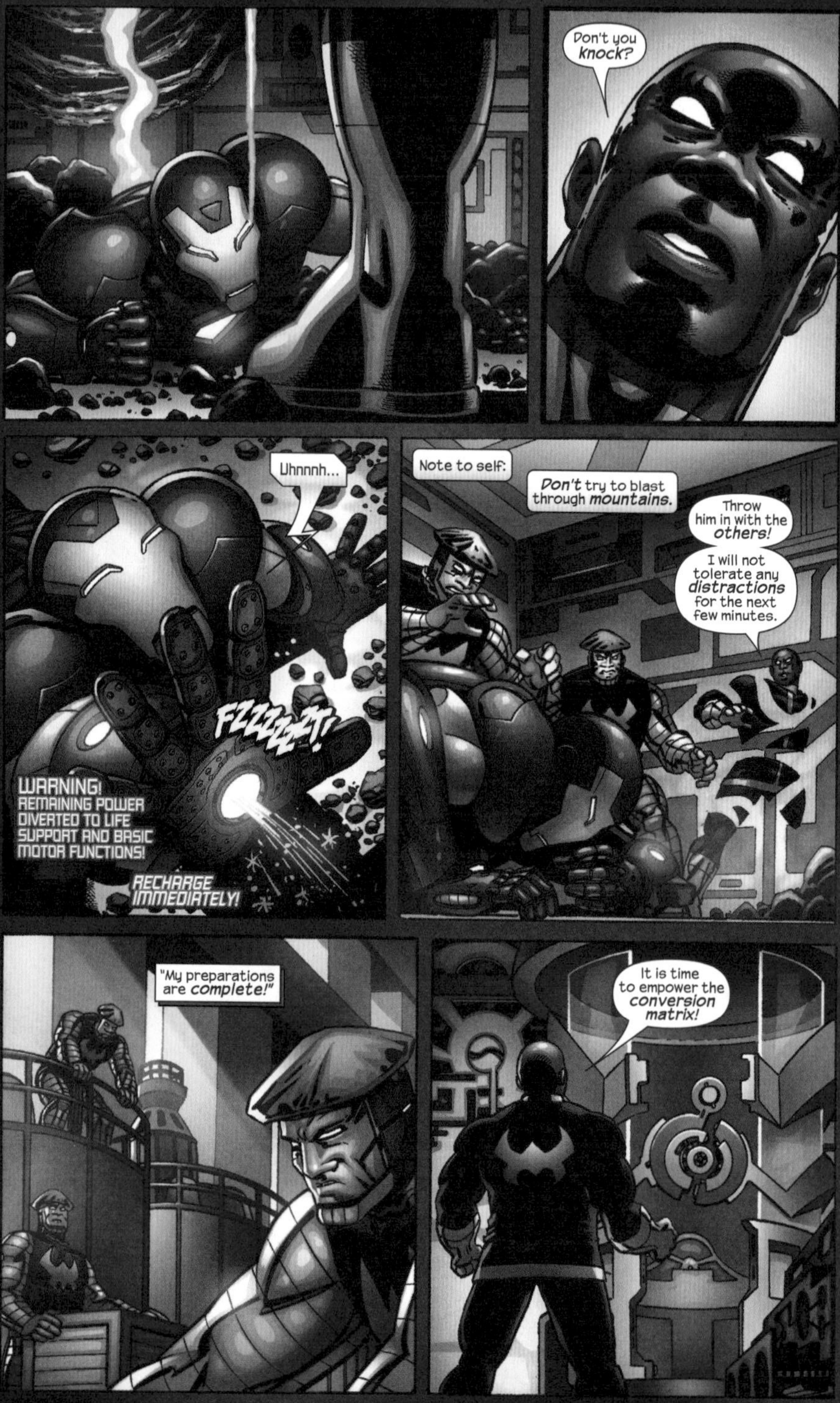

Don't you *knock?*
Uhnnnh...
FZZZZZZT!
WARNING! REMAINING POWER DIVERTED TO LIFE SUPPORT AND BASIC MOTOR FUNCTIONS!
RECHARGE IMMEDIATELY!
Note to self:
Don't try to blast through *mountains.*
Throw him in with the *others!*
I will not tolerate any *distractions* for the next few minutes.
"My preparations are *complete!*"
It is time to empower the *conversion matrix!*

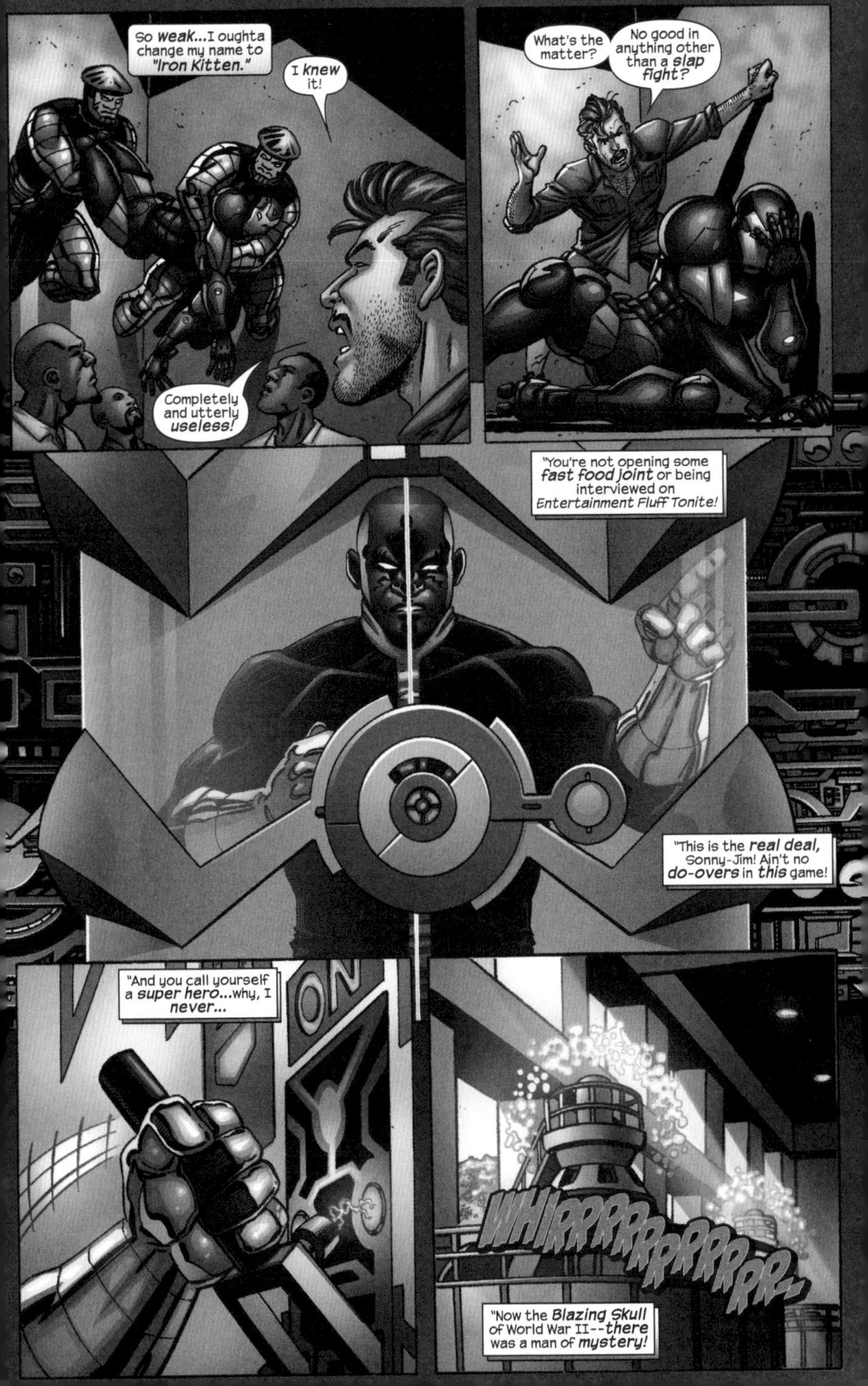
So weak...I oughta change my name to "Iron Kitten."
I knew it!
Completely and utterly useless!
What's the matter?
No good in anything other than a slap fight?
"You're not opening some fast food joint or being interviewed on Entertainment Fluff Tonite!
"This is the real deal, Sonny-Jim! Ain't no do-overs in this game!
"And you call yourself a super hero...why, I never...
WHIRRRRRRRRRRRRRR
"Now the Blazing Skull of World War II--there was a man of mystery!

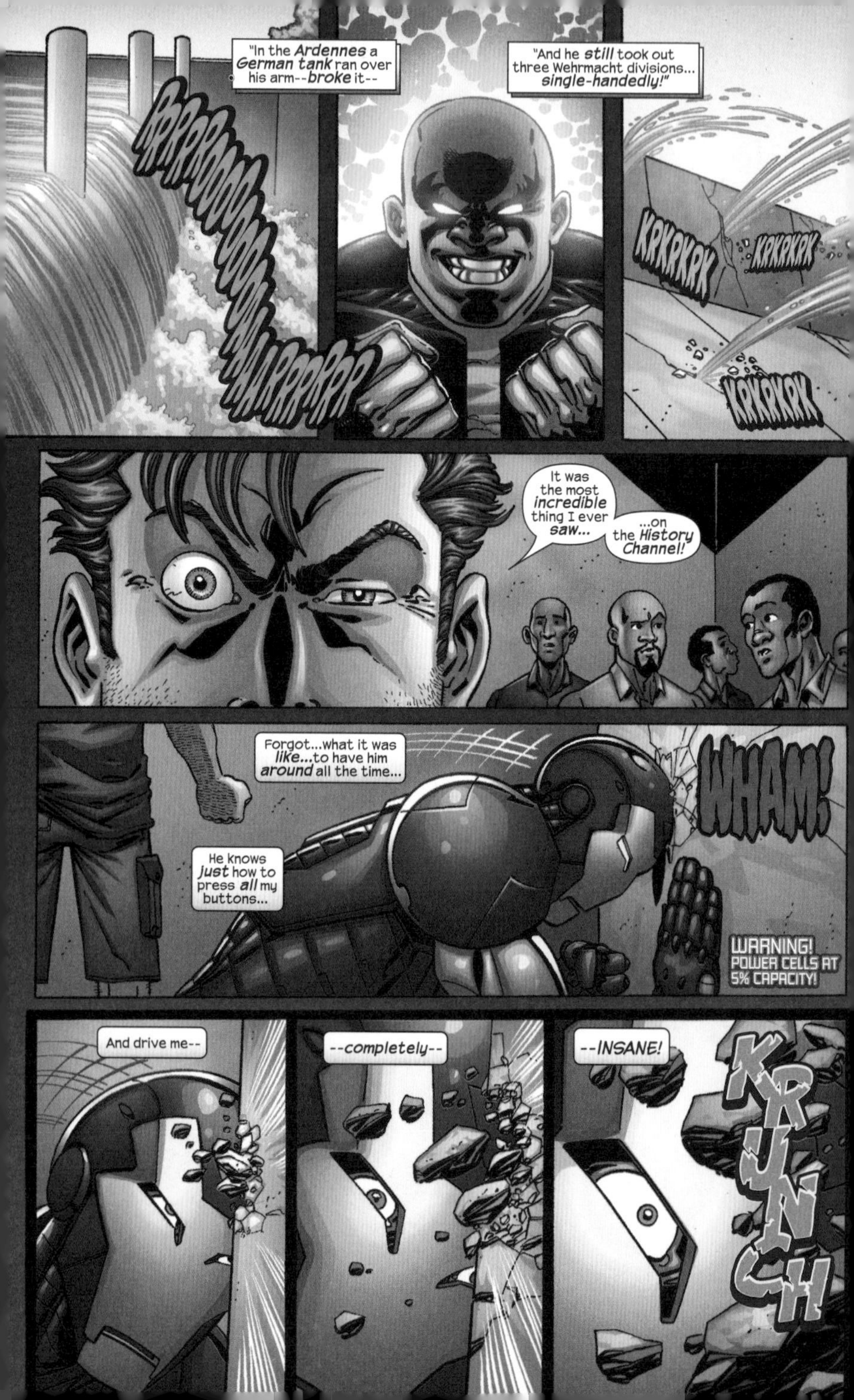

"In the Ardennes a German tank ran over his arm--broke it--
RRRROOOOOOOOOAAARRRRRR
"And he still took out three Wehrmacht divisions... single-handedly!"
KRKRKRK
KRKRKRK
KRKRKRK
It was the most incredible thing I ever saw...
...on the History Channel!
Forgot...what it was like...to have him around all the time...
WHAM!
He knows just how to press all my buttons...
WARNING! POWER CELLS AT 5% CAPACITY!
And drive me--
--completely--
--INSANE!
KRUNCH!

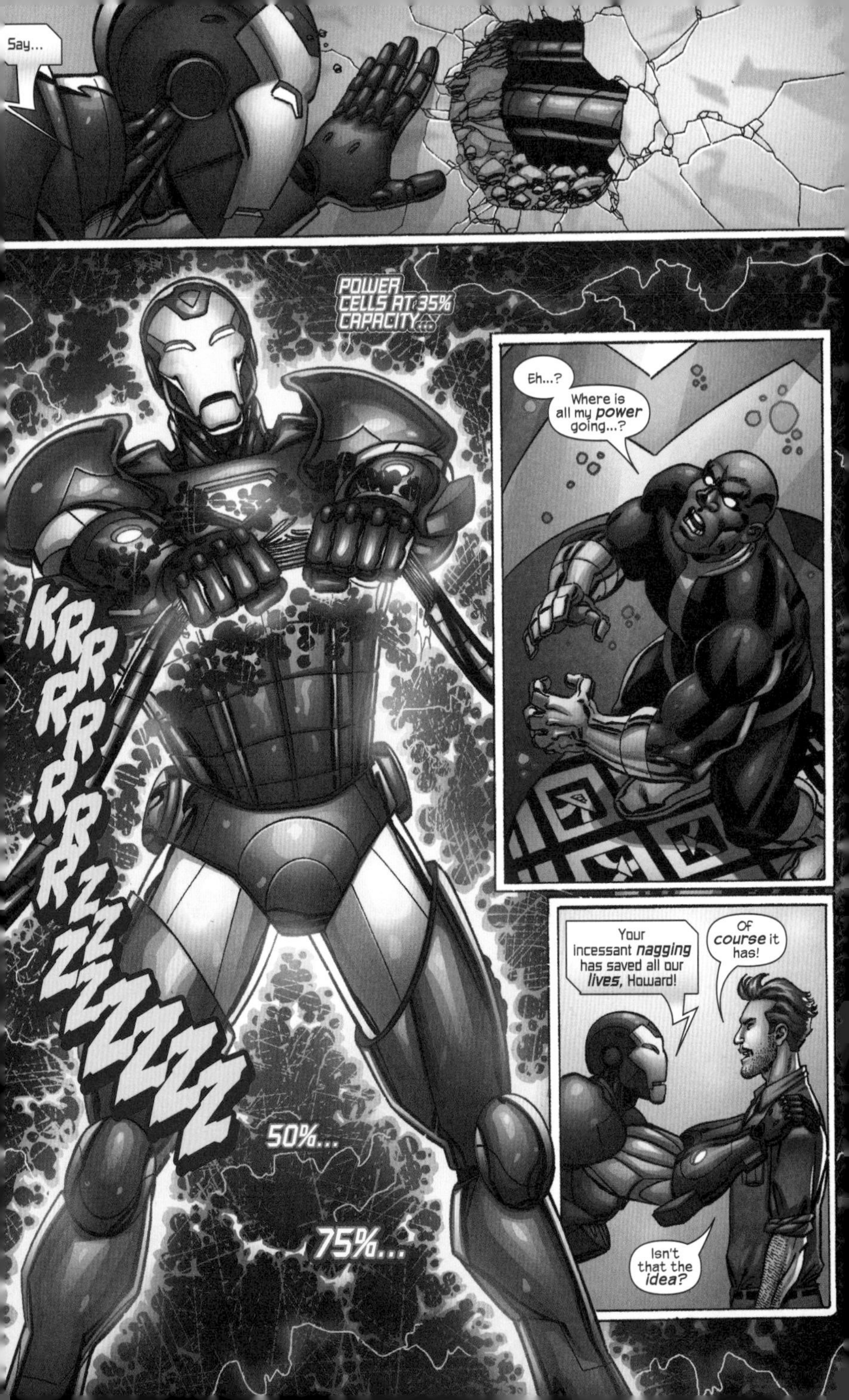

Say...
POWER CELLS AT 35% CAPACITY...
KRRRRRRRRZZZZZZZ
50%...
75%...
Eh...? Where is all my power going...?
Your incessant nagging has saved all our lives, Howard!
Of course it has!
Isn't that the idea?

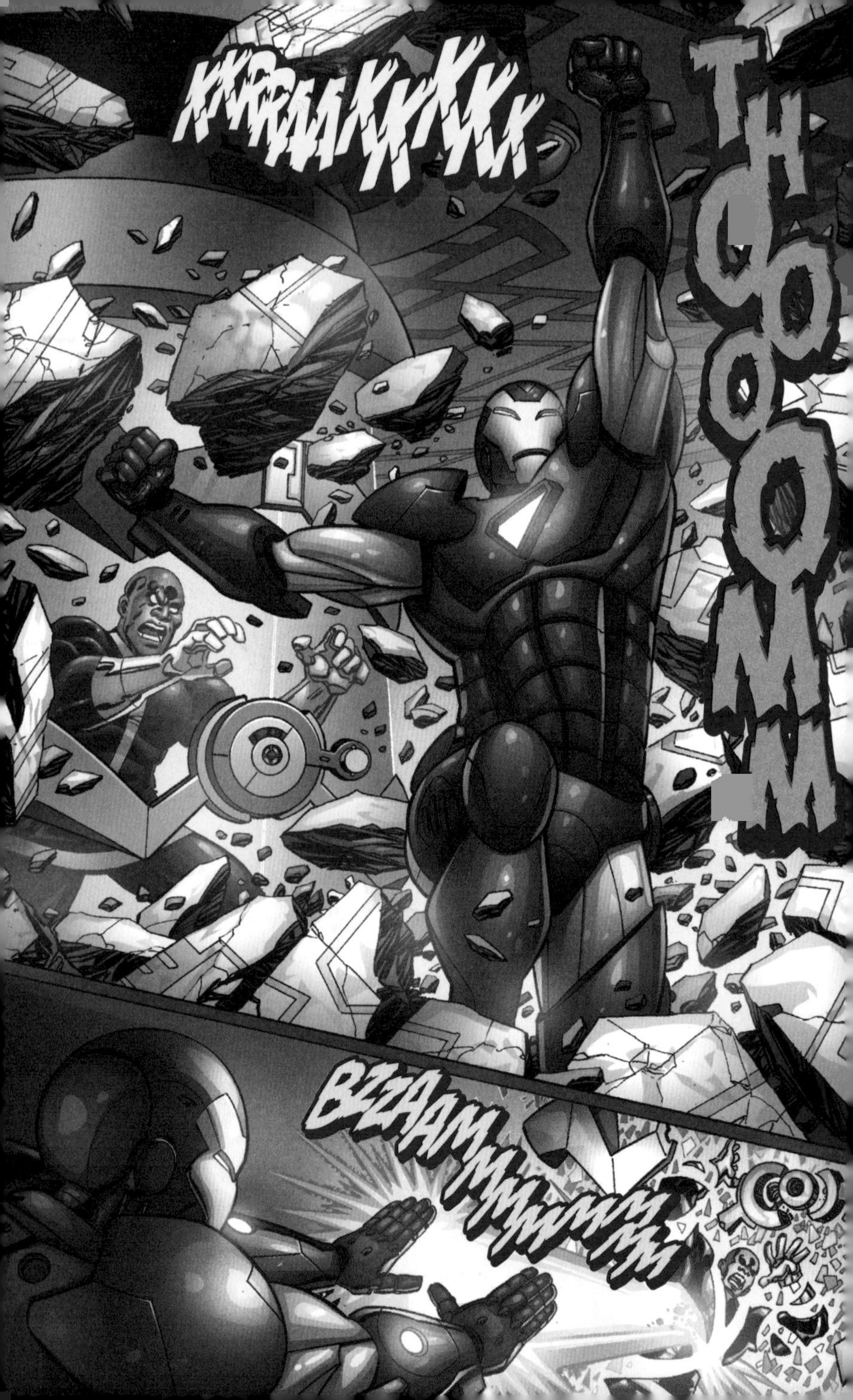
KKRRAAKKKKK
THOOOMM
BZZAAMMMMMMM

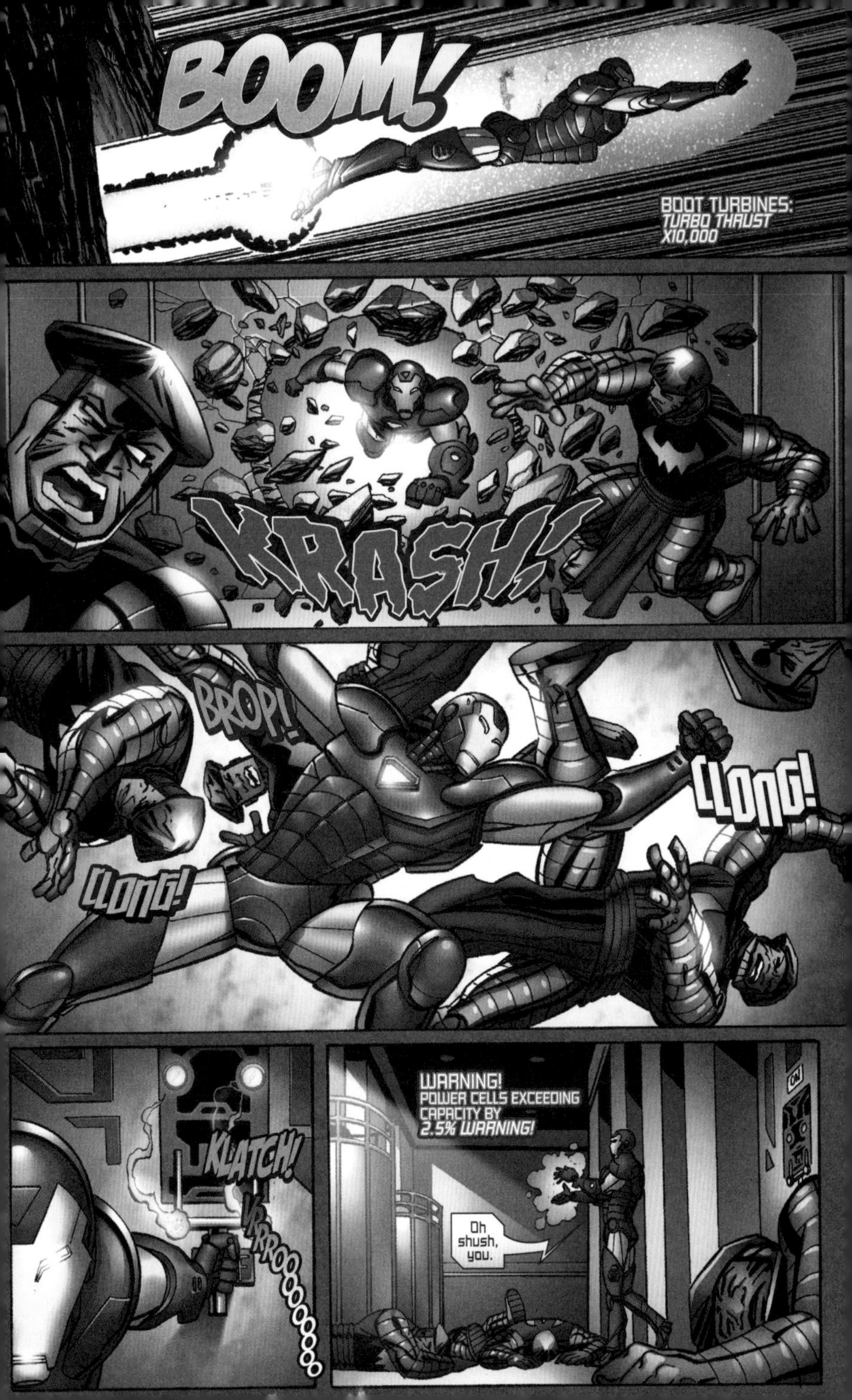
BOOM!
BOOT TURBINES:
TURBO THRUST
X10,000
KRASH!
BROP!
CLONG!
CLONG!
KLATCH!
VRRROOOOOOOOO
WARNING!
POWER CELLS EXCEEDING
CAPACITY BY
2.5% WARNING!
ON
Oh
shush,
you.

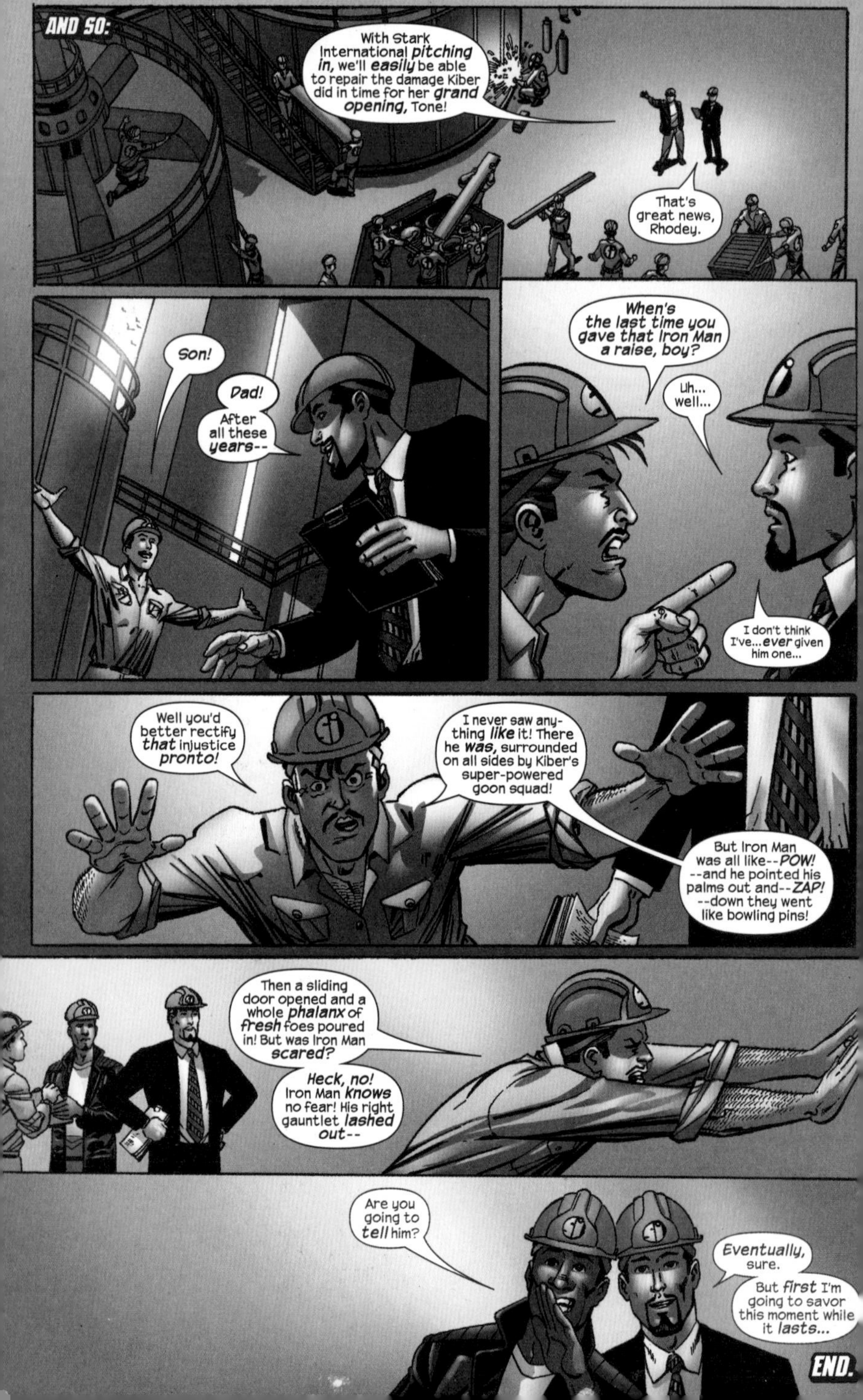
AND SO:
With Stark International pitching in, we'll easily be able to repair the damage Kiber did in time for her grand opening, Tone!
That's great news, Rhodey.
Son!
Dad! After all these years--
When's the last time you gave that Iron Man a raise, boy?
Uh... well...
I don't think I've...ever given him one...
Well you'd better rectify that injustice pronto!
I never saw anything like it! There he was, surrounded on all sides by Kiber's super-powered goon squad!
But Iron Man was all like--POW! --and he pointed his palms out and--ZAP! --down they went like bowling pins!
Then a sliding door opened and a whole phalanx of fresh foes poured in! But was Iron Man scared?
Heck, no! Iron Man knows no fear! His right gauntlet lashed out--
Are you going to tell him?
Eventually, sure.
But first I'm going to savor this moment while it lasts...
END.